Alpha Kaden

Midika Crane

This book is published by Inkitt – Join now to read and discover free upcoming bestsellers!

Chapter One

I pull the edge of the curtain slowly back from the window and peer out onto the street. It's getting dark out, the moon illuminating the deserted sidewalk. To any other eye, the scene might appear innocuous – peaceful even. Everyone's doors are closed, their curtains drawn. Their gates are locked and their kids are safely inside.

But everyone is on high alert, like they are every night.

I sigh deeply, my breath fogging up the window I look through. I rub it with my sleeve so that I can see again. Except there is nothing to see. There never is because, unlike other packs, all life on the streets ceases at night here.

Why? Because my werewolf pack, the Purity Pack, is afraid of the Vengeance Pack. Not precisely the Vengeance Pack, perhaps, but their leader, Alpha Kaden. He destroyed the balance we had established between equality and riotousness within our pack. He stole everything. Especially our freedom.

Our pack isn't loved. It is situated centrally in the Pack Quarter, on the cooler side of the equator. Surrounded by a thick wall meant to keep us safe, we are protected in our small world of religion and peace. Kaden disrupts it.

And we have good reason to fear him. He has kidnapped many innocent girls from our pack. No one knows what has happened to them, but many think he kills them or sells them to his pack members, who have earned equal disgrace. Perhaps he makes a business out of it. We don't know for sure. He also kills our criminals, too. Anyone who breaks the law is the Discipline Pack's business. But anyone who kills is Alpha Kaden's business. He has made that obvious.

1

"Mara, get away from there!"

I am pulled back from the window by my shoulder. I stumble backward as my mother angrily pulls the curtains shut again. She turns to me, hands on her hips.

I love my mother, but sometimes she can be way too protective. She has lived her life believing only in one thing: the Moon is our savior, and always will be. She believes the Goddess controls everything that we do and decides our futures through some type of voodoo magic. Despite growing up in this pack, I don't believe in it. I respect it though.

In school, they taught us a little chant to keep the fear of Alpha Kaden alive in us: "Lock your doors, seal them tight. Close your curtains, every night. Don't look out, in case he's there. Always live in total fear. Even if it means sacrificing your mate, don't let Alpha Kaden seal your fate."

Even my mother condones it.

"Mother, it's fine," I assure her. "No one saw me."

She sighs and runs a hand across her face. Stress is etched into her aging features. She doesn't know how to deal with me sometimes, when I decide to go against her strict rules. I don't mean to do it, but my incessant curiosity keeps tempting me.

"They might have. What if Kaden saw you?" she asks sternly.

I roll my eyes.

"What about our neighbors?" she persists. "You know what they say in church about you, Mara. They act like I'm a terrible mother."

"Well, I wouldn't know if Kaden saw me because I don't know what he looks like," I retort, my voice rising.

Mother narrows her eyes at me. She hates the thought of me knowing anything about Kaden. His identity is still unknown to me. He could walk by me in the street and I would be completely oblivious.

And the worst thing is she won't tell me why I can't know about him. I gather fragments from girls at school, but their parents are just as strict. On a good day, I might find out whether he has killed or not. Sometimes, when it is just mother and father awake, I sneak down to listen in on their conversation. That is how I found out about girls going missing around the town.

"Mara, please. Don't be difficult," mother begs, exasperated.

I fold my arms over my chest. To say I am sick of being holed up every night is an understatement. I've given up on seeing friends on Friday nights. I'm a hop, skip, and a jump away from graduating, but that doesn't mean my mother's rules will be relaxed.

Finding our mate when we are young is essential within our culture. The amount of young males I've even shaken hands with is ridiculous.

"Everything okay in here?"

I turn as my father walks into the room. It has been raining outside, yet I don't remember noticing that when I was looking out the window. He takes off his soaking wet coat and lays it on the bench.

Our house isn't very big, which makes spending most of my time in it even worse. My parents abide by the simple life the Moon Goddess would want. I'm not one for materialistic luxuries, but sometimes I do feel a little deprived.

"Nothing–"

"I caught our daughter peeking out the window again," my mother tells him, cutting me off.

I glare at her. She always seems to be getting me into trouble with Dad.

My father frowns at me.

"Kaden isn't going to be out there," I protest. "You're over-reacting when you say he might be."

I see my father's gaze switch to my mother. He motions with his head for her to leave because he knows how easily she and I argue. When she's gone, he leads me over to the couch so that we can sit down.

"You know the neighbor's daughter? Mandy, is it?"

"Milly," I correct him.

Dad nods. "Kaden took her last week. He stole her right out of her bed, and she hasn't been seen since."

3

I feel my eyes widen. Milly? She is a year older than me, and many times more attractive. The fact that she has been selected to be a part of whatever business Kaden is doing doesn't surprise me in the slightest.

"Why are you telling me this?" I ask him. I like to be in the know, but I didn't expect my father to want that, too.

"I'm worried he might take you. Every morning I'm worried to walk into your room in case I find that he has stolen you during the night."

I shake my head at him. The likelihood of me being taken is slim. If he's taken another girl from my neighborhood, that should mean he won't be back here for another one for at least a month. It's the kind of game he likes to play with people. He lulls us into a false sense of security, until he changes his pattern and shocks us all into confusion.

Dad takes my hand in his and looks me in the eye. Is he going to make me pray?

"We all wonder why he does it, Mara. I promise you, we will figure it out, and stop him as soon as possible." He squeezes my hand slightly.

Dad runs our local church, which leads me to believe his ability to stop Kaden isn't that great. The man we are so scared of is an Alpha of a pack that is notorious for its lack of mercy.

After the Great War that scattered the packs across the land, new forms of society and codes of morality were adopted. Named after our core beliefs, each pack was supposed to keep the peace with its neighbors, and the system proved successful for many centuries. However, with all packs being founded on fairness and equality, it only took one pack to step out of line to destroy the tranquility of all. That was the Vengeance Pack.

"Everything will be fine," I assure him. "Alpha Rylan will sort things out eventually."

That makes my father smile. Rylan is our only hope to end this suffering. If he can't do it, we have no chance.

I retreat to my room and decide to go straight to bed.

4

When I enter the room, I am hit by the cold. My room isn't usually this chilly. I switch on my light and look to see where the cold is coming from.

I have a small room, with a simple closet, desk and bed. Nothing too flashy or extravagant. The source of the chill is pretty obvious: my window is wide open. It's never open like that. Ever. My mother would kill me if she saw that my curtain was pulled back at night. I would surely be grounded if she found out. One time, when I was younger, she even started escorting me back from school after I stayed out to play with my friends till the sun was setting one time.

Warily, I go to the window. I can hear the patter of heavy rain on the road outside. There's a storm picking up and the sound of thunder can clearly be heard in the distance. The sooner I close the window, the better.

I slam the window shut and turn back to my room. A sudden burst of rain hits the glass, making me jump in alarm. I have always hated thunder and lightning...

I just need to calm down and go to sleep, I tell myself as I pull the curtains closed. I am letting this Kaden thing get to me. I pull my hair tie off and cross to my bathroom. Maybe if I shower, I can wash all this childish anxiety away.

I turn the water to extra hot and strip off all my clothes. As I step under the cascade of water, I am transported to another world, a world where I don't have to listen to other people's rules all the time, where my parents don't dictate every decision I make. I rest my head against the tiles.

"Maybe I am destined for the Freedom Pack," I murmur to myself. "A pack where I can do whatever I want." I'm just thinking how stupid I probably sound when a shadow flits across my vision.

I look up, surprised. I peer out of the shower and look around cautiously. Nothing. I am feeling even more ridiculous now.

I get out of the shower, turning the water off after me. As I wrap my towel around my body, I try to dismiss all paranoid thoughts. The shadow was probably just a figment of my imagination. I am known to have a strong one.

Kaden really isn't someone who usually influences my nightmares. I'm fully aware of the threat he poses to me and my family, but I can't bring myself to fear him in normal circumstances. Yet today, for some reason, the chill dancing down my spine confounds my assumptions.

Wearing just my towel, I stand in front of the mirror and inspect myself. My hair looks brown when it is wet, but it is actually a muted blonde. I look pretty much like every other Purity Pack member. My blue eyes are duller than most people's maybe. My skin is paler, and my cheeks have hardly any color at all. These must be the reasons why no boy has wanted to date me. There are always better options. I still love myself, though. I have no other choice.

A loud crash of thunder from outside makes me squeal with fright. I thank the Moon Goddess that the curtains block out the full brightness of the lightning. I dry myself and go back into my room, where I change quickly into my night things. Then I turn the lights out and hop straight into bed, with the covers pulled right up to my chin. I just want to sleep this storm away and carry on tomorrow without any Kaden plaguing my thoughts.

But the more I try to get comfortable in bed, the harder it seems to banish him from my mind. My inner vision is clouded by strange shadows.

I am just about to doze off to the sound of the rain splattering against my window when I feel a hand slap over my mouth.

I have never been taught self-defense and any idea of what to do deserts me. I swing my arms wildly but find myself in someone's firm and unfamiliar grasp. I struggle as hard as I can while screaming into the hand, even though the sound is muffled.

I kick as I am pulled up and out of my bed. I feel someone applying pressure to my neck and for a second I think I am about to die of strangulation. Well, I won't go without a fight!

My legs are the only weapons that I have. I lash out, trying to connect with my captor's ankles. But each time I miss and meet only air with my bare foot.

"Settle down. Everything will be over soon."

And that soft, male voice is the last thing I hear before I black out completely.

Chapter Two

I feel myself coming to and my eyes blink open. However, I am immersed in darkness, which throws me off balance for a moment. Pain lances through the back of my head, slicing across my vision in an array of bright colors.

Where am I?

I can tell that I am tied to something and the bonds I'm secured with are digging into my wrists. I take a deep breath, trying to gather my wits. The pain is immense, but there is little point dwelling on it.

I have been kidnapped. I know that much. By whom, and why, I can't quite grasp yet. I have an idea of who has done this but I don't address it yet, because it is too horrific to contemplate. All my biggest fears are being realized, and it seems there is nothing I can possibly do about it.

I am sitting on a chair, in a cold room. I try to concentrate on my surroundings, but all I can think about is the feeling of someone watching me.

I pull at the restraints a little harder, but it is hopeless. I am stuck fast, with even my feet tied to the legs of the chair. There is no getting myself free, so I must wait. Perhaps if I remain calm, I'll think of a way to get out of here.

Then I detect footsteps. I freeze, cringing. There is someone in this room with me. Right now. The footsteps confirm it.

I don't struggle, I just remain still. I listen closely to the footsteps, trying to gauge where the sound is coming from and where this person is in the room. Whoever it is, they are close to me. I can feel it, and hear it.

I breathe in deeply and close my eyes. I consider saying something, but just saying something won't get me out of here. Whoever has kidnapped me has a reason... I just need to find out what that reason is. I like to think that I am quite smart. I have always been the one in the pack to consider things before I do them. Now, however, all I can do is worry frantically about what will get me out of the clutches of my kidnapper.

A thick silence fills the room. The footsteps have ceased and I feel my heart start to pick up the pace again. Having my senses toyed with like this is making me more than a little uneasy. I feel terribly isolated; the silence weighs down on my shoulders.

"Lock your doors," a soft voice whispers in my left ear.

I jump, twisting my head around to see who is behind me. I can't, of course, as everything is immersed in complete darkness. The voice is shockingly unfamiliar.

"Shut them tight," the voice whispers again, this time in my right ear. The voice belongs to a man. It's soft and raspy, like nothing I have heard before. Whoever this kidnapper might be, I don't know him. At least, not personally.

"Close your windows," the voice resumes, this time right in front of my face. "Every night."

I struggle in my bonds, squeezing my eyes shut. Fear has exploded and consumed my entire body, chasing away all former reason, until I am left with nothing but the desire to escape. A finger is dragged down my cheek. It's a soft feeling, but there's pressure behind it. It feels like the touch of a slick leather glove.

"Don't go out, in case he's there," the voice continues, sounding further away now.

I want to scream in terror. I want to lash out. I want to run. But I am frozen in fear. I can't move. I doubt I could even if I was standing up with no restraints.

The footsteps draw closer until they stop right in front of me. I can't explain the terrible feeling of knowing someone who could potentially end your life is standing right in front of you, and you can't do anything about it.

"Always live in total fear."

I gasp as I feel his warm breath against my face. He is undeniably close to me.

Suddenly, through all my fright, it dawns on me what he is chanting. This soft, terrifying, melodic voice is reciting the exact poem that has been drilled into my head by my parents and teachers over the years.

"Even if it means sacrificing your mate," the voice drawls, though now coming from behind me. I can feel his breath on my neck, fanning across my shivering skin.

Then I become aware that the bonds on my arms are being cut loose. I am stunned and can't think how to react.

"Don't let Alpha Kaden seal your fate..."

I bend down, my clammy fingers struggling to untie the thick knots around my ankles. My only wish is to get out of here as soon as I can, from whoever is in this room messing with me. No doubt he's enjoying seeing me struggle for survival, but I am not about to give him any more satisfaction.

Once both knots are untied, I jump up and try to move away, my hands outstretched in case I hit a wall. I still can't see a thing, but fear that if I don't move quickly I will surely meet an unfortunate end.

I find a wall soon enough. The wallpaper feels velvety under my fingertips compared to the cold, hard concrete underneath my feet. I rest my forehead against it, trying to get my bearings.

"You can't escape something you can't see," the man's voice says from right behind me.

This time I do scream. A loud, shrill scream as I lash my hands out. But there's nothing there. *Am I going crazy?*

I stumble to the right, keeping my hand on the wall. I must find a way out of here. The laughter coming from the other end of the room is doing my head in.

"Is this a game?" I shriek. I'm not sure if my kidnapper can even see me. He must be able to, I reason, if he knows where I am all the time. Of course, this is a game... a sick, twisted game run by an equally sick and twisted man.

I keep going till I feel the glassy surface of a window pane underneath my hand. A burst of hope floods through me, but I have to think.

My kidnapper would never let me take an easy exit like this. There's probably a catch. But that's a risk I must take. I have no other choice. I bang my hands against the glass, but it doesn't smash. It just bends and flexes under my repeated blows.

I fall to my knees. "Why am I here?" I ask blindly into the air.

Just as the words leave my mouth, a light flickers on, blinding me. I cover my eyes till I can adjust after so long in the dark. After blinking a few times I begin to see what's around me.

The room I'm in is larger than I expected. The chair I just escaped from is right in the middle.

And on that chair sits a man.

I can't see much of him. He's wearing some sort of hood that shadows his face. The rest of his clothes are all black leather, but I can still see that he's a big man, with a powerful frame. Seeing my kidnapper for the first time in front of me like this is unnerving. At the same time as being hideously afraid, I have the urge to run at him and attack him.

He lounges comfortably, twirling a piece of rope in gloved hands. The same rope, I presume, that was used to keep me bound to the chair.

"You want to know why I only ever take girls from the Purity Pack?" he asks.

His voice is soft and smooth, yet I hear every word. I haven't time to think what I should say, so I blurt out the first thing that comes to me.

"Because you're a coward."

He gives an amused chuckle then tosses the rope casually over his shoulder and stands. I watch nervously as he approaches, his gait suggesting he's almost floating over, his steps are so soft. I back myself as far into the wall as possible.

11

"This has nothing to do with being a coward. It doesn't even have anything to do with your Alpha. He is a rather pleasant man," he tells me. He's standing over me now, looking down at me. But I still can't see past the shadow that masks his face. He folds his hands across his front. "I hate pleasant."

He kneels in front of me, to get on the same level, and my breath catches in my throat. I hate it that he's anywhere near me. I hate not knowing who he is. And I hate not having the guts to lash out and hurt him.

"I kidnap girls from the Purity Pack because they are weak, pathetic, and believe in some bullshit being that lives in the sky," he tells me.

So there it is. Somehow, I expect no less from him. I give him my hardest glare, despite my fear.

"Well, I find it amusing," he responds, laughing.

I want to slap him for saying such things, but I'm not even sure if he has a face. And that scares me the most.

"So, what… am I your pet now? Or are you going to sell me off to one of your other desperate pack members?" I demand angrily. I have never wanted to hurt someone as much as I want to hurt this man. How could he do this to me? Or anyone else for that matter. He's stolen my life before I've even had the chance to live it.

"You're not going to share the same fate as those other girls. Rest assured, you will not even see my pack, like they have. No, I have a different proposition to make," he tells me slowly, as if I have a choice in the matter. "I have been watching you for some time now. I know you aren't normally afraid of me." He brings his hands together. "Though maybe you are right now…"

I decide to go for it. I launch myself at him, trying to hurt him in some way. But he just grabs me before I can do anything. My skin makes contact with his leathers for several long seconds as he holds me by the wrists, then he tosses me carelessly from him like I am a piece of trash. I land hard on the ground and curl up in pain.

"You're feisty," he remarks drily. "Are you sure you're from the Purity Pack?"

I remain hunched on the ground, nursing my bruises.

"What you need to understand," he tells me patiently, "is that I am an Alpha, and you are my game. I am not yours."

Is he setting ground rules? Am I being warned not to try anything like that again? If I wasn't at his complete and utter mercy, I would attempt another attack on him right now to show him what I think of that. I still have a voice though.

"I will *not* be your slave," I growl.

He laughs.

Kaden laughs... I am in the presence of the deadliest Alpha in the world. He hasn't shown mercy to anyone, so why would he show mercy toward me? I knew it was him the second the lights turned on. Who else would kidnap a girl from the Purity Pack?

"Your fate shall be a little more interesting than that of a slave," he murmurs.

He comes back over to me and holds his hand out. I don't want to take it, but I know that if I don't he might do something bad to me. I let him pull me to a standing position. He's over a head taller than me, yet I still can't see under his hood. All I see is shadow, a darkness I already yearn to light a flame under.

"I would like you to meet someone special," he says.

He claps his hands together and I back away as a set of doors on the far side of the room opens. If I'd gone the other way in the dark I might have found them and been able to escape. Whatever was on the other side of them, it could only be better than this.

A younger looking man walks in, with quite a swagger. He has dozens of scars and scratches on his bare arms, and some on his face. He's clearly another member of the Vengeance Pack. I can tell by the wicked look in his dark eyes that I will get no help or sympathy there. He looks as though he's been beaten, or fallen from a great height. He even hobbles a little.

"Mara, I would like you to meet my brother. Kace."

Chapter Three

Kace eyes me silently. I match his gaze. Why is he here? I don't care if he's Kaden's brother. His existence only interests me if he's going to help get me out of here.

"You better get used to him," Kaden says.

I don't know why Kaden is hiding his face from me, when Kace is making no attempt to hide his. Curiosity stirs at the back of my mind, willing me to find out more.

"Why?" I snap.

"Because you're to be his wife."

My jaw drops. A hot wave of anger washes over me, masking the shock. *Wife?* Is that why he stole me away from my family, to make me some stranger's wife? But not just any stranger. This is the Alpha of Vengeance's brother!

Kace smirks. He planned this. He wanted a Purity Pack member as a wife, to abuse and degrade. I can see it now, written all over his disgustingly scarred, smug face.

I glare at them both. I want to slap the pair of them, but they'd probably both just slap me back.

"Go to hell," I growl.

Kace steps toward me, holding his arms out to me as if he expects me to walk willingly into them. I take a step back out of instinct, wanting as much distance between us as I can get. But Kaden grabs his brother's shoulder, restraining him.

"Leave your soon-to-be wife with me. You'll have a submissive mate by the afternoon," Kaden whispers to Kace, as though he thinks I can't hear him.

If he thinks I would ever submit to him, he's crazy. I'd rather die. Kace gives me a last glance then leaves the room.

I stare at the floor, refusing to look up at Kaden as he walks around me, watching my every move. At this point, the floor at my feet seems strikingly more interesting than him.

"I will *not* marry him," I tell him after a good few minutes' silence.

He doesn't reply. Instead, he carries on circling me, sizing me up as if I am his prey. It feels like that, anyway. The silence eats at the back of my mind. He is using it to manipulate me.

"And I sure as hell would rather die than stay here..." I add bitterly.

I know he will kill me if I don't do as he says. It's how he works. He is a psychopathic murderer. I finally see that now. I should have listened to my parents.

He stops in front of me and I glare up at him.

"You're not going to die. Well, unless I change my mind," he responds smoothly.

I can't tell if he's looking at me now. His face is completely covered. I decide to challenge him about it. "Why won't you show me your face. Scared?"

He chuckles and steps closer to me. I don't back away, knowing that he will think that I'm weak if I do. I stand my ground, trying to see beneath the shadow, but it's impossible.

He reaches a gloved hand out to touch my face. I remain unmoving. His finger glides down my cheek, then he cups my chin. Maybe I should bite him or something.

"I'm scared of no one," he murmurs.

"Then show me."

"I can't show you. You may be attracted to me if I do," he says lightly.

There is an underlying seriousness in his tone that spikes my curiosity. Now I want to rip that hood off, to prove to him that I couldn't possibly be swayed by anyone's good looks. If my assumptions are correct, he is hiding himself from me because he is afraid.

I shake my head at him, but I am restricted as he still holds my chin. "Sorry to say, murderers aren't my type."

He laughs. "Has anyone told you you're not very nice?"

He releases my chin. I can't help but wonder what everyone else was like, those he has kidnapped in the past. Are they dead? Did he *really* kill them? This man is infuriating – I have gathered as much simply from the few sentences we have shared between us.

I remember a girl from my school that got kidnapped. I knew her. I liked her, even. She stuck up for me, until Kaden snatched her in the night.

"Back to the subject of Kace..." he begins.

"I told you. I'm not marrying him," I tell him firmly.

Somehow, I can sense his smile without even seeing it.

"You don't have a choice, my dear."

We don't speak for a moment, we just look at each other. Eventually, he pulls away and motions to the seat behind me. "You might want to sit down for this."

Instantly, I do. I believe him. He is about to tell me something that I'm not going to like, and I don't want to be the kind of person that collapses on the ground in despair. Giving him that satisfaction would pain me more than listening to his commands, which I really don't want to do right now.

"You shall be proposed to in front of my pack tomorrow evening. The news will quickly spread," he explains.

I frown but stay silent.

"After you say yes, your real job will start," he tells me.

I ask him what, but he shakes his head at me. It's stupid to bother, since Kaden obviously likes to do things on his own terms. There is no way he is about to listen to some Purity Pack girl.

"You will find out the rest later. For now, you will sleep," he says airily.

16

I flick my hands dismissively as he turns to go. He stops and glances back at me.

"This hasn't made me want to stay at all."

Kaden grunts. "Would you like to try your luck and escape, Mara?"

"You can't keep me here forever," I retort.

I will be defiant to the end. If he thinks he can keep me here by my own will, he is crazy. I won't stop trying to escape and make it back to my rightful pack. I will try to climb over every wall and pick every lock to get out of this place. I *won't* be staying.

He walks behind me, but I don't turn around on the chair, though I'm quivering. I'm not going to say he doesn't frighten me, as that would be lying. He lays his hands on my shoulders, making me start.

"You have no idea how much control I have over you," he mutters in my ear. He has leant down, so I feel his warm breath against my neck again. I feel even more intimidated. I hate the feeling. For some reason, the fact that I can feel him near such a vulnerable part of my body makes him seem so much more real.

"You're very defiant," he observes. "I love it. Why? Because everyone else from your pack is pathetic." His words make me shiver even more. "You, on the other hand, intrigue me."

Intrigue him? That's got to be a bad thing.

"But we are still so different," he continues.

"Why?" My voice is shaky and I know it is stupid of me to expect an answer.

He walks back around so he is right in front of me and kneels again, bringing his shadowed face close. This time I can almost see the outline of some of his features.

I reach my hand out to touch his face, to find out if he really is as attractive as he makes himself out to be. Instead, he grabs my wrist before I even get close. He pushes it hard into my chest, making me wince.

"Because I've done more things in my life than you could imagine," he whispers harshly.

The man's mad. Why did I even think of daring to touch him?

17

"I've been further than you," he goes on.

I clench my jaw. He is twisting my arm in such a way that pain surges up the back of my head. It's just another way to degrade me.

"I've learnt more than you," he continues gruffly

I refuse to give voice to my pain. I won't let him have the fun.

"I've hurt more than you!"

He twists my arm further, and I let out a desperate whimper.

"And I've killed more than you!"

I don't doubt it. I feel tears forming in my eyes but I hold them back. I am *not* weak. He lets go of my wrist and I refrain from rubbing it, though it burns fiercely. He is simply trying to make me feel worthless compared to him.

"I know you love your family, so don't doubt for a second that I won't bring them here, and kill them before you," he snarls. He pulls away, finally giving me some space to breathe. "And not before taking you against that wall over there first."

"You're sick!" I spit.

He laughs. "But I'll leave that to your husband."

He flicks my hair up. I gather it back and hold it over my shoulder.

"What kind of brother would I be if I taught you how much pleasure you could have with me, compared to him?" he jokes.

I don't say anything. I'm scared he will kill my parents. A horrible daughter I would be if I got them killed because of my smart mouth. They don't deserve any of this. They are good people.

Kaden seems to take notice. "I see you've gotten my point. Wouldn't want your parents to join mine in hell."

I look up at him. I knew his parents were dead, but the way he said it was as if he couldn't care less.

"My parents are great people," I say under my breath. I don't expect him to answer so it's a surprise when he does.

"And so were you. Until you decided you wanted to run away and marry Kace, your secret lover," Kaden says.

I suddenly realize why he expects me to go along with all this. It makes my heart sink. "Is that why you picked me? Because you knew I wasn't afraid of you?"

He gives me a curt nod. "And look how the tables have turned."

I hate him. I truly, deeply, despise the man in front of me.

"Now, it's time for you to go to bed. Shall I accompany you to your room?" he asks, suddenly polite.

He holds his arm out for me to link mine around. With the thought of my parents lingering in the back of my mind, I comply, and we leave the room together.

Chapter Four

I've hardly slept. They brought me to a room they've apparently allocated to me and since then I've tossed and turned on the bed, trying to think of how to escape. It's proved impossible to keep my mind still for more than five minutes at a time. How can I sleep when my family is out there, probably wondering where I am? Knowing them, they'll be assuming the worst, and this time, they will be right.

I think I did manage to slip off for at least an hour's sleep a while ago, but when I came to I became instantly aware of where I am and my heart sank in my chest once more. I am being held captive by the Vengeance Pack, my pack's sworn enemy...

I slide out of bed. Last night it was dark and I could see very little of where they had brought me. Now, though, my breath catches in my throat as I realize where I am.

I stand up and stumble around. This is *my* room! Everything I know and love is in this room right now. I remember picking out the color scheme, hanging the pictures and choosing my duvet set. *It's all here!*

I run to the door, but it's locked.

I feel disorientated. Has it all been a bad dream? Am I home? No, I can't be... I remember being kidnapped, and I remember talking to Kaden. But could this be a dream? Something triggered by my parents' warnings? A flutter of hope fills my chest.

I bang on the door. "Mom! Dad! It's me, let me out!"

There is no answer to my calls. I turn back to my room. Everything is the same. The gray carpet, the blue walls... I wander over to the photographs of my mother and father. They look so happy. A tear falls from my eye and onto the glass, covering my mother's face.

What am I doing? This *can't* be my room! This is all a hopeless lie, and my parents aren't here to save me. I'm on my own.

Falling back on my bed, I close my eyes. I can't tell what is real and what is fake. I can't tell if I'm at home or still with the Vengeance Pack. I feel like I'm floating between two realities.

This is *his* fault. Kaden. This is another one of his games. He wants me to feel confused because confused is vulnerable. Suddenly I hate him even more than ever. My mother told me never to hate, but this burning in my chest can't be suppressed.

I stand, closing out the familiarity around me, and try the door again. This time it opens, but toward me. I stumble back as someone enters.

A young man stands in the doorway, looking in. He looks like what most Vengeance Pack members look like, with dark hair, dark eyes – very luminous and attractive. Basically, the opposite of any Purity Pack member. Not dull. Not boring.

Instantly I feel nervous and out of place. I'm dressed only in a thin, white nightgown I vaguely remember putting on last night. It was the one thing in the wardrobe that wasn't day clothes. This man, on the other hand, wears full-out leather armor, including gloves. *Why does everyone here wear gloves?*

He raises an eyebrow at me as I back slowly away.

"Mara?" he asks. He has that typical Vengeance Pack accent as well. Deep and exotic. I nod cautiously. What does he want with me? I notice how he doesn't come past the door. Respectful, at least.

"Who are you?" I demand, sounding ruder than I intended. I'm blaming it on the stress. Right now, though, anyone from the Vengeance Pack is my enemy, and I need to keep it that way. When I escape, I'm going to leave every one of them behind.

"You may call me Coen," he says gently. He holds a hand out to me, and I stare at it. It's encased in leather, the side of his gloves decorated with small blue gems. Curious.

I swallow. "I hate leather."

He retracts his hand and looks at it for a moment. He's quite handsome, I hate to admit. And, so far, the least intimidating person I've met here.

"Fair enough," he comments. He pulls his gloves off and tucks them inside his jacket pocket. His jacket is just as marvelous as the gloves, studded with the same gems. He offers his hand to me again.

This time, I take it. His warm fingers close around mine, and then I let him lead me out of the room and down a dimly lit hallway.

"You will have breakfast with your..." He trails off, unsure what to say. Kace and I aren't mates. Marriage is for royalty, and I'm not that either. He seems uncomfortable. "...with Kace," he finishes.

My stomach clenches and I begin to feel sick. Being in the same room with Kace was bad enough, but eating with him? Perhaps they will give me a knife... but I wouldn't know what to do with one even if they did. Violence is a sin.

I decide to try to question my escort. "What are you to him? Kaden, I mean."

He sighs. "A personal guard."

I frown. Personal guard? Who knew the most feared Alpha of them all must have a personal guard? I can't think of anyone who would dare to hurt him.

I bite my lip. "And where is Kaden?"

I don't really care, but I'm still curious to know. I wish I had the confidence to abuse him for what he's done to my bedroom. He's doing it on purpose, so I will never forget what he's taken from me.

"He's dealing with business with other packs," Coen answers.

Of course, always harassing other packs rather than looking after his own.

Coen catches me rolling my eyes. "You have every right to despise him, but bear this in mind – he likes his women submissive."

I grit my teeth in disgust. "Luckily, I'm not his."

When we reach the dining area, we find Kace already there. He's poking at a piece of pineapple on his plate. He's dressed casually, as if we are already a married couple that has been meeting for breakfast like this for years. Are we expected to share a room after our union?

He looks up as we walk in and meets my gaze. I return his look of disdain with a glare. I sense he doesn't want to be paired with me almost as much as I don't want to be paired with him. At least we have something in common.

I sit down at the end of the table. I'm not hungry, but Coen goes to get me something anyway. So, I'm left alone with Kace.

"I can tell you don't want to propose to me tonight," I tell him.

He clenches his jaw and lowers his gaze. Does he not want to admit it to me? He is very expressive with his emotions, so there's no point him trying to hide anything from me.

He drops his fork. "You don't know anything."

"I know that you can get me out of here. If I leave, you can have whoever you want."

He slams his hands on the table, making the cutlery clatter, then stands. I look nervously up at him. I'm walking a dangerous line.

"Don't you understand? You *can't* escape him. He will find you, and he will lock you up so you never see the sunlight again," he tells me.

My heart drops at his words. I believe them.

Kace slumps back down and runs a hand down his face. "It doesn't matter anyway. The girl I want tried to kill me."

I look at the cuts and bruises on his face and wonder if this girl he's talking about did that to him. How could he still want her after she did something like that? I wouldn't know, of course. I've never experienced love.

"And she loves another man anyway," he says gruffly, shoving a piece of pineapple into his mouth.

Coen comes back into the room, holding a plate of fruit. I have to wonder where the Vengeance Pack get their fruit from. He places it in front of me and stands back. Is he my guard now?

"You could do better," I tell Kace. He ignores me and carries on eating. I guess exactly what he is thinking.

23

What's the point? What's the point of hoping for someone when you're being forced to marry someone else? That's not love.

I start to wonder what my potential love life is going to be and shake my head at the conclusions I reach. But the Moon Goddess has evidently decided this is to be my fate, so I must accept it and deal with it to the best of my abilities. If I don't have to see Kaden, staying here may not be *too* bad. But I will still try to escape, to see my family and pack again.

Even if it kills me.

Back in my room, I run a brush through my hair and stare at the picture of my parents at the corner of the mirror. They smile brightly. I wonder what they are doing right now. They can't be as happy now as they are in this photo. They must miss me... right?

I put my brush down, wishing my hair shone as nicely as other girls' did. Some makeup would be helpful too. My pasty complexion is not attractive in the slightest – especially not this morning with my cheeks all blotchy from crying last night.

I've been told that my proposal will take place in the next hour. Sitting in this room, just like the one at home, is strangely calming. It's having exactly the opposite effect to the one Kaden no doubt intended it to have.

A knock on my door makes me turn in my seat. Coen is supposed to be posted outside, making sure I don't try to escape while at the same time giving me some privacy. I thought I would be able to get out through the window but when I pulled the curtain back there was only a blank wall.

The door swings open and I'm greeted by the hooded Kaden. Immediately I'm annoyed by his presence, rather than scared. I'm tempted to grab him by the neck and strangle the life out of him, only I can't see anything of it to get hold of.

He's changed into a suit, I notice, although he's still wearing leather gloves. I resist the returning urge to pull his hood back to reveal the face under it. How he has managed to attach a hood to his suit is beyond me.

"What do you want?" I ask coldly.

Shouldn't he be outside, partying along with his other pack members? The thought makes me sick. They celebrate while neither Kace nor I want to go through with it. Vengeance Pack members have no heart. I must remember that.

"I came to ensure you're going to be on time. I see you got the dress I had made for you," he says. Like Coen, he remains outside my door without crossing the threshold, as if it will kill him if he does.

I glance down at the dress I've been instructed to wear. The thick, dark purple material clings to my body. The bodice is glittering with gems I could never have afforded myself. It really is very beautiful and if I was anywhere else I would enjoy wearing it. In the Purity Pack, we aren't allowed to wear rich, dark clothes like these. It signifies a belief in Fate, which none of us is permitted to ponder.

"Do you expect me to run away?" I challenge him.

He goes silent for a moment. I wonder if, under his hood, he is like everyone else in this pack. The same features? The same exact look perhaps?

"I do," he responds.

I frown. As if I could do that. How could I escape the most notorious Alpha and his pack? But I still ask the question. "Why?"

"Because you seem stupid enough to do it."

I scowl at him.

"You also don't seem to have gotten it into your head that I can kill you. And your family," he continues. He holds his right glove up, wiping non-existent dust off it with his other hand. "You don't have to worry though. I won't kill you." He holds his arm out to me, willing me to take it.

I stare at it. What is the point of rebelling now? There is none. So I go to the door and link my arm in his.

He leans down to my ear. "Yet."

Chapter Five

Kaden lets go of my arm. Even though he is my sworn enemy, his absence as I find myself about to walk onto a podium in a big hall unnerves me. I'm suddenly too nervous to care who accompanies me, even if it is my least favorite person in the world.

He brushes past me and climbs onto the stage in front of his assembled pack. They are all cheering and chanting his name. After a few moments, he manages to calm them down somewhat. To my eyes, they are nothing more than savage beasts under the rule of an equally savage man.

"Good evening everyone," he murmurs. A microphone is unnecessary as his mere presence on stage brings everyone to attention. Kace is on the opposite side of the stage to me, waiting for his cue to meet me in the middle. He doesn't bother to look at me.

I can't help but wonder what would happen if I ran away right now? I wouldn't make it out of the building before one of Kaden's pack members found me and dragged me back to him. Maybe I wouldn't even make it back to Kaden alive.

"I have a very special announcement to make," Kaden states.

Everyone answers with shouts and howls, excited that something interesting is about to happen. Many of his members are criminals from other packs. That's what he does. He lets them live here, in a place where they can do no harm to anyone but themselves.

I notice that even now Kaden covers his face. He must show himself to his pack, right? No one seems to expect him to take off his hood, however, so maybe they are used to it.

"A guest will be joining us on stage," he says smoothly. He turns, gesturing at me to come to his side. It takes me a second to move my feet. To commit.

Nervously, I uncover myself and walk onstage so everyone can see me. The silence that falls over everyone is immediate. It is obvious no one expected a Purity Pack member to be here today. The awe on some of their faces is intriguing.

I stand beside Kaden – not too close though.

"This is Ma–"

The crowd surges forward, cutting Kaden off. They claw at the edge of the stage, all pushing each other away to get a better view. I had no idea they would react this way. If I had, I might have considered running away as the sensible option.

Kaden grabs my arm and pulls me behind him. I'm pressed against his back, my cheek against the muscle and sinew, and I can feel the warmth coming through his shirt. This is the closest I've ever been to a man other than my father, although fabric still separates us.

"Back off! No one touches her!" he yells at the crowd.

They cower away. Kaden's voice is so loud and his tone so vicious they immediately obey his command. Once they are all at a safe distance, Kaden draws me out from behind him. I anxiously return to my spot, staring at the ground so I don't have to see the feral looks in the soulless eyes of the pack members.

Kaden then proceeds to ask Kace to walk onto the stage. He takes up his position on the other side. The look of indifference on his face is frightening. Why can't he just stand up to his brother and stop all of this?

"We are gathered here to celebrate our position over the Purity Pack," Kaden announces.

My heart sinks. The crowd goes mental, responding to Kaden's words with primal enthusiasm. The way they are behaving makes it pretty obvious how they feel about my home pack.

They hate us.

"Accordingly, I announce the union of this young lady from the Purity Pack to my brother, Kace," Kaden declares.

27

I feel tears welling up in my eyes, but I fight to keep them from spilling down my face. He doesn't even tell them my name. That is how little I mean to them.

Everyone cheers. I catch Kace's gaze. He looks mad or conflicted at least. Maybe he is thinking twice about carrying on with Kaden's wishes.

Please.

Kaden stands back and Kace crosses to me, holding his hands out to me. Knowing I have no choice, I take them. I can feel him trembling and I'm surprised to find he seems even more nervy about it all than I am.

"Mara, of the Purity Pack," he mumbles, "will you marry me and, in the future, become my mate?"

The silence around us is heavy. I want to say no and escape all this. Nothing would make me happier than to be able to just walk away.

Instead, I say, "Yes."

Kace's jaw clenches as the audience screams its approval, clapping at the same time. I turn and glance over my shoulder, to see Kaden nodding. Then Kace leads me off the stage, his hand resting on the small of my back to guide me.

"And that's it?" I ask, once we are safely offstage.

Kaden, who has followed, shakes his head at me. "No, we are to have dinner in the main hall in a few moments."

I bite back my automatic response. Lashing out seems like a great idea in theory, but in practice I'm sure it wouldn't go down as well.

I'm led down a corridor I haven't been down before. Then again, I didn't know this whole place existed until now.

The dining hall we enter is already filled with people discussing things in subdued voices. The conversation ceases as we come into the room. Everyone stands, bowing their heads as a sign of respect.

It was exactly what would happen back at my pack with Alpha Rylan.

Kace has his arm linked with mine, so it looks like we are actually getting engaged, and mated. It makes me feel sick...

Kaden sits at the head of the table without acknowledging anyone else in the room. While he does this, one by one, the others approach Kace and me.

"Congratulations," one young man says, shaking Kace's hand. He doesn't even look at me before walking back to sit down. The others do the same. They walk up, shake Kace's hand, congratulate him, smile, and retreat without a single glance in my direction.

"They're ignoring me," I whisper in Kace's ear.

He smiles slightly and nods at me. "It's because you're a Purity Pack member."

I'm taken to sit down in a seat beside Kace. On my other side, a man I don't know takes his place beside me and stares blankly ahead. I decide against even bothering to spark up a conversation with him, or anyone else. I don't want to be here as it is.

Dinner is soon served and I eat it slowly. I'm not hungry and my stomach is filled with regret and disdain. I know there was nothing I could do, but thinking about how I said yes to Kace makes the bile start to rise in my throat.

I am eating a potato when I feel something brush against my thigh. I know instantly that it's Kace's hand. He lays it firmly on my upper thigh, his fingers digging into my skin. I glare at him, but he doesn't even look at me.

"Get off!" I snap, trying to slap his hand away.

But he doesn't move. The more I try to pry his fingers off me, the more I feel him resist.

"Why?" he demands, finally turning to look at me. "You're going to be mine officially very soon, Mara."

I have an overwhelming urge to slap him across the face, but I refrain, knowing it will attract attention. I just add it to the many reasons I have for hating him.

Once dinner is over, and I have finished saying my goodbyes to the others, I am ordered to my room to get ready for bed. Kaden announces that it is his duty to escort me.

"Shouldn't my fiancé be doing that?" I query as we walk.

The hood rustles as he shakes his head. "You may be engaged, but intercourse is forbidden until you are married," he informs me.

I'm so startled I come to an abrupt halt. He stops a few steps ahead of me and looks at me. At least, I think he's looking at me.

"You're certainly very upfront about the way you do things," I observe coolly.

He nods. "I'm just being cautious."

We walk the rest of the way to my room in silence. Instead of opening the door, I turn to face him.

"I know I'll never get out of here," I inform him defiantly, "but I want you to know that I'll never want to be here."

His head bows and I wonder if he's looking at his feet. *Is he ashamed? Does he feel remorse? Of course not. He is a monster, and always will be.*

"I can't make you like it here, Mara," he says softly. His voice is oddly strained, as if he's struggling to get the words out.

He makes as if to walk away, but I grab his sleeve and he freezes.

"Why won't you show me your face?" I ask him.

He sighs gruffly. "I thought I told you... you'll be attracted to me if you look into my eyes. You won't be able to help yourself."

He says it so seriously I almost believe him for a second. But then I realize that that could never possibly happen to someone like me.

"You're lying," I retort.

He laughs lightly. "You don't have to believe me. But you're not seeing my face, no matter how much it irritates you."

His arrogance infuriates me – and he knows it.

"Do you let your pack see you?" I ask.

A nod is his only response. He opens my door and motions for me to go inside as if I'm annoying him as much as he's annoying me.

"You should sleep, Mara," he mutters.

Sighing, I enter my room, closing the door behind me. I lied when I said I knew I couldn't get out. I will try. I will go on trying until the day I die.

Chapter Six

I sit on the edge of my bed for what feels like hours, unable to sleep. I put it down to the combination of the heat in my room and the nerves still bubbling in my stomach. Saying yes to Kace like that will forever be a terrible memory burned into my mind. The photos of my family around the room are doing my head in. Why can't I get them out of my mind?

I stand up and pace about for a few moments. I have a naturally curious nature and the need to get out of this room right now is pressing – just to explore, not necessarily to attempt some sort of escape, because I know I'll only fail at that. Though if an opportunity presents itself...

Building up some semblance of courage, I try the door. To my surprise, it swings open and I realize no one has locked it. I peer out, looking down the hallway. I expect to see Coen there, but the place is deserted. I feel a wicked smile hover on my lips. Time to make my move.

I stalk down the hallway, keeping my footsteps as light as possible. It would be a real disappointment to be discovered before I've found anything out. What surprises me most though is that the place is so still, with no sign of life anywhere. It makes me nervous, like I am walking into some sort of trap.

I pad down some stairs, checking left and right. The coast is clear and I choose to go right. My route leads me into darkness, the lights getting dimmer the further I go. The feeling is eerie.

The fact that I could be caught at any moment brings me a feeling of exhilaration. I've never stepped out of line in my life and this is the first risk I have ever dared take.

I descend two more flights of stairs. The first one is wooden and clean and I am in danger of slipping with every step. The next flight of stairs has one light illuminating it and the steps are stone.

I know I should stop now and retrace my steps, go back to my room and sleep, but curiosity pulls me along like a dog on a leash. The further I go the more I want to go on.

I pause. A strange sound comes up from below, making me shiver with fright. The sound can only be described as a loud banging noise, like metal on metal. It raises goosebumps on my skin and makes my blood run cold.

I have to investigate, or else I'll be spending all night in my room wondering what it was.

Moving slower now, down the steps and with a lot more caution, I make my way toward the sound. It gets louder as I go further down. By the time I'm at the foot of the stairs, the sound is threatening to burst my eardrums.

Down here the temperature is a lot higher and I can feel sweat on my forehead. I pull my hair off my face and keep moving. I still have no idea what I'm about to find down here. A normal person might turn back at this point but I have nothing to lose so I keep going.

I pass several doors, checking each room as I go by, and work out that the sound is coming from the end of the hallway I'm in. I find myself before a partially opened door and hear someone moving about inside, banging things around. I don't know what I might find, and I know I could be risking my life going on. If that's the case, I tell myself, then at least I'll be put out of the misery of being kept prisoner here.

Biting my lip, I creep closer, on tiptoe. Praying I don't get caught, I peer round the edge of my door and gasp at what I see.

A man. Naked. Well, nearly naked.

My eyes start at his feet, then follow up his black trousers, and to his bare back. Intricate lines of ink adorn the tanned muscles on his back, bathed in a light sheen of sweat. My gaze dances up his muscular arms, which wield a large steel mallet of some sort. I even take in the dark mess of midnight hair upon his head.

The stranger swings the mallet down onto something metal with a crash, making me jump. I want to see what he's doing and, as he has his back to me, I slip inside the room. I know it's stupid but I can't stop myself.

Now I see that the walls are covered with weapons. There are swords, daggers, all manner of other blades, all of them shining and deadly. I definitely shouldn't be here. This man's probably a psychopath who would kill me if he found me in here. I'm tempted for a second to grab one of the weapons to use against him but, again, I know I don't have the guts to do it. And it's against my religion. I find myself wishing my parents had at least taught me some self-defense.

I turn for the door, but my foot catches on something – a tool box of some sort or maybe an uneven bit of flooring – and over I go. I scramble to my feet but I'm too slow to make a clean getaway.

"Stop right there!" the man yells.

I jump in terror. The voice sounds instantly familiar, and it chills my heart. I pause, the door and safety only inches away. Slowly, I turn on my heels, holding my hands up as if he's pointing a gun at me.

My gaze is held by a pair of obsidian black eyes. They are so dark I see my horrified reflection within the irises. They stare at me from below a thick layer of hair hanging over his forehead. He looks at me through the scraggly strands, sizing me up.

His face is something I can't describe in words. I want to touch it, to feel every contour of the supple skin, but I keep my trembling fingers at my side. I can't stop looking at him, drinking in every detail of his defined abdomen in awe.

What really gets my attention, however, is the tip of the sword he is holding so close to my face.

"Mara," he whispers, his voice hoarse.

And I know for sure who it is... I can hardly breathe as the shock consumes me. I know exactly who this unfairly attractive man is.

33

"Kaden."

His jaw tightens – a well-shaped jaw, I can't help noticing – as he tosses the sword aside with a clatter onto his workbench. I remain stock still, unable to take my eyes off him.

To say his appearance is not what I expected is an understatement. I had assumed he hid his face from me in shame, just as he was, or should be, ashamed of his whole life and want to conceal it from me. I expected him to be ugly, maybe even disfigured.

I couldn't have been further from the truth.

"You shouldn't be down here," he mutters.

I struggle to tear my eyes away from his and finally manage to divert my gaze to the floor. I am conscious that I probably look ridiculous to him, padding about the lair of the Vengeance Pack in just a light nightdress.

He sighs and grabs a cloth from the bench to wipe his forehead.

I lick my lips and, looking up, finally find my voice. "What are you doing in here?"

His gaze follows mine to the wall of weapons.

"It's a hobby of mine. Turning something as horrifying as a weapon into a piece of art," he tells me. His tone is grudging, but I sense the pride in his voice. This is what really matters to him. I try to do my best not to surrender to my utter vulnerability.

"Deadly art," I mutter under my breath.

Kaden stares at me then sweeps up his leather gloves and slips them over his hands, without once taking his eyes off me. I can't stress how scared I am of the devilishly handsome man standing in front of me. Especially with all these cruel blades within easy reach.

"You shouldn't be down here. I should have you bent over the side of my bed right now for your behavior," he growls, wringing his hands.

My heart skips a beat at his words.

Then he holds his hand out to me. "Too bad that's my brother's job."

At the same time as being sickened by his words, I'm relieved that he isn't threatening my life or something. I've risked it enough, having already dangled it in front of him and all his weapons.

I take his hand and I hope he doesn't notice how I'm shaking. The feel of the leather between my fingers is unnerving.

"Why do you never touch me?" I blurt out as we leave the room. I regret the question almost as soon as I've asked it and I bite my lip.

He gives me a veiled look. "We *are* touching," he says, squeezing my hand.

Suddenly bold, I roll my eyes. "I meant, what is it with the gloves? Why won't you touch my skin?"

He grunts. "Why? Craving my touch?"

I shake my head, and he barks a short laugh as we start to climb the stairs.

"I'm just curious," I tell him honestly. And it's true. All of a sudden, I don't regret my curiosity. Look where it's gotten me. That makes me think for a second – would Kaden ever have shown me his face if I hadn't pried?

"Curiosity brings punishment," he growls darkly.

I feel my eyes widen. "Punishment?" I squeak. He *can't* seriously be thinking of punishing me for this? Then again, I remind myself, he is the Alpha of the Vengeance Pack...

I repeat my question several times but he doesn't answer me until we are on the top floor, nearing my bedroom. In fact, he seems completely oblivious to anything I say until I am standing before my bedroom door.

"But seriously, why can't you touch me?" I ask, exasperated. I don't understand why Coen freely took his gloves off and touched me, yet Kaden won't.

"Trust me, if I touch you, you will be attracted to me," he says quietly.

Is he serious?

35

"That's what you said about your face, but I've seen it now and don't feel a thing," I tell him roundly. I can't tell if I'm lying or not. I do know I could stare at him for a very long time and not get bored.

He suddenly lurches forward, grabs my arm, and pushes me up against the wall, one hand holding my wrists above my head. The other pushes my hip against the wall, so no inch of his skin touches mine.

"Don't play me, Mara! Not when I'm seriously considering either slitting your throat or ripping your clothes off," he hisses. His lips are so close to mine, I feel his breath on my skin.

I don't say a word, but I fancy my harsh breathing is giving him all the response he needs.

He lets go of me and pushes me into my room. I stumble backward, trying to regain focus.

"Punishment starts tomorrow," he mutters, before closing the door on my stunned face.

Chapter Seven

"I'm never going to find my mate now," I complain, digging the seeds out of a slice of watermelon.

Kace looks up from his breakfast with surprise. It's the first time I've spoken since I walked into the dining room. He sets his coffee mug down and glares at me.

"Mates don't exist," he answers.

I sigh. We don't break eye contact as I cut a chunk of watermelon and shove it in my mouth. He doesn't say a word as I chew. Vengeance Pack members don't believe in the Moon Goddess like the Purity Pack does, which means they don't believe in mates either.

Mates is the one thing I do believe in. My parents are mates, and their relationship is one I would love to have one day.

"Yes, they do exist," I inform him, once I've swallowed the fruit.

He coughs and leans back in his chair. Coen is in the other room, eating his breakfast with the other guards. "How can you be so sure?" he asks. He sounds curious, which takes me by surprise.

I push my plate away. "True love exists..."

"True love is a joke."

"Just because your true love tried to kill you doesn't mean it doesn't exist," I snap.

He flinches, narrowing his eyes. I probably shouldn't have said that. Sometimes I wish I had a roll of duct tape stuck in my belt always, so I can keep my mouth shut when I need to. He stands, his facial muscles taut. I try hard not to appear intimidated.

"At least I don't believe in some bitch who lives in the sky!" he spits.

Suddenly I don't regret anything I have ever said to him.

"The Moon Goddess will have heard that," I retort viciously. "She will punish you."

Kace raises his eyebrows. "Oh, kinky."

I push my chair back and stand, confronting him. I try to stare him down, conjuring up as much hate in my glare as possible. He only smiles in response.

"One day, Kace, I'm going to hurt you!" I swear.

He shakes his head in wonder.

I feel a hand on my arm. I spin around to find Coen looking down at me with gentle but warning eyes. He is the only one of them I feel I can trust, or at least hope to. If I don't like something, he understands and doesn't push me too far. For someone living in the Vengeance Pack, he is so... normal.

"Take her away," Kace orders.

Against my will, Coen leads me from the room. I hate being told what to do and the power everyone seems to have over me here disgusts me. He releases me as soon as we are out in the hallway and lets me brush myself off. He even has the courtesy to allow me to catch my breath before I punch someone. This is how I know I'm mad... because I know I'd never actually resort to violence.

"Kaden wants to see you," he says after a few minutes' silence.

I groan. Kaden is the last person I want to see right now, but after last night I have no choice but to follow every command he gives.

I follow Coen through the maze that is the den of the Vengeance Pack, much of which remains unfamiliar to me. This place will be my home for the rest of my life, but I still don't know the ins and outs of it yet. It's probably because every hall I walk through looks the same as all the others. I assume Kaden will never really let me get used to it. He likes his mind games and any chance I get to escape seems fated to be stolen by him.

I'm led into a small room with a concrete floor. Coen closes the door behind me instead of following me in. Deprived of his company, I suddenly become nervous.

There's a seat in the middle of the room so I go and sit on it. It takes twelve minutes – I count the seconds in my head – before Kaden wanders in, as casual as you like.

He's wearing his hood again, which makes me narrow my eyes. *Don't tell me he's going to ignore the fact that I saw his face last night! It's something I can't ever forget, no matter what tricks he tries to pull.*

"Good morning, Mara," he says softly, coming to stand in front of me.

"You're looking good today," I mutter sarcastically.

He sighs, pausing before he flips the hood back so I can see his face. For a second, I'm distracted once again by his attractiveness. I hate that. I try to focus on his cold, black eyes.

"So, what am I doing here?"

Kaden circles me. "You did something very bad last night." He drags a gloved finger across my shoulder, over the back of my neck and to my other shoulder.

I shiver in response but stay quiet rather than test my luck with a snarky response.

"I like games," he tells me.

"I'm aware," I mutter. How could I not be when he's been playing games with me since the day I've come here?

He comes to a stop in front of me once more and looks down at me like I'm his prey.

"I have a riddle for you."

Great.

"If you answer the riddle correctly, I'll excuse you from further punishment." The leering smile on his face is making my stomach turn queasily.

"And if I get it wrong?"

He laughs. It's a mean, almost maniacal sound that sends shivers down my spine.

"That's a surprise," he informs me.

I frown. For a start, I don't like surprises. And I like riddles even less. In class, I was never one of those girls who could answer those things. And I wasn't under the kind of pressure I am right now.

Kaden stoops down beside me, and I hold my breath. I'm tempted to beg him to choose something else, but I don't want to give him even that satisfaction.

"This will be easy," he tells me.

I nod slowly.

"If it's information you seek, come and see me," he begins. "If it's pairs of letters you need, I have consecutively three," he finishes.

I tilt my head and exhale. "That doesn't make sense," I mutter, my mind churning. *How does this relate to anything?*

His lips curl. He thinks he's stumped me. "You have ten seconds. Ten…"

"Wait!"

"Nine."

"I need more time!"

"Eight."

I slap my hand against my forehead. He's not going to stop.

"Seven."

Consecutive paired letters… what could that possibly mean?

"Six."

"Give me some more time!" I beg.

He shakes his head. The triumphant look on his face is sickening.

"Five."

I cover my ears so I don't have to hear his voice as I watch him count down past five. The sinking feeling in my stomach is unbearable. Jumping off a bridge right now seems better than whatever fate Kaden has in store for me.

"One," he finishes, when I take my hands off his ears.

We sit in silence for few moments, while I brace myself.

Kaden just stares at me with glistening eyes. "The answer?"

I shake my head helplessly.

"A bookkeeper," he tells me softly.

Of course.

While I sit there and think what an idiot I am, Kaden goes to the door and opens it. I look up as someone comes in.

Milly. Looking miserable and frightened – the last girl Kaden kidnapped before me. I know instantly it's her from her platinum blonde hair and slender figure. She was the girl every boy wanted back home, despite their belief in mates. Right now though she is a picture of terror and ill-health. She must have been here for weeks, and who knows how Kaden has treated her…

A guard I don't recognize pushes her in, her hands tied behind her back. She looks malnourished and is dressed practically in rags. She stares at me as she staggers in. Her eyes seem dull and there are dark circles under them. She looks terrible.

Kaden leads her to me, smiling at the disbelief in my eyes.

"Mara," she stammers, "what are you doing here?" Her voice is scratchy, like she hasn't used it in a long time. She looks genuinely saddened by the fact that I'm here as well as her, although I'm sure I look in much better condition. I've been treated like royalty in comparison. I can't tell her I am marrying the Alpha's brother…

I go to speak, but Kaden cuts me off.

"She had the opportunity to save you," he tells Milly.

Her eyes widen, a glimmer of hope glowing in them.

My heart sinks.

"But unfortunately, she failed," Kaden continues smoothly, the smile on his face etching itself into my mind forever.

Milly frowns in confusion, looking at me for back-up. If I had the opportunity to get one of us out of here, I would pick her.

The guard who brought her steps into the room behind her. Milly turns and begins to panic.

"What's happening?"

41

"I'd like you to think about Mara when you're in your cell," Kaden says.

Despite my protest, the guard grabs Milly and begins to drag her from the room. I run forward, hoping to protect her innocence from these monsters. I deserve this, not her!

Kaden grabs my waist and pulls me back. I punch at him angrily and try to prise his fingers loose, but I can't get a grip on his leather gloves. How I hate those things.

"Let me go!" I yelp, watching the door close and Milly disappear from my sight.

Kaden holds me back, no matter how hard I struggle.

"Mara, calm down."

"What are you going to do to her? She's innocent – unlike you!" I yell. I'm hardly listening to the sounds coming from my mouth.

"Listen–"

"You listen! You're a disgusting person! You won't even touch a girl, yet you allow an animal like that to do whatever he likes to her!" I scream at him. I'm only just registering the tears streaming down my cheeks, as I think of what might be happening to Milly. It makes me want to throw my breakfast up on the floor.

"You're angry. Good," Kaden responds quietly. "Take that anger and turn it into vengeance," he murmurs in my ear.

I push at his chest, and this time he lets me go. I stumble back, wiping the tears from my cheeks. He wants me to be like him! I'm not like him! I never will be like him!

"That's what you want? Me to be like you?" I question, my voice wavering.

He sighs. "No, not like me. I want to help you to belong, that's all."

I fall to my knees and sob into my hands. I can't describe my hate for Kaden. He's a monster.

And he wants to turn me into one too.

Well, he can try beating me into submission, but I won't do it. For the sake of girls like Milly, I can't give up.

Chapter Eight

Kaden left the pack to their own devices the same day as my punishment, and he hasn't reappeared for days now. I've been stuck in my room the entire time, reading the odd book Coen brings me. This entertains me for about half the day before the ink blurs before my eyes and I have to set it down.

I meet Kace three times a day for meals. He remains silent despite my questions. I ask him what he does all day. I am ignored. I ask him when we are supposed to be getting married. Ignored again. I ask him where Kaden is. Ignored.

These past few days have been so boring, I've resorted to scraping patterns into the wallpaper with my fingernail, creating memories of home on the soft blue wall. Sometimes I pray. For my home. For my family. For freedom.

Other times I just cry. For Milly. For myself.

I'm entertaining myself by braiding my hair when Coen opens the door. I have just finished a French plait, using an elastic band I found under my bed to keep it together.

He looks as magnificent as ever, in a cloak that reaches his feet. It whispers around his legs when he walks. He doesn't have his sheathed sword today, which makes me slightly apprehensive. Never would I have thought the lack of a sword would worry me.

"Good afternoon," he greets me.

I smile back at him, glad to have contact with someone else. "Come in."

He takes in a deep breath and looks torn. I realize that he's not meant to come into my room. Obviously, some strict new orders have been put in place without me knowing.

He surprises me, however, by seeming to come to a decision and walking right on in. Instead of sitting beside me on my bed, he stands awkwardly in the middle of the room.

"I have come to keep you company. Even though I'm not a female–"

"Well, thank you, Coen," I say honestly.

He smiles slightly. He never smiles with his teeth, I notice.

"Come and sit," I say, patting the spot beside me on the bed.

He stares at it as if it's a dragon about to breathe fire on him if he gets too close.

I tilt my head in confusion.

"Sitting on an engaged lady's bed is unforgivable," he tells me. He looks down at his feet, but I still catch the blush that creeps onto his cheeks. Of course, I shouldn't have been so forward. If Kace or Kaden found out, he might lose his job, or even worse…

I decide to slip down onto the floor, crossing my legs over. Coen chuckles slightly at my way of meeting in the middle, and sits down in front of me.

"Do you believe in mates?" I ask him, after a few moments have passed in silence. My words seem to have a great effect on him. It's as if a huge burden has settled on his shoulders, weighing him down.

Did I say something wrong?

"I do," he tells me.

This surprises me. From what Kace has said, it doesn't seem like Vengeance Pack members are accustomed to believe in mates, or even true love for that matter.

I decide to go for it. "Do *you* have one?"

He nods slowly, his eyes glazing over. He stares into space for a while, delving back into memories I'm not aware of. I stay silent, watching him curiously. There is always a specific look in someone's eye when they have known love and lost it. In Coen's case, it is written all over his face.

"I do."

He sounds so sad, it makes my heart ache. Mates should bring you joy and happiness. Maybe Kaden forbids him from being with her?

"She rejected me," he explains before I can ask.

I cringe. How stupid could I be to bring this subject up when it's obviously something he doesn't want to talk about. Being rejected by your mate is a terrible experience that no one should have to go through. I feel heartsick for him.

"I'm so sorry–"

"Don't be. She found someone else, and that's it," he says, a look of defeat in his eyes. He suddenly looks pale and sick.

I shake my head. "I don't understand. Whoever it was, if she was in love with, you she should have lost the ability to be interested in any other man." That is what I have been taught. Those were the words of Alpha Rylan.

He shifts uncomfortably. "She was already in love. There was nothing I could do."

"Can I know her name?"

"Althea."

"Of the Power Pack?"

"Yes."

His words make me sad. This is a horrible fate.

"You know, it just means the Moon Goddess wants you with someone else," I tell him, trying to give him some hope in the dark. "Maybe someone who lost their mate like you did."

Coen stares at me and I can see he's never considered this before. He grabs my hand and even manages a smile.

"Thank you, Mara. You're the only one who understands," he says warmly.

His words depress me, however, when I consider my own situation. I'll never find my mate in this loveless society – not while I remain confined in this pack by that killer Kaden.

We sit in silence for a while.

"You'll find someone too," he says gently.

Our eyes meet. His are so warm, compared to Kaden's, but I shake my head.

"Perhaps. But not with one of the Vengeance Pack."

He squeezes my hand. His comfort is helping right now, but it isn't filling the dark hole that seems to have formed in my heart.

"It just isn't fair. You don't deserve to be here," he says softly.

This makes me sigh. He's right. I didn't do anything to deserve this fate. I look up and I can almost see the wheels turning in Coen's head, like he's thinking how to get me out of this.

And he is.

"I could help you escape," he says suddenly.

I give him a look. *Is he being serious?* His eyes are alight with excitement. He jumps to his feet, not letting my hand go so I'm forced to stand up with him.

"The wall!" he says, the smile on his face like no other.

I tilt my head. "What wall?"

"The wall that keeps the Pack inside. I know a way out. Kaden uses it, and doesn't believe I know the passcode!"

My heart leaps. If this is true then I may have a means of getting back to my family. Suddenly I am as excited as he is, hope finally shining at the end of the tunnel I thought had been filled in. I could even find help for Milly.

"Are you sure about this?"

"Yes. We should go now, before Kaden gets back. I am expected to take you to dinner," Coen says hurriedly.

I nod. If Kaden finds me trying to escape, I'm likely to get in the biggest kind of trouble. But if he finds Coen aiding me in my escape, then he might kill him.

My fingers still entwined with Coen's, I let him lead me through the door. He doesn't seem to be worrying about there being any other guards about, as if he knows the coast will be clear. This makes me wonder if they are with Kaden – and where that might be.

"The Highway's on the other side of the wall," Coen explains. "You should be able to flag someone down to take you back to your pack."

The Highway. It's the only part of this world co-owned by all the packs. No one can claim it as their own; it is open for everyone to use, whenever they choose. Someone would be sure to take me back to the Purity Pack.

Coen leads me through a maze of halls I've never seen before. This disorientates me, but the thought of going home gives me a sense of purpose I have never felt before.

We make it into daylight soon enough. I sigh with relief, feeling the sun on my face. I haven't been outside in so long. I even take the time to notice that the grounds we pass through are neatly tended. Kaden must hire someone to garden for him, since I can't see him getting his hands dirty in that way.

"This way," Coen prompts, tugging my hand. He's anxious to get me out of here.

The wall is massive. I've never noticed it before because back home we never talk much about the Vengeance Pack and their quarter. It seems to go on forever. Coen leads me across the grass, going as quickly as possible.

"Where is this door?" I ask him. I'm examining the wall ahead of us but can't see a door handle or button of any sort.

Coen laughs lightly. "Right here," he says.

He presses several bricks in turn. I realize they have numbers scrawled on them and that he is pressing them in a given sequence. I watch in amazement as the first brick falls backward and disappears into the wall. Suddenly, other bricks start falling back, away from my view. Then I see that they are not falling but are being retracted by mechanical arms, which pull them back to create a space through which we can pass.

And I can see the outside world beyond.

I start forward, but Coen grabs my arm. "Wait."

"Are you coming?" I ask him.

His face falls, and he shakes his head solemnly. "I can't. I must stay and serve Kaden. It is my job. And anyway, I wouldn't survive out there. Not without a pack. I have a terrible memory," he tells me. He lets go of my hand, and it falls heavily to my side. I can't believe what he's saying. I can't let him stay here with that monster Kaden.

"What if Kaden finds out you helped me escape?" I ask.

Coen's mouth tightens. "He won't." He pushes me toward the exit. "Now go, before it is too late."

I lean forward and wrap my arms around Coen's shoulders. He hugs me back, although a little apprehensively.

"Thank you," I whisper. A feeling of loss fills my heart, but I try to push it away. Coen wants to stay here. He was born here and, like he said, he must serve Kaden as he promised. I know now that I don't have the time to stay and convince him otherwise.

"I'll see you again, Mara."

The grass brushes across my legs as I clamber through the wall and set off at a run toward The Highway. There are quite a few cars on the road, as automobiles have increased in number since the Wisdom Pack brought them into fashion. I'd never imagined these death traps might one day be the key to saving my life.

When I make it to the side of the road, however, no one stops. I wave my arms above my head, hoping someone will see me and offer me a lift.

But no one does.

Some of the drivers look at me, it's true, but none of them stop. Don't they see how desperate I am to get out of here?

Suddenly a black truck-like vehicle indicates to the left and pulls over to the side of the road. I let out a deep breath, hugely grateful that *finally,* someone has turned up to the rescue. I'm sobbing with relief as I reach them.

The window is wound down and I stick my head to thank the driver. Then my heart plummets to my feet.

It's Kaden.

Chapter Nine

"Well, what do we have here?"

Kaden sits smugly in his seat, staring at me through the open window. He looks as if he's just won the biggest prize in the lottery by stealing someone else's ticket.

I take a moment to assess the situation.

I could run. I want to run. If I head off down the road, I won't get more than a hundred feet before he catches up. If I go back across the grass I'll be faced with the Vengeance Pack wall, where he can easily corner me. If I get in the car, I'll die. If I dash across to the other side of the road, I could make it to the woods, where I *may* have a chance of getting away.

But I need to make sure he doesn't expect it.

"What are you doing here?" I ask, trying to gain myself more time to think.

"I was about to ask you the same thing," he muses. His lips crease in a smile that can only be described as evil. He is evil. And he knows it.

"Leaving," I state defiantly.

His expression turns to one of shock, like he can't believe I'm actually sticking up to him. He probably expects me to run. That is what I want him to think – that I'm truly standing up to him, rather than plotting my escape.

Then he grins. "I see. Without my permission?"

I stare. His *permission*?

"Does your husband know?"

"We aren't married yet."

He suddenly leans over the passenger seat and pops the door open. It's like an invitation. Cool air from the air conditioning blows onto my legs, enticing me with icy fingers.

"Yet," he says, tasting the words on his tongue.

Does he seriously think I'm going to hop into his car and ride off into the sunset with him? If so, he's seriously lost it, because that's the last thing I'm planning on doing.

"Great," he tells me. "That means you're mine for today. We have a lot to discuss..."

"Discuss? I'm not interested in another one of your games," I counter.

He sighs deeply, looking ahead of him. Cars whizz past, hardly noticing what is going on here at the side of the road.

"Games are fun," is all he says.

"Funnily enough, I don't find your punishment fun at all."

"Get in the car and I'll show you how much fun my punishments can be," he says, with a devilishly handsome smile on his face. I grit my teeth in disgust.

Then an idea pops into my head. "I will, on one condition."

He narrows his eyes at me. I can tell he is curious. A condition is something he can manipulate; I can tell that's what he's thinking. But this is something he could never manipulate...

"Give me a drink bottle."

He frowns. He has no idea what is swimming around in my mind right now.

"You want water?"

"Yes, please."

He grunts. "You're wasting my gas."

"And I will continue to until you give me what I want."

"I could walk out of this car and ruin your ass in front of everyone on this road right now," he says.

A low growl of anger surfaces in my throat.

"But since I'm enjoying your antics, I will give you what you want." He leans over to his cup holder, which contains a half empty bottle of water. He tosses it to me and I manage to catch it.

I screw the lid open and take a swig. He's watching me carefully, so I pretend that's all I've been wanting this whole time. Just a drink of water.

I slip into the car, but don't close the door after me. The leather of the seats clings to my warm skin as I sit down. Kaden watches me with caution.

Taking him by surprise, I throw the water into his face. Then, without staying to see his reaction, I'm out the door and sprinting across the road, dodging the traffic and praying I come out of this alive.

"I'm going to kill you!" I hear him shout from behind me.

Okay, so I may not live through this...

My throat starts to burn, as well as my thighs, as I rush through the undergrowth on the far side of The Highway. I'm unfit, but I'm running on adrenaline. I push through the grass, the edge of the woods in sight. If I can reach it I can find a tree to climb and wait it out till Kaden gives up.

I twist my head around to see if Kaden is coming after me. I don't see him. I'm not that surprised – he probably doesn't want to cause a scene in public.

I make it to the woods and feel some degree of relief. Despite my lack of local knowledge and my unfit condition, I weave quickly through the trees. Luckily for me, it's much cooler under the leaves and there's a lot of cover. My heart is still pounding furiously in my chest, however.

When I turn again to look over my shoulder I still don't see Kaden behind me. Have I lost him?

I twist around a tree, then press my back against it and close my eyes. All I can hear is the sound of my panting as I attempt to regain my composure. If I don't calm down, he's going to hear me.

I hold my breath for a moment, listening for footsteps. Nothing.

"Mara?" I hear his voice say. It's coming from somewhere to my left and it seems a good distance away, yet still too close for my liking. I let my breath out slowly. I need to climb one of these trees and hide.

"You know how I like games?" I hear him calling.

I try to block out his voice. He knows I'm in these woods somewhere, but hopefully he can't work out where exactly.

I glance up, but can see no bough available to grab and hoist myself up on. I say a few words no Purity Pack member should utter, even under their breath.

"Hide and seek happens to be my favorite," Kaden calls. He sounds closer this time.

I tread quietly toward the next tree. It too lacks any branches I can reach. Another curse.

"I'm not going to put a bet on it, but I think I'm going to win this game," I hear him taunting me, sounding much closer now. "Which means..."

He breaks off, and suddenly the world goes silent. Five seconds, ten seconds... It's as if the birds stop singing, and I can hear my own heartbeat.

"You owe me."

A pair of gloved hands grab me round my waist, making me scream.

"Let me go!" I yell, struggling in his arms. I can feel his breath hot against my neck. He's probably smiling that sick smile of his.

"I've let you have your fun," he mumbles in my ear. He twists me around and presses me firmly against the tree.

I feel as if the breath has been knocked out of me and am unable to move.

His handsome face is so close to mine, I can see every curve and line of it. His skin looks so smooth, I want to touch it, want to feel it under my fingertips for the first time.

Seeing a monster up close makes it impossible to deny it's real.

He presses me more firmly against the tree, but it doesn't hurt. I'm distracted by Kaden's proximity and the look he's giving me. For a second, I think I get a glimpse of a soul in his eyes.

He leans so I can feel the energy between us. It seems to be drawing us closer, his lips tantalizingly near. I am conscious of his hips pressed against mine, ensuring I have no chance of escape. And, weirdly, just for a moment, I don't mind.

I'd only have to move an inch to kiss the most infamous killer in werewolf history.

His eyes are on my lips, and I wonder if he feels the heat between us as much as I do. It's warming my face, my whole body.

I fancy I detect an internal fight going on behind his eyes. It's like I can see devils dancing on his shoulders, arguing with him over what is wrong and what is right. I'm not allowed devils, however, being a Purity Pack girl, which allows me to recover myself before he can and to push him firmly away.

He stumbles backward and I take the opportunity to start running again. Except my legs are weak after what just happened – something that I don't understand.

The pull between us was like nothing I have ever experienced. We didn't have to touch for me to feel the most pleasure I have ever had.

It doesn't take more than a few long strides for Kaden to reach me and to pull me back in anger.

"No one escapes me a second time!" he grates. Despite my struggles, he keeps a strong grip on me. I'm not getting out of this again.

"Kaden, please–"

"Yes, keeping saying my name like that. I love it when they struggle," he taunts.

I shake my head furiously.

Suddenly, I feel his fingers against my neck and I realize what he's doing. But it's too late for me to do anything before I black out.

Chapter Ten

A sudden surge of fear awakens me. My eyes flutter open. The position I am in is all too familiar. I'm on a chair. Tied up.

I roll my head around and hear my neck click in protest. How long have I been out? It takes me a moment to get my bearings, but when I do, I realize someone is sitting right in front of me.

Kaden.

He's on a chair, just inches away. His hands are clasped together and he's staring at me. I can't work out what his expression means. It's as though he has a switch and can turn off his emotions whenever he wants. His hair is still wet from being splashed by the water. It sticks to his forehead, some strands hanging down over his eyes. His jaw is clenched tightly. My heart sinks as I realize the position I'm in.

"Do you have any idea how mad I am at you right now?"

I swallow. He'll have some form of punishment in mind, of that I'm sure.

"I don't know what you expect from me," I mutter.

He runs a hand down his face. There's angst in his frown, etched deep between the faint lines around his eyes, in the way he bites the edge of his lip.

"I need to tell you the *real* reason why you're needed," he confides.

I shudder. There can't be many things worse than having to marry Kaden's brother, and if there are I don't want to know about them.

"I don't understand…"

"You marrying Kace is just a ploy to get your family off our backs, to stop them from finding out why you're really here." His voice seems almost reluctant, like he wishes he didn't have to tell me about his plan. "I want you to do something for us."

I don't like the way this is headed.

"What?"

"Someone, not so long ago, betrayed my brother," he tells me solemnly. He looks into my eyes, daring me to question it.

"And...?"

"Her name is Althea. I want you to deal with her."

My heart sinks to my feet. Coen's mate? Does he mean he wants me to kill Coen's mate? "I can't hurt her... she's Coen's mate," I blurt out.

Kaden shakes his head. "No. She is not to die."

That's something, at least. But I can't help wondering how this Althea girl dug herself a hole so deep. She rejected Coen, but he seems like he might get over it now. At least I think he will. But if she tried to kill Kace or something...

"What do you want me to do then?" I ask apprehensively.

Kaden rubs his hands together. He looks ill at ease.

"Althea is having the child of Alpha Landon of the Power Pack."

I hesitate. "So?"

"I think you can guess..." His voice trails off.

A lump forms in my throat, so big I almost choke. He can't seriously mean what I think he means.

"You want me to kill it?" My heart feels numb. The thought of killing a child makes me want to cry, or throw up, but I can't. I won't.

Kaden purses his lips. "It's the only–"

"This is Kace's idea, isn't it?" I say, rising to my feet. "And you don't care, because that's what Vengeance Pack members are like."

Kaden stands up, avoiding my eyes. "It needs to be done."

I stare at him in utter disbelief. "Curing cancer *needs* to be done, not this!"

55

"That baby is a product of lies and hatred."

"You're a product of lies and hatred!" I snap back, folding my arms over my chest.

Kaden takes a step toward me but I match it going backward. I don't want him anywhere near me.

"I don't think you understand how important this mission is," he murmurs.

My teeth are clenched so hard my jaw begins to ache. How can he stand there and say these things with that impassive look on his face?

"I don't think you understand how I'm not going to do it."

Kaden takes a deep breath in. "I knew you would do this."

I wait for him to go on.

"I don't want to keep threatening your family, Mara. Do you want me to kill Milly? I have her in a holding facility, and I'm not afraid to do so, if you don't comply."

I'm so angry now I can barely restrain myself from attacking him.

His gloved hands reach toward me and fasten on my biceps. Instead of tossing me away like a pathetic doll like last time, he holds me firmly in his grasp.

"She will be set free, along with you, if you do this," he bargains.

I look up at him, trying to ignore the physical contact between us. "You'll free me?" I ask in disbelief. "And Milly?"

He nods slowly.

I feel a tear roll down my cheek. "Tell me what I have to do."

***

That night, I wonder if I have made a huge mistake, making Kaden think I'll go along with him. I'm not going to do it, of course. He may think I have agreed, but he is insane if he thinks I would ever even consider doing something so despicable.

I sit up and swing my legs out of bed. The air is much cooler tonight and it soothes my bare legs and arms as I venture out of my room.

Last time I did this, it resulted in punishment. But I can't stay in that box and think about how I agreed to murder an unborn child. So, an adventure of sorts it is. And by adventure, I mean wandering around the den, looking for inspiration and avoiding trouble if I can.

I pad down the corridor, my fingers brushing against the wall, going in a different direction to last time. The rooms I pass through are almost bare and there seems to be no one about.

I emerge into a large foyer and see a set of stairs leading up to the floor above. They are covered in maroon and gold carpet. A rope is clipped to either side of the banisters, a subtle way of saying "keep out".

I consider it for a moment. Okay, maybe avoiding trouble just isn't something I do.

I slip under the rope and feel a surge of excitement run through my body. I take the stairs two steps at a time.

At the top I have a choice of three corridors. I settle on the middle corridor. As I walk down it, I can't help wondering where Kaden's sleeping quarters are. The thought only pops into my head because this area seems to have that same soft scent that he does.

"I know."

A voice coming from a room somewhere ahead of me makes me freeze. It's familiar, but it's not Kaden's. I place one hand on the wall to brace myself. My heart is beating wildly in my chest.

"Do you though? This is important."

I recognize Kaden's voice. I'd know that huskiness anywhere.

"I still can't seem to grasp why I *have* to though," says the first voice.

I go further down the corridor toward the voices. The sound of hands slamming against a hard surface makes my heart skip a beat, but I keep going.

"Because I'm still your Alpha, Kace! And you have to listen to me."

So it's Kace who's with him. Hmm. What are they talking about?

"You may be my Alpha, but she will be *my* wife very soon."

My eyes widen. I'm almost at the room they're in now. The door leading into it is partially open and I go as close as I dare. This is surely going to get me killed, I warn myself, but I push the thought away.

"Do you know what she is to me?" I hear Kaden say.

I bite my lip.

"You always told me that it's business before love," Kace retorts.

Staying as low as possible, I peek cautiously round the door. I can only see a small sliver of the room. They are in an office, Kaden standing behind a desk. Kace is out of my sightline.

Kaden looks glorious, I hate to admit. The shirt he wears is a white button-up, but it's loose, showing his torso. I try not to stare too long at the muscles and tattoos that are exposed. I notice he looks stressed and his dark hair is tousled from him running his hands through it.

"Do you know how hard it is?" he asks. His voice is strained. This is the first time I've witnessed emotions from him that I'm sure are real. I can see in his eyes how desperate he is. It tugs at my heart a little.

"You killed my real mate!" Kace snaps.

If only I could see his face too – he sounds so angry, so hurt and torn.

Kace's words make me pause. *Kaden killed his mate?* I thought they didn't believe in mates...

"You wouldn't know what hurt feels like, Kaden."

Chapter Eleven

I sit silently, staring out the window. Coen sits in the driver's seat, going steadily as if he too is in no rush to arrive where we are going. I'm grateful for that.

I can't believe this is happening. Kaden has ordered me to be escorted to the Power Pack, for me to start my mission. If you can even call it that... missions are supposed to be done by spies, professionals.

"How much longer?" I ask, breaking the silence that settled between us hours ago. We neighbor the Power Pack, yet it's still a long way. I feel my legs begin to cramp from sitting in the same position for so long.

"Not long," he murmurs.

Not long? What does that mean?

Coen has been awfully silent all this time. It's unnerving... the reason seems obvious, but I decide to investigate further.

"What do you think about this mission?" I demand. The word mission tastes sour in my mouth. What kind of mission involves killing an unborn child? Maybe I should ask a Discipline Pack member, since they are usually the only ones who do this sort of thing.

Coen's expression darkens and his fingers tighten on the steering wheel. The sigh that comes out of his mouth evokes extreme depression rather than anger. I can only imagine how he is feeling right now.

"It doesn't matter what I think," he mutters. I get the impression that's all I'm going to get. It's as if he's shutting himself down. I have never wanted to look inside someone's mind so much before. The brooding look in his eyes spikes my curiosity.

On arrival at the Power Pack, I'd assumed they would make us stop and check our ID at the very least. This is supposed to be the strongest pack of them all and they probably intend to keep it that way. But they wave us through without a word. I give Coen a questioning glance.

"They know this is Kaden's car."

I'm struck by the look of the place. The large wall that separates the pack from the outside world does a good job of concealing the treasures hidden within. The road we drive onto is surrounded by exotic greenery. I only find the plants foreign-looking because I haven't grown up here, I know, but it all seems very different here to any pack I've ever seen before. After being cooped up in the Purity Pack all my life, I can safely say this is my first foreign adventure, my kidnapping aside. Winding the window down, even the air feels different somehow. I'm also impressed, not in a good way, by the number of security guards milling around.

"Where exactly are we heading?" I ask, trying not to meet the gaze of one of the guards as we drive past. The stone-cold look in the man's eyes makes me shiver; it's obvious how serious they take their jobs.

"To Alpha Landon's estate," Coen informs me.

My heart gives a jolt.

"Isn't that on the edge of a cliff?" I ask, trying to remember my geography classes back at school.

Coen nods slowly. "The same cliff Althea threw Kace off."

I think for a moment. So this Althea is definitely the same girl Kace said he was in love with... I glance at Coen, but he doesn't seem at all fazed to be telling me this. How could two males so close to each other fall in love with the same girl? It makes sense that Coen would, since she is his mate – but Kace?

"Kace loved her... your mate," I remark, fumbling for a way to get something more out of him.

Coen's eyebrows rise and he speeds up a bit, making me grip my seat. I remember the look in Kace's eye when he talked about Althea. Even though she broke his heart.

"You'll see why soon," Coen says.

Driving deeper into the territory of the Power Pack, we pass a series of towns. It takes us around an hour to reach Landon's estate. Strangely, there seems less security the closer we get. *Do they assume he can look after himself?* The thought makes me shiver.

Without warning Coen swerves, nearly making me smack my head against my glass window. He comes to a halt at the side of the road and turns the engine off.

I blink a few times.

"You must walk from here," Coen tells me. "Do you know what you've got to say?"

For a brief moment I can almost see a glimpse of Kaden in his eyes. I find myself nodding.

"I think I'm lost. I can't remember who I am, but I think my name is Mara." The words sound so ordinary coming out of my mouth. They are what Kaden told me to say.

Coen nods approvingly. Then he gets out of the car and motions to me join him.

"We need to make it look as if you've been through a lot to get here," he mumbles.

He suddenly grabs my T–shirt sleeve and rips it clean off at the seam. I yelp and push him away.

"Are you kidding?"

Coen grins sheepishly, then drags me further away from the road to where a shallow drain has been dug out. It is filled with murky water, which I eye dubiously.

Coen kneels and dunks his hand in the water to scoop up a large handful of mud and debris. Then he turns to me.

"What are you doing with that?" I ask nervously, making sure my gaze stays on his hand so he doesn't try anything.

"I need to make it look as if you've trekked for miles..."

"Don't you dare–"

Before I can finish he has launched himself at me, his hand aiming for my face. I scream in protest but I'm too slow. I can feel the muck running down my face and neck. Pushing him away now is easy because he's doubled up with laughter.

"You're disgusting!" I shout at him. The feeling of the mud plastered on my face and neck makes me want to gag.

"I'm disgusting?" Coen gasps through his laughter. "You should see yourself!"

It is only with an effort that I stifle the profanities that rise to my lips.

Coen recovers enough to grab a handful of grass. "Rub this on your legs or something... you don't look grubby enough."

"I'll show you grubby," I grumble. I take the grass, however, and rub it on my legs till they are covered in green stains.

Coen nods in approval, then leans forward.

"Wait..." He ruffles my hair, ignoring the glare I'm giving him. "Done."

"Now what?" I ask.

Coen points down the long road ahead of us. It seems to go on forever, without a building in sight. I sigh in resignation.

"I have to walk?"

Coen nods and steps back toward the car. Exasperated, I watch him get in and turn the engine on. He winds the window down.

"Kaden will see you tonight."

And with that he drives off, blowing a cloud of dust into my face. Coughing, I swing my hands around, trying to clear it.

I've got a long walk ahead of me.

By the time the estate comes into sight, I'm close to exhaustion. I just want to get inside somewhere so I can shower this dirt and muck off my body. My skin itches and I just hope I can get all the stains off.

Surprisingly, the gates to Alpha Landon's estate are unattended and unlocked. No guards, nothing. Nervously, I stroll through, waiting for someone to jump out at me.

A smooth path leads me up to the front door. The whole place is more extravagant than I expected, but I suppose the best is the only option for an Alpha.

It takes a few moments for me to gain enough confidence to knock on the door. The sound echoes, making me even jumpier.

When it swings open, I'm surprised by who I see at the door. I expected a guard, or even the Alpha himself. Instead I'm facing a dark-haired girl not much older than me. She stares down at me with dark eyes set in a beautiful, heart-shaped face.

She frowns as she looks me up and down in some confusion.

"Who are you?" She speaks with an unfamiliar Power Pack accent.

I take a deep breath. "You're Althea," I hear myself saying. I probably shouldn't have said her name... now I've blown my cover for sure.

She nods slowly.

"You didn't answer my question," she says, a little sourly.

I look down. The fact that she is pregnant is obvious. It makes my heart skip a beat. In there is the baby I'm supposed to murder...

"The fact is... I don't know who I am."

Chapter Twelve

At first, I think she's going to shut the door in my face before I can give her the rest of my story about why I am standing on her step. Instead, Althea's face softens and she opens the front door wider.

I'm so surprised I don't move immediately.

"Are you lost?" she asks softly.

I nod, not knowing what else to do. She motions for me to step inside, and I obey, trying to avoid looking at her belly, which gives every indication I need to tell she is pregnant.

"I don't actually live here anymore," she explains as she closes the door behind me. "I live with my mate."

"Your mate…" I echo sourly. I cringe, scolding myself from saying it aloud. But I can't help thinking of Coen and the hurt she has caused him. Power Pack members are all for selecting their mates, rather than letting the Moon Goddess decide for them, so I shouldn't really be so surprised.

When I turn to face her, I see she is looking bewildered.

"His name is Landon…" she begins, then shakes her head. "I should really be asking about you."

My gaze drops to my feet. As a Purity Pack member, I find it nearly impossible to lie to someone's face. Maybe if I can keep my head down, I can do this.

"I don't even know who I am," I mumble. My ploy must be working, as she steps closer, her hand touching my shoulder gently. I glance up and meet her gaze. "I might have hit my head or something because all my memories seem jumbled up."

Like a knife digging into my heart, I see how genuine her sympathy is. Her eyes are so soft and warm, I want to cry in her arms and beg her to send me home. But Kaden's face lingers in the back of my mind, his threats a taunting reminder of the position I've been forced into.

She has no idea.

"Are you from this pack?" she asks.

"I think so," I say breathily. She should be able to tell, surely, from my accent and appearance that I'm not from here, but she doesn't question a thing.

Althea is obviously worried about getting too close to me, in case I'm deranged and lash out at her or something, but she still takes my hand and gives it a brief squeeze.

"I'm about to walk home. Would you like to come back with me? You can shower there, and we can try to find your family."

I catch her checking my neck with a quick glance. She's looking for the bite mark, checking to see if I've been mated.

I nod my head, a little too eagerly. She crosses to a large box by the door. When I offer her help, she shakes her head in dismissal.

"I may be pregnant, but it doesn't mean I'm not capable," she says with a short laugh. She props the door open with her foot and points with her forehead for me to go out first.

The sun is starting to set outside, and everything's drenched in a soft golden glow. I breathe in the balmy air, while Althea slams the door behind her. Then I follow her back down the road. My legs ache from walking so much and my skin is itching even more than it was before.

"How long have you been walking?" Althea asks me after we've been going a good ten minutes.

I give her an honest answer of about an hour. I refrain from telling her it was in the hot sun as well.

"You must be tired. Do you know why you can't remember anything?" she asks breezily.

My forehead creases as I pretend to think. The lies that come out of my mouth make me feel like I should spend every day from now on praying for the Moon Goddess's forgiveness.

I shrug. "I woke up on the side of the road with hardly any memories."

At least she doesn't have to know my name. I'm sure if she heard it was Mara, she would alert Alpha Rylan of the Purity Pack. They are bound to be looking for me.

Althea holds off asking me more questions. Maybe she is as exhausted as I am.

Her home turns out to be a quaint, decent-sized cabin in the woods. I hold her box for her as she unlocks the door.

"My mate, Landon, is out right now," she says.

The door creaks as it opens and I step inside. The house is bathed in warmth, and now that it's dark out, it's very welcoming.

I place the box on a table in the middle of the room we have come into. Everything in here seems to be connected. The kitchen and the lounge are combined into one space. Does an Alpha seriously live here?

When I turn around, I freeze in sudden fright. Althea stands just inches away, holding a knife perilously close to my neck.

"Who are you really?"

I take a deep breath, wondering if it will be my last. The warmth in Althea's eyes has turned to ice. Almost as cold as the blade that's pressed so close to my neck. I glance over her shoulder and register that she has closed the door... damn.

"W-what do you mean?" I stutter.

Her jaw clenches and she looks me up and down in disgust.

"Don't act like I can't smell Alpha Kaden on you," she says bitterly.

My heart sinks. It's over. She knows.

"Don't do anything, please," I beg. "He will kill everyone I love otherwise."

Maybe she sees the genuine fear in my eyes, because she lets go, her face softening. I let out a lungful of air.

She tosses the blade on the table. "What has he done now?"

"He's sent me here..." I trail off. If I tell her, and Kaden finds out, my father will be murdered. I must do what I can to protect him. "To spy for information."

The excuse is pathetic, but it's something. She's much more likely to kick me out if I tell her I'm here to kill her unborn baby. Her face contorts in surprise.

"Kaden is threatening your family?"

I nod and she closes her eyes in annoyance.

"That son of a bitch."

"Please don't kick me out. If he finds out, I'm surely dead," I plead.

Althea looks sympathetic. How many altercations has she had in the past with Kaden to know him so well?

She motions to a chair for me to sit down. I do so.

"Where are you *really* from?" she asks.

I can't tell her the truth... "The Freedom Pack."

"Can we help send you back there?" she inquires gently.

I swallow. Milly is in Kaden's custody, but I can't even tell her that. I'm beginning to regret saying anything at all.

"Maybe. Will you let me stay?" I ask hopefully.

"Until we can get you back to the Freedom Pack, where you belong."

My heart flips. I've never even been to the Freedom Pack, let alone lived there. I don't know a single soul from that pack, since they tend to keep to themselves. I have heard that civilization there is simple and a lot of the pack members are uneducated.

I thank Althea many times. Her generosity might just get us both killed, but in the meantime, the plan is working, and my father is safe.

"You must be tired," she says at last. "You can shower and sleep in the baby's room. There is a spare bed in there."

She also warns me that getting Landon to agree to my staying will be harder. I don't blame him for that. I wouldn't want a spy in my home if I was an Alpha.

I shower quickly, scrubbing off the dirt and grass. Althea has lent me some clothes, which fit me surprisingly well. It's a nice room she's given me. I don't deserve any of this.

I am just settling into the bed when a sharp knock on the window makes me jump. Unable to see a thing, I stumble to the window, hoping to see who is outside, although I have a feeling I know exactly who is out there.

Kaden. Of course.

I slide the door open, letting in a cool breeze.

"Good evening, Mara," Kaden murmurs.

I scowl at him. Sure, Coen warned me he was coming, but it doesn't mean I'm pleased to see him. His gloved hand comes through the window, and I know it's not an invitation. I take his hand, and he helps me through the window, one leg at a time.

"You look delectable," he observes. The clothes Althea has given me are perhaps a little too tight fitting, showing off a figure that I've tried to hide from males back home. I suddenly notice a wound on his face.

"What happened?" I ask.

Blood is seeping down his chin and neck from a deep cut on his cheek.

He curses under his breath. "Alpha Landon happened. He ambushed me by the border. Him and his useless guards."

"He did a number on you," I murmur. For some reason, my first reaction is to sit him down and offer him aid. He's a killer, I remind myself; he's done much worse to other people. The wound looks nasty, though something tells me he couldn't care less.

"Stay here," I order.

I quickly clamber back into the room. Creeping to the bathroom, I rustle around in cabinets until I find something of use to Kaden. I manage to find some antiseptic cream and bandages and grab some tissue on the way out.

Kaden looks dumbfounded when I return, loaded with aid for him.

"What in the world...?"

"Sit," I tell him.

Kaden furrows his brow but then sits down on a fallen log. I lay the things out in front of me. Tissue bundled in my hand, I go to dab the blood from Kaden's face, but his gloved hand grips my wrist.

"You can't touch me," he says heavily.

I roll my eyes. He tears his gloves off one by one, then hands them to me, and I slip them on. They are too big for me, but I don't mind. As I dab the blood away, he winces. I attempt to smother my smile, but it doesn't work.

"Does that hurt the poor little Alpha?" I mock, kneeling before him.

Kaden gives me a dangerous look, but I brush it off. I finish by dabbing the wound with the cream and patting a bandage on his cheek. I have to admit that the finished result looks rather comical.

I'm finished but he doesn't move away. Neither do I. Our proximity would be unnerving on another day, but for some reason, I don't feel close enough to him.

Slowly, I reach my hand up and touch his face. He lets me, because of the gloves. I run my fingers down the side of his face without the bandage, as if I can't help myself.

"I don't understand why you're so afraid of touch–"

"Not today," Kaden interrupts, looking grim. He peels the gloves off my hands. Solemnly, I watch him ease his own hands back into them, like he's placing them in a coffin.

I decide not to tell him that Althea knows. *What's the point?*

Kaden helps me clamber back through the window.

"Sleep well tonight, Mara. I shall see you tomorrow."

69

Chapter Thirteen

My gloved fingers tap rhythmically on the steering wheel. The bandage Mara placed on my cheek last night is long gone. It's the next day, and my wound has healed already. Healing is no problem when you're an Alpha.

I watch from a distance, my car concealed behind a mass of trees just off the side of the road. Mara is leaning against a tree, talking to Althea. The pair of them seem to be getting along fine, which means the plan is going as planned.

I shift in my seat as Landon walks out of the house. For a young Alpha, he's strong; I must keep an eye on him.

He glances at Mara as he goes to Althea's side. The three of them start chatting, and I gather that this is the first time Landon and Mara have met.

If he tries something funny, I swear...

The two shake hands. Then Althea says something that makes Landon's face darken. He takes a step toward her, and I instantly sit up, straining my eyes to ensure he doesn't hurt her. Althea comes between Landon and Mara, pushing Landon back and yelling at him. I wish I was closer so I could hear what they are saying.

Althea and Landon move away from Mara to talk privately. It's obvious, even from here, that they are wondering if they can trust her.

The look on Mara's face, as she stands there alone tugs at my heart. I *hate* that. I can't stand the fact that she is making me feel things. My reign as Alpha has taught me to expel all emotion. The only release I get is with desperate females of my pack, whom I discard the day after. I hate myself even more for doing that.

I turn the car and back it up. I need to get out of here before I am tempted to intervene. Mara needs to do this on her own. That's why she is here.

I wait for darkness to fall before I even dare approach Alpha Landon's house. Parking my car out of sight, I stalk toward it through the woods.

Mara plays in my mind. I keep seeing her soft blonde hair, her bright blue eyes. I shall not admit she's beautiful, for that will cause me weakness. And weakness was my father's downfall, or rather, the reason why he was taken from my life.

I sit on the fallen log below Mara's window, waiting. Knocking on her window is pointless; she knows I'm here.

Suddenly the window slams open and a body lands disheveled at my feet. Then it giggles.

"What are you doing on the ground?" I demand. I kneel down and help Mara up out of the dirt. She looks at me in the dim light, her cheeks glowing and her eyes glazed over. A tentative hand reaches out for my face, but I'm quick to catch her wrist in my gloved grip.

"I think I fell," she says, her voice slurring strangely.

I come to a grim conclusion. "You're drunk."

I help her to her feet, and she falls against my chest, giggling, like what I've said is the funniest thing she's ever heard. She's so small, it wouldn't surprise me if she got drunk after just a couple of decent drinks.

"I've never been drunk before!" she exclaims. She pauses, and for a moment I think she's going to cry, but she proceeds to burst out laughing.

She's lost it.

"Why would they let you get drunk?" I ask her. Anger brews in my chest as I think of Landon deliberately getting her completely wasted. What would happen if she spilt the plan I forced upon her to him?

Suddenly her eyes widen, and she clamps a hand over her mouth. She backs away but I match her step for step, daring her to try to run away.

"What are you hiding from me, Mara?"

"I'm not hiding anything..." she says loudly.

I narrow my eyes at her. I've known Mara for only a brief time but I know when she is lying, her face is so expressive.

"Lying to me isn't going to get you anywhere," I mutter.

Her face contorts and she turns pale. She turns around suddenly and vomits straight into the bush behind her. Surprising myself, I rush forward and grab her hair, holding it back. I concentrate on the moonlight glimmering on her head, as I rub her back rhythmically.

When she's done, she straightens and leans against me. I lead her away from the bush and sit her down on the fallen log. She looks dazed.

"You shouldn't have let yourself get into this state," I scold her. I know it's pointless; she won't remember in the morning.

She giggles again. "Are you going to punish me?"

Her words send a streak of heat down my body, but I'm quick to dismiss it. Why does she do this to me? I kneel in front of where she sits, taking care to stay a safe enough distance away so I can stop her if she tries to touch me.

"Why, do you want me to?" I ask her softly.

She pauses and I think she is angry with me, or will slap me or something. Instead, a sly grin appears on her face and she moves closer on the log.

"I've always wondered what it would be like to *be* with an Alpha," she purrs, leaning closer.

I hold her shoulder to steady her. Yep, she's definitely drunk.

When I go to stand, she reaches out and grabs my knee. "Where are you going?"

"You need sleep," I say pointedly.

She shakes her head furiously, giving me a desperate look. It makes me pause.

"But... I thought you were going to kiss me."

My heart freezes. *Kiss her?* Is this how she has been feeling....? I swallow. No. She's drunk.

"Not now, Mara."

She stands up, swaying on her feet. Again, she tries to reach out toward me, but I enclose my hands around hers. If only I didn't have my gloves on. Then she would know...

I can't let her touch me. Yet knowing she craves my touch brings me inconceivable pleasure.

She lurches forward suddenly, clasping my shirt in her fists. Flinching, I eye her carefully. She brings her face close to mine, smiling lazily.

The urge to kiss her consumes me – to strip our clothes off and to get rid of all the space between us, to finally claim her as my own. But I can't... if she knew, my plan would be reduced to shambles. I gently push her back, the pain in my heart eating away at me.

"I want you," she whispers. The three words almost amount to "I love you". But she won't remember this... this is just the drink talking, and drink has no memory.

"I shall put you to bed," I tell her. Maybe if I tuck her in myself, she will sleep. A spark has lit in her eyes, and she's getting too close again, stumbling over her feet. The look on her face makes me nervous.

"To bed, huh?" she leers, her tone too suggestive to ignore.

I grab her arm and lead her to the window. I pour her through, her limbs going everywhere, then follow her myself, trying to keep quiet so Landon doesn't hear us. To compromise the mission would be devastating.

Mara trips over the rug on the floor, but I manage to catch her before she thuds against the ground.

"Quiet, they might hear!" I urge in a hushed voice.

She looks shocked, then grins wildly and pulls away to stalk across the room with exaggerated care.

"Mara–"

"Quiet!" she snaps, mocking me.

Rolling my eyes, I watch her burst into a fit of giggles and fall face first onto the bed. After a few moments of her lying motionless there, I approach her. I poke her shoulder, and when she doesn't respond, I roll her over onto her back. She's completely passed out, her eyes shut. She looks so peaceful. A smile starts to form on my lips but I smother it. I pull the bedsheets up to her chin and sit down on the edge of the bed.

She is the most innocent person I've ever met. As she lies there in the oblivion of sleep, she has no idea what this is all about. No idea of my past, or even my present. To share it with her would be too cruel. To taint such innocent beauty with my issues.

Slowly, I pull my gloves off, laying them beside me. I stare at my hands, hating them.

She will never know. Gently, I run a bare fingertip across her cheek, feeling the trail of sparks that follow. She is so soft. Why is that I have been paired with this beautiful creature? My hand caresses her cheek and she whimpers faintly in her slumber.

"Why me?" I whisper. I will continue to intimidate her, so she won't know how much she intimidates me.

My thumb brushes over her lower lip, and she sighs. If I thought this spark I feel was real, I would pick it up and crush it between my fists, so I could torture it the way it tortures me.

"Kaden," she mumbles in her sleep.

I can resist no longer. Lowering my head down so it's level with hers, I pause. Should I? Should I close the distance and cement what is truly between us?

Fighting my inner demons, I lean down and press my lips against hers. I savor the brief moment of pure bliss; the feeling of my mate's lips against mine.

Then I swallow and pull away. I would do anything to stay here with her, to have her wake up in my arms and realize who she truly belongs to. Instead, I pick my gloves up and slide them back over my hands.

With one last longing glance at her, I stand.

"One day, Mara. One day, you'll know."

Chapter Fourteen

My eyes drift open slowly.

A throbbing pain in my temples forces them closed again. I let myself get drunk... how could I help it when Landon was drinking, and I was doing my best to fit in, to soothe his uneasiness about me?

Last night we talked. A lot. But the problem is that I hardly remember what happened. Did I spill Kaden's plan to them by accident? I hope I didn't say anything to ruin the plot. Perhaps Kaden visited me yesterday. He would have been mad to see me drunk though.

Peeling the covers off my body, I drag myself from the bed. Getting drunk is a sin in the Purity Pack. I should feel ashamed right now, but I don't detect any shame in me. The only thing I feel is pain and concern that I have acted stupidly.

As I clamber into the shower, I notice something. There is dirt all over my palms. I frown. What was I convinced to do last night? Or maybe I did this myself. I even have a sour taste in my mouth that I don't even want to begin thinking about.

Focusing upon the task at hand, I quickly wash it all off.

When I enter the kitchen a few minutes later, I'm faced with an elated-looking Althea. She sits at the dining table, breakfast in front of her. She even stands when she sees me.

"Are you ready for our plan to commence?" she asks.

I frown, drawing a blank. Out of the corner of my eye, I notice Landon in the kitchen, stirring something on the stove. Althea seems to register my confused expression.

"You must have got pretty drunk last night. It was only three small drinks..." She breaks off.

I blush. The problem with being part of the Purity Pack is that I've never been allowed to drink. The second glass Landon offered me tipped me over the edge. That is about all I can remember now. "What was our plan again?"

"We are sending you home!"

For a moment, I get excited. Back to the Purity Pack? Then I realize she must mean to the Freedom Pack. I wish lying wasn't so difficult. I wish I could tell them the truth now, so I could be sent home, to my real home. Yet Kaden would surely find me there, and I can only guess what would happen then. The more I think about it, the worse the idea of going home becomes.

I clear my throat. "Right... when?"

Althea glances over her shoulder. "Landon can drive you there tomorrow morning. It will take a couple of hours."

Perhaps I should feel disappointed, but then a devious thought creeps into my mind. If they take me there, Kaden won't be able to find me, right? The Freedom Pack occupy the largest territory of all the packs and it's mostly desolate, so it should be easy to get lost in it. If I disappear, Kaden will never think of looking for me there.

"Sounds good," I say, feeling brighter.

Althea smiles, and Landon wanders over with a bowl of oatmeal for me. We eat in silence. It is obvious Landon is still unsure about me by the way he keeps glancing up at me with a suspicious look on his face. Althea, on the other hand, eats happily in my presence.

Once we've finished, Althea takes my plate to the kitchen and Landon follows. I watch the two of them with genuine interest. He wraps his arms around her from behind, resting his head on her shoulder. She turns her head and kisses him softly. The sight tugs at my heart.

I can only wonder if I will ever find love like that.

It is past noon when Althea asks me if I will accompany her to the woods for a walk. I agree, wanting to clear my head before I see

Kaden tonight. I'm not the best liar, but hopefully he won't see through my façade.

"You're very pretty," Althea tells me as we saunter through the trees. "I'm surprised men aren't after you all the time."

I glance at her, wondering if she is being serious or is just pulling my leg to see how I'll react.

"I've always thought all the other girls in my pack are much better-looking than me," I tell her honestly. "I don't know why. Maybe it's their confidence."

The shade from the canopy we stroll under cools my skin and makes me shiver. But I wish I could stay here a little longer.

"When you say 'your pack', I take it you mean the Purity Pack?"

My eyes widen.

"Trust me, I knew the moment you opened your mouth. And anyway, Freedom Pack members are always naked." She laughs.

Oh, great...

"You're not going to send me back there, are you?" I ask. I would be more than happy to see my family again, but at what expense? Kaden finding me and murdering me, probably.

Althea chuckles. "Running from something?"

"Only an Alpha with murderous tendencies," I mutter.

Althea pauses and rests her back against a tree. She warned me before we set out that she might have to take small breaks.

"Right... I keep forgetting why you're *actually* here," she muses.

Thankfully, she doesn't know why I'm *actually* here, so I try to divert her line of thought. "If I go to the Freedom Pack, he won't find me there."

Althea nods and sighs. "You should know that the Freedom Pack isn't entirely safe. The Alpha, Grayson, is flighty and unmated."

I'm not scared at the revelation. Perhaps it's because I have been in worse situations, with Kaden dangling my very life before my eyes.

"I will be fine," I assure her.

We start walking again, aimlessly. A conversation I'm not sure I should start itches at my throat. "What do you know about Kaden?"

I give Althea a sideways glance to make sure she doesn't suspect my motives in asking such a question. Instead, she seems to be pondering her answer. She must have met him, I'm thinking, with her mate being an Alpha.

"I don't know him personally, only what Landon has told me," she tells me, stepping carefully over a fallen branch. "Apparently, he was good as a child."

I find that hard to imagine...

"His father was cruel," Althea continues, "but Kaden didn't believe in the same values as he did. But one day, he completely changed. It was after his parents mysteriously died. He's been utterly cold-hearted ever since."

I nod thoughtfully. Kaden having a dark past doesn't surprise me. I did know his parents died, but I thought he had been trained to be cruel since he was young. It doesn't seem plausible that it happened overnight.

"Do you know if he's ever..." I pause.

"What?"

"Had a lover?" I blurt out. My face instantly stains bright red and I regret saying it. Especially when Althea gives me a knowing smile. Why do I care? I shouldn't even be asking a question like that, since it would take an equally sickening girl to fall in love with him.

"I wouldn't know. Why do you ask?"

I frown. "No reason, just curious."

Althea doesn't continue the conversation. Maybe she knows it's stupid. Or maybe, because she knows Kaden, she ignores the possibility that I would ever have a chance with someone like that.

***

I have to sit and wait for a long time for Kaden to show up.

The log I'm sitting on is becoming really uncomfortable by the time he finally saunters toward me from the trees. He smirks when he sees me there.

He looks so handsome. He is wearing his usual black coat, but instead of it being buttoned up, it's open, revealing the thin, black shirt he has on beneath.

"Good evening," he murmurs, standing in front of me.

I look up at him, meeting his dark eyes. Every time I consider them, I wonder what secrets lie behind them. Dark ones, no doubt, like the one I found out about today.

"Did you have a good evening last night?" I counter. I fancy a flicker of alarm crosses his features, but he smothers it quickly. I frown. "I can't remember a thing about it, but did we meet last night?"

He lets out a deep breath, and I wonder what he is hiding. When he nods slowly, I fear the worst.

"I didn't say anything… embarrassing, did I?" I ask, my heart in my mouth.

He scrunches his nose up for a second, and I almost consider it cute. Almost.

"You insulted me a few times, vomited, then went straight to bed," he informs me.

I groan inwardly. I did that, in front of him? He must think so badly of me now. Well, at least I didn't try to seduce him or something.

He rubs the back of his neck. "Kace sends his–"

"If you say 'love', I may vomit again," I warn him.

Kaden chuckles. "Nothing of the sort. He just wants you to know that your wedding is scheduled for the moment you step back into my pack."

The thought fills me with a strange sadness, until I remember my plan for tomorrow morning. That fills me with a little more confidence.

"So that's me settled then. What's your plan for the future?" I challenge him bitterly. Murder, murder, and maybe murder again probably.

80

His eyebrows crease as he thinks. I'm surprised to see he is taking my challenge seriously. "I'm not sure. Every day is a different one, I suppose," he mutters.

It occurs to me that this may be the last time I see him. Before I can even think about it, I have taken a step closer. His eyes widen a little as he gazes down at me.

"What if I just disappeared?" I demand, trying to keep my tone of voice level as though it's just an innocent question.

Kaden frowns. "You couldn't."

"How can you be so sure?"

"You can escape all you want, but I would hunt you down. I would use all my resources to find you. And when I find you..." His voice trails off. "Not that it shall ever happen, I'm sure."

I don't reply. He has no idea how I'm going to make him eat those words, how I'm going to show him exactly how wrong he can be.

"I have something you'll need," Kaden comments, changing the subject.

He slips his hand into his front pocket and pulls out a slim vial filled with a watery red substance. I stare at it for a few moments. You don't have to be an idiot to know it's poison.

"A couple of drops in her drink will be enough. To affect the baby, not her," Kaden tells me.

I take the vial gingerly between my index finger and my thumb. I wouldn't ever do it... and I don't have to anymore, though he doesn't need to know that.

Instead I'll go to the Freedom Pack, and finally be free.

Chapter Fifteen

"Do you remember everything I told you?" Althea questions me. She leans against the car I'm sitting in, looking in at me through the open window. Landon sits in the front seat, staring straight ahead.

"Not really," I admit.

It's early the following morning. We have decided to leave early in the day, since it's a long drive to the Freedom Pack and, at Landon's suggestion, I can sleep most of the way. The plan is to arrive before midday so I'll have plenty of time to find shelter before darkness falls.

"The first thing I suggest you do is find somewhere to stay," Althea advises me. "Many of the houses there are abandoned, so stay in one of those if possible. Eventually, I'm sure Kaden will lose interest in finding you, and you can go home."

I nod and hope it will work, despite my doubts.

"Whatever else you do," Althea continues, "stay as far away from Alpha Grayson as possible. He's not the most... put-together Alpha out there."

"She will be fine, Al," Landon says gruffly, cutting Althea off.

She sighs and leans into the car to kiss my forehead in farewell. I suddenly feel as though I'm going to miss her much more than I expected. I came here to kill her baby and now I'm leaving a good friend in order to find a new place to call home.

We depart quickly. I can't help looking out the window for Kaden. If he sees us, I'm dead...

There's no sign of anyone following, however, and eventually the motion of the car lulls me to sleep.

"Mara..."

My eyes shoot open and I sit up, only to be restricted by the seatbelt. Landon is looking at me from the driver's seat. He appears weary and his soft brown eyes are rimmed red. It's obvious he's been driving for quite some time.

"We're here," he tells me.

He's right. Outside, I'm faced with a massive wall. Unlike the Power Pack wall, this one is crumbling, with cracks running straight through. To my left, there is even a large gaping hole in its structure. It fits with everything I have been told about the Freedom Pack. Anyone could walk in here.

"It's a bit of a mess, isn't it?" Landon remarks.

I glance at him and try to suppress my misgivings. The Freedom Pack is another pack that isn't discussed often. They are considered a bad influence. Anything that was good about them was destroyed the moment Alpha Grayson took over. We were often told that if there is anyone worse than Kaden, it's Grayson. It wasn't that he was criminal so much that he was neglectful of his duties toward his pack.

"What can you tell me about Alpha Grayson before I go in there?" I ask.

Landon thinks for a moment. "I can't say I know him very well. What I do know is that he was the youngest Alpha until I became one. But he's the most immature one, that's for sure."

His words make me think.

"It's probably best to just stay well away from him, like Althea recommended. He likes new things and might not let you go for a while if he gets his hands on you," he warns.

I swallow nervously, not liking the sound of that at all.

"Okay," I reply, "I think I get it now. Find shelter somewhere and stay as far away from the Alpha as I can."

Landon nods, smiling, then pops the door open for me. "Good luck," he murmurs.

Once I have closed the door behind me, Landon takes off pretty quickly. I hoist my backpack onto my shoulder and head toward the gaping hole in the massive wall.

It's hot here, hotter than it was where I was staying with the Power Pack. But instead of it being burning hot, it's humid and sticky. I'm sweating buckets as I reach the wall and start to clamber over broken concrete.

Before a minute more has passed I'm officially in Freedom Pack territory. As soon as I'm through the wall I'm hit by a wave of heat. It's suddenly obvious why they all live naked here.

Stalking through the tall grass, I look around for some sign of civilization, but to no avail. It's too hot for there to be much vegetation, but sparse trees provide a degree of shade from the midday sun.

"Hello?" I call to no one in particular.

No one answers. I was hoping that perhaps someone might be within earshot and hear my call.

I walk for hours, the sun beating down on me. The heat drags at my feet like shackles, and sweat pours down my face. No matter how far I go, it seems there are no settlements anywhere. Every ounce of optimism is drained from my body. Eventually, I slump against the wide trunk of a tree, my hand over my heart.

The sun is setting over the horizon and, despite the haze of negativity that has settled over me, I have to admit that it's a beautiful sight. I close my eyes and allow myself to relax my stiff limbs for a while.

The sound of a twig snapping close by brings me to instant wakefulness. I glance around but I can't see much. Darkness is spreading like a disease across the land, limiting my vision.

Then I see him.

He's stark naked, not twenty feet away, leaning casually against a tree. Only gentle shadows cover his crotch and a smile of pure juvenile excitement dances upon his face. Eyes as sharp as silver stare at me, searching for any sign of vulnerability.

"Oh, great," I mutter under my breath.

He steps forward, and I avert my eyes from his lower body, which he now reveals fully to me.

There's something about this man's presence that tells me exactly who he is. An Alpha. Alpha Grayson.

"I smelt you the second your foot stepped within my walls," he says. His voice is laced with that exotic Freedom Pack accent that's impossible to acquire unless you've lived here your whole life.

"I didn't realize you cared who came and went around here," I reply, with a little more sass than intended.

Grayson raises an eyebrow at me. The color of his hair is that of rich, dark wood and in the twilight it seems to shine with an inexplicable brilliance.

He chuckles at my taunt. "Only if they smell as sweet as a member of the Purity Pack."

I consider running. If I run, will he bother to pursue me? If I shift into my natural wolf form, then he will surely smell me for miles, which wouldn't leave me much of a chance of outsmarting him. I will have to escape on foot then – perhaps hide up a tree. Although that didn't seem to work with Kaden.

"So, tell me, Angel eyes, what brings you to my pack?" he asks.

I wonder if he seriously thinks the nickname will be enough to charm me. Despite my best efforts at averting my eyes, there is something about the cut of his abs that keeps directing my attention to his crotch. He notices and laughs. "See something you like?"

"You should put some clothes on," I grumble.

His face twists in amusement and he takes a step closer. "Would you be less disrespectful if I told you wearing clothes is not a part of our custom here?"

I get the urge to sneer at him. Since when has he cared so much about custom? Only one law prevents this pack from slipping into anarchy: the one that states that everyone has the right to freedom.

"Would you be more respectful if I told you that modesty is the foundation of our customs where I come from?"

"You're in my pack now, remember."

I hold back a snarky remark and try to get my bearings without him noticing. Alpha Grayson so far fits the definition of nonchalant, so perhaps my salvation lies within his own flaws.

"That reminds me, I have somewhere to be," I tell him, pretending to notice how late it's getting as the sun finally disappears below the horizon.

I turn to go but Grayson grabs my shoulder and forces me to face him. His large hand is warm, sending shivers down my body.

"No, you don't."

"I do."

"No."

"Yes."

"Pretty sure you don't..."

"Can we stop acting like children?" I snap.

Grayson tilts his head at me, and his eyes sparkle with youthful exuberance.

"You first."

I sigh deeply and shake his hand off my shoulder. Then I turn around again and start walking away. I only make it a few feet before I'm forced to stop again as his hand descends on my shoulder once more.

"Would you–"

I pause. His eyes are no longer that shining silver... now they are a dangerous red. His jaw is clenched and his muscles taut.

"What in the world...?"

"Go, before I hurt you!" he rasps.

I back away, watching him warily. He looks as if he's fighting a tremendous battle with a demon under his skin.

"What's happening?" I ask as I stumble in the thick grass.

His head snaps up, and the fire in his eyes frightens me to the core. "The moment the sun falls and the moon rises, I no longer have control over my body..."

I grow impatient, my fingers tapping against my thigh. Where is she? She knows we meet out here every night.

I go over to her bedroom window and peer in cautiously. I see her bed is empty. Strange. I waited until Althea was in bed before I came. So where is Mara?

I pull the window up, ignoring the groan of the lock as it breaks under my strength. Inside there is no trace of her.

She's gone. *Mara's gone.*

A hot surge of anger runs through my veins like liquor, making me clench my fists. I begin to work out how I have been manipulated. Landon isn't here. And neither is Mara.

"That son of a bitch!" I growl, claws involuntarily elongating. Pacing, I try not to rip the hair from my head.

There is only one possible conclusion.

"He's taken my mate..."

Chapter Sixteen

Stumbling over my feet, I witness Alpha Grayson losing control before my very eyes. It's as if a demon is consuming his soul, though he tries his very best to fight it.

"I said run!" he screams at me.

And I do. Twisting around, I run at full speed away from him. Shifting would be like dangling myself on a stick for him; my scent would follow me for miles. So, I run on my two sneakered feet as fast as my unfit legs will allow. Dodging between trees, I hear the wildest howl rip through the night. Whatever Grayson has turned into, I don't want to see it.

It's tough work racing through the thick grass. Faintly, I hear the thud of paws somewhere behind me and I realize with a grim heart that Grayson is in hot pursuit. I don't rate my chances of escaping him very high. Obviously even *he* feared the monster he was about to turn into. These thoughts are like hands on my back, pushing me on.

But he's almost on me.

I don't turn, scared of what I might be faced with. Instead I keep my eyes on the trees ahead, praying I might make it there alive. Then I realize he is right behind me and I'm going to die. I'm going to die. There's no way I'm not going to die.

All at once all noise of pursuit ceases. I've already stopped running, but so has he. I turn cautiously – and there's nothing behind me. Unable to believe in my good luck, I try to catch my breath.

And then a sudden and very violent commotion to my left, just a few feet away, has me shaking like a leaf. Two massive wolves are rolling on the ground in the long grass, snapping and snarling at each other. One is a large brown wolf, and the other a wolf with lighter, almost blond fur. The sight of them clawing and tearing at one another is truly terrifying.

Paralyzed with shock, I watch as the large brown wolf is tossed into the air and slammed into the base of a tree. The sound of the impact makes me turn away in horror. When I look back, both wolves are gone.

I walk slowly toward the scene of their struggle. If they aren't here, then where are they? I begin to doubt that they truly existed in the first place. Did I imagine the whole thing after becoming delirious in the heat?

Then, out of the shadows, emerges a naked figure. I back up slowly, assuming it's Grayson, but instead, I see a head of blond hair. The man's eyes glimmer green like the forest around us.

"Don't be afraid... he's gone," the stranger murmurs.

Something about his voice makes me relax, allowing me to regain my breath.

It's as if I have already trained myself to ignore the nakedness of the men here. Instead, I notice the cuts upon his face and feel stirrings of concern for him.

"Was that you?" I ask, meaning the blond wolf that attacked Grayson.

He nods solemnly. "I heard Grayson leave the house this afternoon and went to investigate. When I saw him chasing you, I had to act," he explains.

I thank him profusely for saving my life while trying not to get emotional about the fact that he very nearly didn't.

He brushes it off modestly.

"You live with the Alpha?" I ask him.

Again, he nods. "He's my brother. Which is why I could distract him long enough for him to come back to his senses."

"His senses?"

"My brother has a condition. We have never been able to find anyone who can cure him of his insatiable need to transform into his werewolf form every night."

By the look in his eyes, I sense that this has been an issue for years. I stick my hand out in front of me, without even really thinking. "Mara."

"Evan."

We shake hands. Evan smiles warmly at me, and I can't help but sigh in relief. I finally feel as if I've found somebody who might be able to help me.

"So, where were you heading?" he inquires.

I shrug in response and tell him that I truly don't know where I'm supposed to go and that I'm actually lost. It's the truest thing I've said these past few days. I don't even know where I will be in a few hours' time.

He gazes at me sympathetically. "The Freedom Pack is a dangerous place. I know somewhere you can stay in the meantime. On one condition..."

I shoot him a suspicious look.

"...if you tell me why you're here. Then I will take you to a dear friend of mine," he promises.

Somehow, I knew this was coming. Bending the truth seems like the only option for me at this point. I hate that lying is becoming such a necessary habit for me.

"I'm running from someone. I thought this place would be the best pack to hide in." *Well, it's true as far as it goes.*

He nods, thinking about it. "You're not wrong."

At his invitation we start to walk together through the gathering night. I let him lead the way as it gets harder to see, trusting him to know where he's going. I want to ask him where Alpha Grayson is, although as long as he's not *here* I don't really care where he is.

And for the most part, I feel safe around Evan.

"You know, they say a mate can cure any condition," I tell Evan, referring to Grayson's strange habit of turning into a killer every night.

90

"It doesn't seem the Moon Goddess has granted him his mate yet," Evan replies.

I can only imagine the burden his brother must be on him. But the fact that he believes in the Moon Goddess is bound to be some consolation.

Few packs believe in the Moon Goddess these days. The Power Pack doesn't, and neither does the Wisdom Pack, who prefer to believe in the evolution of science. The Passion Pack does, but the Devotion Pack lacks the strong belief they used to. The Love Pack does, of course, and even the Discipline Pack has some strong believers. The remaining packs, like the Harmony Pack and the Loyalty Pack, believe it's the behavior of werewolves that fuels their ability to mate.

"I'm sure Grayson will meet his mate eventually," I say, trying to sound positive.

We walk for a while longer before we emerge in a township of sorts. Houses of all shapes and sizes are scattered in all directions. Proper roads and paths are non-existent. Some of the buildings are in good condition, while others look abandoned.

"Who am I meeting?" I ask timidly. I hope he's not sending me to stay with some serial killer or something, like Grayson. No, I trust Evan.

He doesn't answer but instead approaches a quaint-looking home in decent condition. He knocks loudly on the yellow door, and we wait for it to be answered.

A short, youngish woman answers. Her soft brown hair is tied back from her face, showing off her high cheekbones and the silvery eyes that are so common among the Freedom Pack.

A smile lights up her face when she sees Evan and she jumps at him. He responds by wrapping his arms around her. Watching them embrace is not awkward in the slightest. In fact, I'm quite envious of the obvious love shared between them.

When they separate, Evan keeps an arm securely around her.

"Meet my Leia – my mate."

Everything slots into place. Of course... his special friend.

"Leia, meet Mara. I met her in the woods and she needs a place to stay," Evan explains, introducing us.

Leia thrusts out her hand and I shake it.

"Of course you can stay! A Purity Pack member is always welcome in my home," she says brightly.

I never knew it was so obvious that I'm a Purity Pack member. But I'm glad I don't have to explain myself.

"Come in, it's cooling down out here," Leia says.

I follow her inside the house. A fire has been lit in the fireplace, and I see at once it is a simple, cozy home she presides over. Leia seems to carry an aura of contentment around with her, as if she wouldn't want things any other way. She leaves the room to make us tea, and I'm left with Evan in the living room.

"Your mate... you don't live with her?"

The idea seems strange. Mates should be around each other always. If I knew who my mate was, I would *never* leave his side.

"My duty is to look after Grayson. Until he finds his own mate," Evan says, rubbing the back of his neck.

Our attention is drawn to the television in the corner as a news update begins. The Wisdom Pack usually do the news reporting, since they are so tech-savvy. I'm genuinely surprised to find they have televisions out here in the Freedom Pack.

A man and woman sit at a desk. Both have the characteristic Wisdom Pack features, with silky black hair and piercing blue eyes.

"Today, the Vengeance Pack has once again captured the headlines after Alpha Kaden's shocking live announcement today," the woman says.

I stare at the screen with dismayed apprehension.

"That's right, Sally," the man responds. "Today, the notorious Alpha issued the following threat to a girl no one has even heard of!" He glances off, and it's obvious he's checking his appearance in the camera lens.

I have a nasty feeling I know who they are talking about.

"I would have thought the Alpha would have bigger issues on his plate than some girl from the Purity Pack," the woman named Sally remarks, laughing.

I'm conscious of Evan looking at me.

"Anyway," she continues, "here is the footage of Alpha Kaden's shocking announcement."

The reporters disappear and instead I'm looking into the cruel eyes of Alpha Kaden. I have to admit I've never seen him looking like this before. Darkness shadows his eyes, as if he hasn't slept for a long time. His jaw is rigid and his cheekbones gaunt. He looks paler than I remember him to be. There is definitely something wrong with him... it's almost comforting to see the hard glint of cruelty in his eyes. At least that's the same.

"I know you'll see this, Mara," he says softly. His voice is broken – cracked at the edges.

My heart begins to race when he mentions my name. I knew this was about me.

"You did it. You escaped me when I thought no one could possibly do so," he murmurs.

I lick my dry lips.

"You may think you've won. But you haven't. Not yet."

His face breaks into a wicked smile. The old Alpha Kaden is back. The Alpha that scares me more than any other.

"You have successfully initiated another game. And it's one of my favorites."

I bite back my terror.

"Eventually every game of chase comes to an end, Mara."

Suddenly it's as if the screen isn't there and I'm left facing Kaden in person.

"This time, we are *both* players. And I have bets on the winner."

Evan is now standing right beside me as we stare in horror at the man on the screen.

"Let the hunt begin."

Chapter Seventeen

My dreams are haunted by Kaden as I try to sleep in the bedroom Leia has provided for me in her home. I imagine him chasing me, those hateful leather gloves of his laced with poison that will kill me.

I wake up screaming.

When dawn finally rolls round, I am exhausted. Already, Kaden is winning the game.

Leia gives me another fright when she opens my bedroom door. Grateful she doesn't go round naked like most of the other pack members seem to, I give her my full attention. She deserves that much.

"Good morning!" she greets me. "I'm going to the market this morning. Care to join me?"

The thing about Leia, judging by what I have gathered so far, is that she is always optimistic. I'm not sure if it's a side effect of having a mate or not, but she looks at life like it is such a beautiful thing, and I'm envious of her.

"Sure, that sounds great," I mumble, sleep still having a hold on me.

She smiles broadly. "Great, I will lay out some clean clothes for you in the bathroom. I hope they fit you!"

Once she's gone, I lie back down and close my eyes. Perhaps it will take my mind off Kaden, but I was hoping to stay inside in order to lower the risk of seeing Alpha Grayson again.

As it turns out, I don't regret following Leia to the marketplace she spoke about. It comprises a number of stalls clustered in a small area, with people milling around selling, buying, and bartering. The place is alive with color and unfamiliar aromas. Many people I walk past give me strange glances, obviously recognizing me as a member of the Purity Pack.

"I'm just going to go grab some things from the far side. Meet me back here, and don't talk to people if you can avoid it," Leia whispers in my ear.

Nervously, I watch her skip off with her wicker basket.

Suddenly, I feel very vulnerable. Most of the men going past me are fully naked, while the women wear only the thinnest fabric over their bodies. None of them seem the least bothered by it. I feel increasingly out of place in the yellow sundress I have borrowed.

I continue looking around. Lacking money to buy things, it feels like a pretty futile exercise.

Until my eyes meet a pair of silver ones.

Alpha Grayson. What is *he* doing here?

He loiters at the far end of the market, leaning against the wall of an abandoned building. He is fully dressed, in a dark cloak with the hood pulled down to shadow his face, but I know instantly that it's him. How long he's been watching me, I don't know.

Stumbling backward, I try to decide what to do. The crowd is thick, so maybe I can get lost in it and find a place to hide until he's gone.

He seems to realize I've seen him for I notice him coming toward me with a determined stride. I retreat into the crowd, keeping low so he can't see me. I spot a tent ahead of me and aim for it. It's bright purple and has mysterious-looking ornaments hanging from it, but it's shelter...

I slip into it and close the fabric behind me. With a bit of luck Grayson hasn't seen me dive in here.

"Mara," a voice whispers from the shadows.

Turning swiftly, I see an elderly woman hobbling toward me. She's draped in a golden robe and has an unspeakable atrocity curled around her head. Is it a dead animal? I don't want know.

"How do you know my name?" I demand uneasily. Suddenly I'm wondering who's worse – this woman, or Alpha Grayson.

She pauses by a table in the middle of the tent. It's covered in a purple tablecloth.

"I know a lot, Mara," she says. "Now sit down before the Alpha sees you through the crack." She indicates a chair at the table and sits down on the one opposite. Glancing behind me, I see there is a small gap in the curtains. Quickly I move to sit in the seat.

"You're running from two Alphas, aren't you?"

I frown at the woman, who stares straight into my eyes. It makes me uneasy. Her eyes are silver, but a tint of lilac swirls around her irises. She looks truly mysterious.

"Who are you? And how do you know about the–"

"My name is Esmerelda, and I am a Gaze Reader!" she announces proudly.

My eyebrows crease together. I thought Gaze Readers were a myth... I remember my mother scolding me when she caught me with a book about Gaze Readers. Even back then, I had never imagined what it would be like to meet one.

Gaze Readers. Those blessed by the Moon Goddess. Those who can look into a person's eyes and read what they see there. They are said to have originated from the Devotion Pack.

The woman, Esmerelda, leans over the table and grabs my face between her spindly hands. She twists my face around, making me squirm. Her hands feel calloused and aged.

"You have made a grave mistake, running from the Alpha of the Vengeance Pack," she says. As she stares into my eyes, I stare back into hers. All I see are my eyes reflected back. My dull, lifeless blue eyes. Eyes from which Kaden has stolen all hope.

"I had no choice," I stutter.

"You always have a choice... surrender to him, for otherwise he will come for you!" She's speaking very loudly and I try to hush her, but that just makes her cackle even more loudly. If someone hears us, they might wonder what the heck is going on. I need to get out of here.

I stand up quickly, knocking my chair over.

"Gaze Readers are supposed to give good advice," I tell her. What she says could easily get me murdered. Does she not understand what Kaden would do to me if he found me?

"I do give good advice! You must listen, silly girl, for Kaden will not hurt you," she insists, standing up with me.

Frazzled, I shake my head. Kaden is a murderer, and I'm sure the punishment at the end of this game he's playing will not be a pleasant one.

Esmerelda looks crazy right now, her peppery hair sticking up all over the place. She tries to grab my hands, but I snatch them away.

"Please listen, silly girl–"

"Stop calling me that!" I snap.

"You are blind! Do you not see what you are to Kaden?"

I goggle at her. *What is she talking about? I am nothing but a player in Kaden's sick game.*

She grabs my wrist. When I try to pull away, I realize she's stronger than she looks. She frightens me now.

"Stay! Let me tell you *exactly* what you are!" she demands, pulling me further into the tent.

I struggle against her, to no avail. Thinking I'm about to be murdered or something by this crazy woman, I begin to call out for help.

Almost at once I feel two warm hands land on my shoulders.

"Esmerelda, you old hag. Are you terrorizing young girls again with your absurd proclamations?" a man's voice says from behind me.

I freeze as I realize that it's Alpha Grayson who has come to my aid.

Esmerelda curtsies low at the sight of her Alpha.

"Oh, Alpha Grayson. What an honor to have you in my tent," she croons.

Turning around seems like a terrible idea, as I really don't want to confront Alpha Grayson of all people, but he has his hands on me now and I'm sure he's not going to let me go anytime soon.

"Thank you for detaining Mara long enough for me to find her," Alpha Grayson intones graciously. His voice is low and I can tell that he is amused by the entire situation.

My spirits plummet. A feeling of dread settles on me like Esmerelda's golden cape. He knows my name, which means he knows I'm running from Alpha Kaden. He's probably alerted him, and Kaden's on his way here even as we speak.

Grayson fastens his grip on my wrists and leads me from the tent. I don't dare struggle, knowing it would only give him childish pleasure to overpower me.

"Shall we go somewhere private?" he suggests.

He doesn't wait for an answer but leads me from the marketplace. I feel utterly defeated. Does this mean Kaden has already won his game...?

"You look sad," Alpha Grayson observes, noticing my expression after we have halted in a quiet grove on the edge of the woods.

I ignore him and gaze at the ground. Sad? There are many emotions I am feeling right now, and I don't think sad does justice to any of them. The grove we are in brings back disturbing memories from last night. When I look up at Grayson standing in front of me, I shiver. How is that he can change so completely from a handsome young Alpha to such a nightmarish creature of the night?

"You're going to tell Alpha Kaden that I'm here, aren't you," I tell him.

A flicker of amusement shows in his eyes. "I don't owe that man anything. Don't worry, you're safe here."

For some reason, I believe him. And if he is telling the truth, then I am still in the game...

He pulls the hood back off his head, letting his messy brown hair fall out around his face. I'm not entirely convinced yet that I'm as safe as he tells me I am.

"You're cursed," I remind him. "Why should I believe you?"

He smiles ruefully. "Most nights I am chained to my bed. You really don't need to worry so much."

Easy for him to say. He is the Alpha of the most laid-back of all the packs. His life is meant to be free and easy. The life of a Purity Pack member holds many burdens and responsibilities.

He takes a step toward me and I surprise myself by not stepping back. Close up, I see for the first time how attractive he is with his straight-cut jaw and high cheekbones. But I instantly scold myself – this man is not my mate.

"I will look after you here," he murmurs. His tone is very seductive.

He places a hand on my face. I find myself leaning into his touch. The thought of the forbidden fills my body with excitement. Purity Pack members should never indulge in the touch of the opposite sex.

"It's been a long time since a beautiful girl like you came into my Pack," he says softly.

It's as if his words expel all breath from my body as his thumb skims over my lower lip. What is he thinking?

Suddenly, he leans down, but before our lips can meet I turn my head aside. Instead, he kisses my cheek. As he pulls away, his eyes blaze dangerously. For a moment, I think he is going to say something, but then he seems to change his mind.

"I was planning on going for a run. Would you care to accompany me?"

"As..."

"Yes, as wolves. I promise you will enjoy it," he says.

My mouth drops open. I haven't shifted in many years since it's not approved of within the Purity Pack, who consider it a sin.

Grayson registers my reluctance. "Come on, it's fun! Let loose for once."

"You're right," I agree hesitantly. "I'm in a new pack, and my parents aren't here..."

Grayson flashes me a grin and I thrust away my feelings of doubt. Sure, he's probably a bad influence, but I haven't had fun in a long time.

I watch Grayson begin to shift and, suddenly feeling reckless, I follow suit.

I'm sitting at my desk with my head in my hands. My guards have scoured four packs and have found nothing.

I miss her.

Slamming my fists against my desk, I enjoy the pain. So far she is winning. But how? As an Alpha, I have never lost any game I have started. And I am not willing to lose this one either.

But how has she gotten such a hold on me? I weaken by the day. I *need* to find her.

"Alpha?" a voice addresses me from the doorway.

I look up and see my Head Guard, looking solemn. I nod at him to talk.

He rubs the back of his neck. "No sign of her within the Love Pack. We have put posters up and offered rewards like you suggested," he tells me.

I slump in my chair. Another pack where she is not to be found. Good. I'm sure she would have fallen in love with one of the soppy males over there anyway.

"Try the Harmony Pack," I order him.

He nods and closes the door respectfully behind him. My searches are narrowing down the places where she could be. I will not stop till I find her.

Suddenly, a sweet scent invades my office. I stand, breathing in deeply. The scent is so familiar. It belongs to one she-wolf, and one she-wolf only. She has shifted. She has no idea of the scent she releases.

I can smile again.

"Oh Mara, you've made a mistake."

Chapter Eighteen

Skidding to a stop, I gaze around at my surroundings. They are incredible. Grayson has led me deep into the woods to a small clearing. After running for so long I just want to collapse on the fallen leaves below me.

Being able to shift and run without restraint has driven all thoughts of Kaden from my mind, though now we have halted he is already re-entering my subconscious, with his vicious smile and cruel eyes. I wonder what he's doing right now?

The sight of Grayson shifting in front of me brings me back to reality. It's amazing how I have already become used to seeing naked men everywhere.

He gazes at me expectantly, but I shake my head. I am honestly quite happy to stay in my wolf form and keep my naked body concealed from his prying eyes.

He smirks at me as if he can read my thoughts. "Come on, there is no part of the female anatomy that I haven't seen before," he says smoothly.

I ignore him. Does he think *that's* going to convince me?

"Fine. I'll turn away and I promise I won't look," he tells me blandly.

This, I can agree to. I wait until he has turned around so I can shift back to my normal form without him watching. Then, while he's looking elsewhere, I dart behind a tree.

"Mara?" he calls after he turns back and sees I am no longer where I was. "Where are you?"

I pop my head around the base of the trunk behind which I'm cowering, completely naked. "May I be of assistance?"

"What are you doing behind there?"

"What do you think?"

He chuckles and shakes his head. "Fine, be that way. But you're not getting my gift then."

I frown. He never said anything about a gift...

I watch him walk behind another tree and rustle around in a pile of leaves. To my surprise, he produces a dagger from it.

"It belonged to my parents," he tells me. "I wanted to give it to you, because I want to teach you how to fight. In case you need to one day."

I feel my eyes widen. He wants to teach me how to fight? All my life I have been taught that fighting is bad and that it is the last possible thing we should resort to.

Trying to suppress my nervousness, I emerge from the shelter of the tree. Grayson keeps his eyes on mine, not even glancing down at my body, as if he's not even interested. Instead, he just casually hands me the knife.

I twist it in my hand. It's beautiful. The handle is painted with black ink, creating beautiful swirling patterns. And he wants to give this to me?

"I can't accept it," I say, trying to hand the knife back.

He steps back, holding his hands up. "Please do. Tomorrow I will teach you exactly how to use it. You want to win this game, don't you?"

***

Back at Leia's that night, the heat hits really hard. Stepping out of a cold shower, I decide to wear just a loose shirt of Evan's and some of Leia's underwear.

The two of them have been so kind to me since I arrived. As I stroll back to my room after saying goodnight I vow to pay them back somehow when this all blows over, and I can go back to the Purity Pack.

102

I cross to the window and wonder if I should leave it open for a while – not all night, but just long enough to get some air in the room so I can relax. So I do, leaving the perfect gap for the slight breeze to come through.

Sleep finds me quickly. Slipping into a deep slumber, my mind is burdened by thoughts of Kaden. Those eyes, with so many secrets buried deep within the irises, torment my unconsciousness. I never thought one man could plague my thoughts so much... especially not a murderer.

Heat wakes me from my slumber at an ungodly hour. When I glance over, my window is still open and, standing in front of it, is a man, though I can see only his silhouette against the moonlight. Blinking, I try to see who it is, but then I decide it is just a shadow and I let sleep curl its unrelenting arms around me and drag me back under.

I don't know what time it is when I awake again. I recall the earlier hallucination of a man and am about to laugh at myself for my gullibility when I see him sitting on the edge of the bed.

This time, I become fully awake.

I sit up and rub my eyes, then stare wide-eyed at the shadowy figure. Although I can't see his face, it's obvious he is staring right back at me, whoever he is. My first reaction isn't to be afraid of him in any way. Instead, I'm curious, as if I'm still stuck in a dream state.

"Who's there?" I ask, my voice soft and rusty from sleep. The figure raises a finger to its lips, warning me against speaking.

I can't stop the sudden thrill of fear that slices through me as I realize there is no way this is a dream. If this person is here to hurt me, then I should be screaming for help. Yet not a single word comes out of my mouth. Not even when the mysterious room invader looms over me.

A scream hovers on my lips and I am about to let rip when I feel the stranger's bare hand upon my face. And what I feel makes me gasp aloud.

Sparks. The large, smooth hand caresses my cheek and I feel an unrelenting stream of sparks dance on my skin.

Then the man leans down, his lips brushing against my jawline, making me shiver.

My mind is spinning. All I can grasp is one simple concept. The man now leaning over me is my mate. And I can't even tell who he is. Why hasn't he turned the light on so I can see who he is? Surely he can't want to keep this from me.

The stranger deposits soft kisses on my jaw and neck. I can feel how soft and supple his lips are. I try to move my hands, to run my fingers through his hair or trace his facial features, to get a better feel for who he is, but my hands don't make it far before he grasps my wrists and forces them above my head.

"Mate..." is the only word that comes from my mouth, in a breathy mixture of pleasure and desire.

His lips curl against my neck as he smiles. He knows exactly the effect he is having on me.

It's as if my body has already surrendered itself to him completely as if all control has left me. I feel his fingertips dance along the hem of my shirt. Evan's shirt. He gives a low growl and in one movement rips it apart down the middle. The tearing of the fabric makes me gasp.

How am I going to explain that to Evan in the morning? How am I going to explain any of this to myself?

The thought is expelled from my mind as the man tears the remains of the shirt off me and tosses it over his shoulder. I am naked below him, aside from my underwear. I'm suddenly glad it's dark, so he can't see the tint on my cheeks, or my breasts fully exposed to his touch.

He leans over me for a moment, unmoving. It's as if he's looking at me like he can see me. Perhaps he can, as it seems the moonlight falls on me, yet conceals him.

My eyes instinctively close as he lowers himself to me, kissing my face – everywhere but my lips. With one hand enclosed around my wrists above my head, the other trails across my stomach and waist, feeling every inch of me.

Feverishly, he begins to kiss lower, leaving a hot trail behind every touch of his lips on my skin. I feel his tongue against my breasts, testing me. I can't restrain the gasp of surprise that escapes me at his hot mouth against my skin.

His hand toys with the edge of my underwear, while his mouth brings me unspeakable pleasure as his tongue hungrily circles one of my breasts. The wanton inside me begs for this man to release my hands from his grasp, but he does not comply.

Through the haze, it occurs to me that this man does not wish for me to remember him. He wants me to forget all about this in the morning. I will not allow it...

His lips trail lower, across my stomach and over my hips. Slowly, he moves my hands, so they rest on my stomach. But he still holds them firmly, so I can't explore his body like he explores mine.

His other hand parts my legs so he can settle comfortably between them. What am I about to allow this man to do? My mate...

A fingertip runs lightly over my underwear. He seems to have no worry about it not belonging to me, unlike the shirt. I sense his eyes on me as he slides the fabric slowly down my legs.

All that I can gather about this man as I stare at his silhouette is that he seems to assert a natural dominance. I get that from the way he came into my room unannounced and from the way he still pins me down like an animal.

And I hate how I like it.

He leans down again, and I see how the moonlight shines through his dark hair. But that's all I see. I can't help the soft moan that escapes my lips as I feel his hot breath against my core.

Instead of placing those supple lips exactly where I want them, he kisses my inner thigh softly. His slow movements are driving me insane, and he knows it. It's obvious from the way I feel him smile in triumph against my skin.

The closer he gets to my middle, the more I squirm in earnest. At the same time as hating the torture he inflicts upon me, I can't help but love it too. I don't want him to stop. Ever.

When I finally feel his soft lips touch *exactly* where I want them to, I give a loud moan. He freezes, his fingers digging into my wrists is a warning. He's right, I should be quiet. But it's almost impossible as his hot tongue starts to work on me. Whoever this man is, he knows exactly what he is doing, and I have to turn my head into my pillow to smother my gasps of pleasure.

I hook my legs over his back and shoulders. I feel hard muscle and long scars. Scars... why does that remind me of someone?

All other thoughts retreat to the back of my mind as hitherto unknown pleasure takes over my body. All I can seem to concentrate on is this man's tongue against my flesh, and how he knows exactly how to use it on me.

In a sudden rush of feelings, I see sparks fly across my vision. I can almost feel the edge under my feet and I begin to beg for this man to push me over.

But instead, he takes me by surprise. He pulls away.

Gently, he removes my legs from his back so he can get to his feet. I am left there, a mess atop the covers, waiting for him to come back and finish the job. Instead, I see him walking away, his back to me.

"Wait..." I choke out.

He pauses, his head turning to listen.

"Come back," I mutter.

I see him nod, before he slips back out the window, leaving me on the bed...

As if he was never there.

Chapter Nineteen

"You look... tense this morning," Alpha Grayson observes, earning a glare from me.

"I'm not," I mutter.

As a matter of fact, I *am*. Very tense. No matter how hard I try, I can't get last night out of my head. For once, Kaden is pushed to the back of my consciousness as I try to work out who my mate is.

Whoever he is, I'm mad at him. Why didn't he tell me who he is? How could he just come into my room and do that to me without having the guts to admit who he is? I'm his mate. The one person in this world who is meant for me is apparently afraid of me.

"I'm an Alpha, Mara," Grayson reminds me. "We read people with ease."

We are walking side by side into the forest. Today, he's dressed, which is a relief. His gift of a dagger is clutched tightly in my hand. He is going to teach me how to fight. Despite it being something I have never been allowed to indulge in, I'm excited to see how it will turn out. I'm sure I will be useless at it.

I sigh deeply. "My mate visited me last night."

His eyes widen in surprise. Perhaps he can help me find out who this elusive man is.

"And? Who is he?" he asks.

He sounds just as surprised as I am. My mate is in the Freedom Pack, right now, and I have no idea who he is. It's exasperating.

"That's the thing... I don't know," I confess breathily.

Grayson looks confused.

"It was dark," I go on hurriedly. "He didn't say a word to me. He just–" I break off, not wanting to continue. I've grown to like Alpha Grayson, but there are some things that I don't really want to share with him. I hardly even want to admit to myself what I did.

He glances at me expectantly. "He what?"

"Just visited, touched me, and then left again," I tell him. There was a bit more to it than that, of course. I'm not used to lying, but lately I've been having to do it a lot. After last night, I'm mentally reminding myself to pray for my sins. The Moon Goddess can't be happy with me right now.

"We will track him down, don't worry," Grayson assures me.

I smile gratefully at him. Good. I can't let this man escape my clutches, especially after what he did to me last night.

We walk a while longer. The sun is out, and very hot again, so we stay under the trees. The shade against my skin feels nice, and I try to use this sense of freedom to clear my thoughts for a moment.

Until I see it.

A piece of paper stapled against the base of a tree makes me freeze. Grayson sees it too and glances at me before going nearer. I swallow, knowing exactly what it is before I even get close.

A poster. Of me. My face takes up most of the paper, but the photograph is not just any photograph of me. It is of me last night. I sit upon the bed, my mate just a shadow on the edge of the bed. I stare at him, my eyes wide and bright. The moonlight is the only thing illuminating my face.

My stomach in my throat, I rip the paper from the tree. Underneath the incriminating photo of me, is bold, black text.

Worth the Sin?

I'm filled with an overwhelming sense of fear, like I'm being watched. I look all around, feeling myself going pale, only to see Grayson staring back at me in concern.

"He's here," I say breathlessly, my gaze darting around the trees, looking for Kaden.

"Who?" Grayson asks.

I thrust the paper at his chest. As he looks at it, his gaze narrows. I carry on looking around in all directions, wiping my sweaty palms on my shirt. All I can think is one simple thing.

Kaden is here.

"You think this is Kaden's doing? There's no way to tell," Grayson remarks, trying to reassure me.

The thought of Kaden being here in the one place I've felt safe makes me want to throw up or burst into tears.

"Of course, it's his doing! He's taunting me," I reply, my voice strangled.

Grayson still looks confused.

"Only Alpha Kaden would ever do something like this! He meant for me to see it," I insist. I grab the poster from Grayson's hand and rip it into pieces, then throw them into the air.

As I watch them blow away in the breeze, I spot another poster on a tree a bit further away. I drag Grayson toward it. It's the same poster, with the same picture, but a different caption at the bottom.

I Wonder Who He Is?

I toss the paper over my shoulder in anger. He knows who my mate is. And something tells me he's going to use it against me.

Grayson picks the paper up to look at it himself. "He probably doesn't know either."

I shake my head furiously. "He would *have* to know. He was there taking pictures," I point out. My words make my heart sink. I'm sure I'm right.

Grayson grabs my hand again and squeezes it gently. The look on his face suggests he is worried about the Kaden situation as well. Why wouldn't he be? The Alpha of the Vengeance Pack hanging around is like a bad omen.

"I think I see another," he murmurs.

From that point on, they just keep coming. Picture after picture of me with cruel, sadistic captions underneath, written to taunt me.

One of them is particularly unsettling.

Watch Your Back, 'cause I'm Watching It Too.

"I have to go," I say.

If I stay here, Kaden will drag me off to the Vengeance Pack and I'll be back where I started. All the help I've been given will have been for nothing, and I will never be able to save Milly.

"No, stay here," Grayson counters. "My estate is not too far from here and I promise it's safe."

I hesitate. Would even Kaden dare to steal me from Grayson's own home?

I sigh and let the poster fall from my hand. "I just feel like so much of a burden. And I'm not sure what Kaden would think about me staying with you, another Alpha."

I don't doubt for a second that Alpha Grayson can look after himself, but how long will Kaden leave it before he acts? Do I even matter enough to him to bother continuing the pursuit? Maybe if I'm out of his reach he will give up trying to get to me.

"I have guards and the place is fairly well enclosed," Grayson goes on. "You'll be safe there."

I nod slowly. "Okay, I'll do it."

He grins, but then the pleased expression on his face falters and he goes pale. I turn around to see what he is staring at. It's another photo, fixed to a tree behind us.

There are two scrawled, handwritten words on it.

I win.

***

I smile to myself.

How could I not be pleased, when I'm winning? I knew I would win... Mara is my mate, and there is no possible way anyone could keep her from me.

Except, possibly, Grayson.

That young, stupid Alpha. I heard what he said to Mara in the woods today. He thinks that he can keep her from me? When my

110

family is the reason he is cursed. He is challenging me, trying to provoke me into action.

I will get to her, despite him. Like I did last night.

The thought makes me shiver. Last night, I acted on impulse, and it was stupid. I had never intended going into her room like I did. It was my own need taking over from what should have happened, and now she is aware that her mate is close by. The optimism it's going to give her makes me anxious.

I can still taste her sweetness against my lips and it makes me crave more. Leaving her hanging was a way of ensuring I keep control over her. She will want more... She's desperate. I'm desperate. Yet she can't know.

Now I sit in Grayson's home, waiting. The moment I heard him say he would protect Mara I came here to prove him wrong. He can't keep her from me, however much the heroic side of him would like to.

She's not in my arms right now because I'm having too much fun. That's what I keep telling myself.

I hear them come into the house. It's only a few minutes before Grayson wanders into the room where I am. I hate how men here think it's okay to be naked. There is no way I want to see that.

"Kaden," he mutters in disdain when he sees me lounging casually in his seat. His silver eyes are glowing bright, and I know, as the sun starts to set around us, that I have limited time to make my claim.

"Grayson," I respond. "Grown up, I see." I offer him a half smile.

He sets down a bunch of papers, which I assume are the posters I put up in the forest. Warnings.

"What do you want?"

I stand. He knows what I want. And I bet he wishes he didn't. I see it in the way a small tremor goes through him. He has every right to be afraid of me, and I like it that way.

"I want many things. But right now, I want Mara," I say smoothly.

His jaw clenches. "You're her mate, aren't you?"

"Ah, I see you're getting smarter also. Yes, and I would like her back," I tell him.

He sighs audibly and I see him try to gather up the courage to defy me. As the second youngest Alpha, he has a lot to learn.

"She doesn't want to go back to your pack. If she knew it was you that visited her last night she would be disgusted."

His words jab my heart. It makes me mad that he may be right. "That's not the point—"

I'm suddenly cut off as Grayson's eyes begin to turn red. He's changing into a monster and there is nothing I can do to stop it.

"Why should I give you your mate," he growls, "when you still have mine?"

Lexia. Of course. His mate, whom I kidnapped from the Discipline Pack. She still doesn't know that I took her and placed her within my pack in order to have something over the Alpha of the Freedom Pack. She doesn't even know they are mates.

"Lexia will not be yours until Mara is mine," I say coolly.

I can see he is on the verge of shifting, and the look in his eyes spells out a warning... I need to get out of here.

"Tomorrow, Grayson... sleep on the fact that I will kill for Mara."

Chapter Twenty

Breathe.

With every step I take, my nerves get tauter. I'm such an idiot for doing this, but it's the only option.

I need to find Kaden.

This morning, Alpha Grayson told me that Kaden visited him. He threatened him, with his mate, and now I feel like I am responsible for what has been done. Now, I must do what a Purity Pack member would do.

Leaves crunch under my feet as I wade deeper into the forest. The gift of a dagger is tucked against my palm. I am as ready as I ever will be to finally face this monster of a man. For the last time...

My plan is simple. Make him bleed. Make him beg for his own survival until he strains for mercy. Then I will leave him for Grayson to find and lock up.

Even with this plan etched into my mind, I'm still having doubts. The element of surprise is what I'm striving for, but what happens if he gets the better of me? I have spoken of my plan to no one... no one will arrive to ruin this moment when I can prove I have a valiant heart.

For once, I want to be one step ahead in this game.

I come to a stop in a place that I think is suitable. I'm positive Kaden will hear me and come for me the moment I show myself. *He is here, isn't he?* He is probably waiting for the perfect moment to strike. And I'm giving him one.

"Kaden!" I scream.

My voice echoes off tree trunks and radiates through the woods like a siren. I make myself sound desperate and in need of help. Perhaps Kaden will get here faster if he thinks that I am vulnerable.

"You win, okay! I surrender..." *That's bound to get his attention, wherever he is.*

Nothing. For five minutes I wait for my calls to be answered, but nothing happens. Resting against the base of a tree, I pray to the Moon Goddess that my plan will work.

Hope has almost died within me when a hand comes out from behind the tree I lean against and hauls me round to the other side. Gasping, I'm pressed up against a hard, warm chest. When I look up, I meet the cruel, dark eyes of Alpha Kaden.

He's smirking, of course.

"You called?"

My plan was to stab him straight in the heart and run. But the moment I feel his body pressed against mine, I'm left breathless, and my mind is flushed of thought.

"I–I," I stutter incoherently.

Slowly, he backs me up until I feel the base of the tree against my back. He holds one of my wrists against the tree, while my other one is tucked behind my back. He clearly hasn't realized I am holding a knife in that hand.

"I've missed you, Mara," he murmurs.

For a moment, I almost believe he's serious. But the gleam of amusement in his eyes convinces me he's tricking me. And it's for the last time. My fingers tighten on the handle of the dagger.

"The feeling isn't mutual," I snap.

He chuckles deeply. "Ever the smart talker. Did Grayson teach you nothing?"

His mention of Grayson stiffens my resolve. He told me of his mate trapped within the Vengeance Pack. I will do anything to stop myself from ending up in the same situation.

"So, tell me, Mara, why did you call for me, when you've put so much effort in getting away?"

114

This is the moment I've been waiting for. All it will take is one jab in the chest with the knife to wound him enough to disable him. Not to kill him, of course.

Yet his proximity renders me useless. As his free leather-gloved hand strokes my arm, I can't help but relax. I need to clear my head.

"I want you to release Grayson's mate," I say confidently. Truly, I do want that, but it's not the reason why I am here.

Kaden raises an eyebrow speculatively. "Lexia? You want me to release her?"

I swallow and wish I wasn't so bad at lying. "I do."

"Well, you don't seem as though you're in a very good situation to barter for something like that," he says, shaking his head slowly.

He's right. I'm pressed up against a tree, with an Alpha who could murder me at any second.

But I refuse to be afraid.

"Please..." I beg, my voice trailing away. I'm not quite sure what I'm begging for, but I'm filling up time because I'm sure my hand is stuck behind my back.

He smiles wickedly. "You might just have to... convince me," he murmurs in my ear.

My jaw clenches, as I force myself to stare into his eyes. I want to see the surprise on his face as I stab him in the chest with my dagger.

"How?" I ask, my voice just a breathy whisper.

He smiles and suddenly it dawns on me how close his face is to mine, so close in fact that his breath is mixing with my breath. I start as his free hand squeezes my waist roughly.

"Beg me," he whispers in my ear.

I squirm in his grasp. "Never."

"You seem to think you have some choice in this," Kaden remarks, cockily.

I'm not sure what he's insinuating... I don't even want to think about it.

"Just let me go," I mutter, trying to ignore the fact that his hand is beginning to wander down from my waist.

115

The amusement in his eyes is evident. "Why?"

I grit my teeth against the feeling of his gloved fingers on my inner thigh.

"I'm not here for you to touch me like that," I mumble.

"What are you here for then?"

I am about to answer with a snarky remark — something about winning the game — when Kaden's fingers reach into the part of my body reserved for my mate. I gasp with indignation and try to wriggle away but the pressure of his fingers only increases. And by the look on his face, it doesn't seem he's about to stop.

"You have tested my limits, Mara, now it's my time to test yours."

His words make me shiver involuntarily, and I know that he notices. Slowly, I feel him begin to move his fingers against me.

"What do you want from me?" I hiss, turning my head so I don't have to look at him. His eyes will only make me weaken.

"Say my name. Tell me I've won and I'll give you the release you so desperately crave."

"Never," I growl. I squeeze my eyes shut and try to think of something other than the tips of his fingers tracing firm circles against my delicate skin.

He laughs softly in my ear, and it's obvious he's enjoying this. How could he not? The power he has over me is apparently complete. My hand is tight on the dagger. If I could just get my mind clear, this would be much easier to execute.

Instead, I find my legs tightening around Kaden's hand as his gloved fingers massage me through my clothes. I hold back the moan that threatens to escape my lips. I refuse to give Kaden the pleasure of hearing it.

"Surrender yourself to me," he insists.

It's that one word that does it. Surrender.

Never!

In one fluid movement, I pull the knife out from behind my back and sink it deeply into Kaden's chest.

116

He stumbles back in surprise, letting me go. His hands fly to the knife embedded in his chest. Then he yanks it out and what I see makes me want to scream.

The knife is not covered in red blood as I expect it to be. Instead, I see it is a mixture of red and black fluid that drips from the blade — and I realize, with a sinking heart, what I've done.

I haven't just stabbed the Alpha. I've *poisoned* him.

What disturbs me most though, is the look in Kaden's eyes as he falls to his knees in front of me, dropping the dagger onto the grass.

"No... no, no!" I stutter.

I fall in front of Kaden, grabbing onto his shoulders. Whatever poison Grayson has laced this dagger with, it's working fast.

"I swear I didn't mean to do this!" I say desperately.

I had meant to wound him, just enough to weaken him. Not to kill him with poison.

He smiles weakly before toppling to the ground, face first. I'm quick to pull his shoulder over, so he's lying on his back. He stares straight up at me, betrayal swirling deep within his eyes.

"What do I do?" I demand frantically.

I press my hands against the wound on his chest in an attempt to stop the flow of blood. It's the only thing I can think to do through the fog of fear across my mind.

"Tell me you love me..." he gasps.

I pause and gaze into Kaden's face. It's deathly pale, and I sense the poison overwhelming him. He's dying, right in front of me.

"What do you mean?" I ask, not sure I heard him correctly.

Weakening by the second, he reaches his hands up and strips one of his gloves off. I watch it hit the grass in front of me. Then I meet his pleading eyes.

"I can't die until you know," he mutters, his voice strained and breathless.

His bare palm is extended to me, making me stop for a second. He wants me to touch him...

117

And I do. I take his hand within my own, wrapping my fingers around his cold, dead ones. And I gasp.

Sparks.

Chapter Twenty-One

I stare at Kaden's body without moving.

Kaden lies on his front on the bed, white hospital linen covering his lower half. His eyes are closed and his lips are partially open. He looks peaceful. Almost...

"Why would you do it?" I question, my voice rough and unsteady. I've hardly spoken these past four days. I've spent most of my time bent over Kaden, praying that he'll wake up. But he hasn't.

Why he lies on his front, I'm not sure. They just put him that way, despite the wound on his chest that has so far refused to heal.

"How was I supposed to know that you would stab him?" Grayson responds airily.

We are standing just outside the room, looking through a glass panel in the door. My breath keeps fogging it up and I have to keep wiping it clear, but I resolve to stay where I am. I don't want Grayson in there with him, though I'm not sure why. I've been very protective concerning Kaden even though it's me who has put him in this state.

"Poison," I murmur. "Classy."

"Knife to the heart. Classy," Grayson echoes.

I glare at him. I'm feeling very grouchy. How could I not be when I can hardly sleep for fear that he'll die. I'm on the verge of collapsing. I rest my forehead against the glass. I can feel the sympathetic look Grayson's giving me as well as the hand he rests on my shoulder.

"If I wanted him dead, Mara, I wouldn't have answered your calls and brought him back here for the best doctors and nurses to work on him," Grayson reminds me pointedly.

He's right, but his words don't sink in. All I feel is guilt. I want Kaden to wake so I can plead for his forgiveness. Yet the fact that he has kept so much from me still rankles in my mind. I should be mad at him, but I can't be when I see him on the bed like that.

"I'm going in," I say.

I push through the door and enter the room, which smells clinical and clean. Kaden remains unconscious and unresponsive. Sitting down on my seat beside his bed, I resume the position I've gotten used to lately. I lay my arms on the bed and rest my head on them as I watch him breathe.

I imagine him in some kind of dreamland, happier than he's ever been here. I contemplate his calm expression and pray that the Moon Goddess is taking care of him as best she can, despite everything he has said about her, and my little belief in her.

Gingerly, I run my fingertips across his soft, flawless skin. The sparks it gives me reminds me that no matter what this man's past entails, he is my mate, and I shall care for him as long as I can. At the same time, of course, I want to strangle him for what he has done to me.

"He loves you," I hear Grayson say from behind me.

I turn and see that he is looking at Kaden. He looks hurt, broken almost. It means a lot to me that he truly does seem to care, despite what Kaden has done to him.

"It won't seem real until I hear him tell me himself," I reply quietly. Turning back, I begin to trace the scars down Kaden's back.

"Why doesn't he wake?" I ask.

Grayson sighs deeply. "I promise you that my best doctors—"

I jump up as Kaden shivers under my fingertips.

"He... I–I think he's waking," I stammer.

I look closely at him but his face remains impassive. I glance at the tubes running from his body and inspect the bag of poison that's slowly been filtered from his body and replaced by clean, healthy blood. It's full to the brim. For one knife, a lot of poison has spread through his body.

"How do you know?" Grayson queries, coming over to stand by my side.

I pull my chair back and shake Kaden's shoulder gently. He doesn't respond. I squeeze my eyes shut. Maybe I was hallucinating and he didn't really move after all. Maybe he is really gone...

"Hey, everything's going to be okay," Grayson murmurs. He turns me around, before wrapping his arms around me.

I feel tears begin to well up in my eyes as I stuff my face into Grayson's shirt.

"Get your hands off my mate..."

I spin on my heels to see Kaden staring straight at me, having twisted his body around enough to look at us. I'm so startled I nearly collapse to the floor.

In a second, I have wrapped my arms around his body, holding him as close to me as possible. His groan of pain is the only thing that makes me pull away. I need to remember that I have just stabbed the man in the chest.

"Sorry," I murmur, releasing my hold but still remaining as close as I possibly can.

A lazy grin spreads over his features and I feel my racing heart begin to calm a little. Using whatever strength he can muster, he pulls himself off his stomach and rolls over onto his back.

The expanse of bandage wrapped round his rib cage makes me feel both guilty and nauseous at the same time.

"Good morning beautiful," Kaden says, his voice rough and barely audible.

"It's actually the afternoon," I correct him, taking his hand between mine. The sparks are undeniable. He glances at me, feeling them too. When I imagined my mate, I had no idea it would be the man who had terrorized an entire pack and kidnapped me. Had anyone said so, I would surely have told them they were crazy.

"You look terrible," he mutters, probably noticing what lack of sleep can do to someone.

I roll my eyes. "Can't say you look any better," I retort, giving his fingers a squeeze.

He chuckles. It's a familiar sound that makes me want to sing and dance for the first time in weeks.

"Whose fault is that?"

Silence descends. Stupidly, I had hoped we could put all that behind us. I look down down at my feet, suddenly unable to meet his eyes.

"Mara... it's okay," he mumbles.

I dare to look up as he struggles to pull himself into more of a sitting position. I want to scold him for putting himself under any strain while he is so weak but I force the impulse down.

"If I knew that we were... well... mates, I wouldn't have stabbed you," I whisper, picking my words carefully.

I'm embarrassed by my own timidity, but then I notice that Grayson isn't there any longer and I wonder at which point he left.

Kaden manages another grin. "I would like to think you wouldn't."

"Speaking of mates..."

I break off, prompting Kaden to raise an eyebrow, probably predicting what I was going to say.

Do I want to yell at him for keeping it from me? The fact that we are mates? Yes. Heck, I wanted to punch and kick him when I first realized what he had kept from me, but I don't want to now. We can talk about it later maybe, when he feels up to it.

Without warning, he pulls me toward him, clasping his arms around my back. I brace myself against the crisp sheets, afraid of crushing him.

He smiles at my mortified expression. "Can we just kiss now and talk later?" he asks.

I place a finger on his lips and shake my head. "Not when you've just woken from a coma." I sound terribly motherly, I realize.

He cocks his head. "I can see down your shirt, by the way."

I shriek and pull back, automatically pulling the top of my shirt closed. He gives a delighted laugh.

"Charming as ever," I mutter.

"Come on, you're my mate – remember?"

I sigh in defeat and collapse into my seat beside the bed.

Kaden looks warily at me. "When was the last time you ate?"

"This morning..."

"Slept?"

"I think I slept at least an hour last night."

Kaden narrows his eyes and I'm suddenly aware of his disapproval. I've never seen this caring side of the dreaded Alpha before. It's strange.

"That's why you look like you do. Perhaps you should be in bed with me," he says. He sounds like he is joking, but I can tell he is serious about the sleep thing.

My lips twitch but I refuse to smile too broadly. Instead, I run my fingers through his soft black hair, watching it fall around my fingers. For a man who hasn't washed his hair in four days, his hair feels awfully soft.

"Seriously, though, you need to sleep," Kaden tells me. His eyes go hard, as he stares at me expectantly.

As if I would stand up and walk straight out the room without a goodbye.

"And leave you? Not an option," I say stubbornly.

"Mara. Please. It would bring me nothing but comfort to know my mate is safely tucked up in bed," he explains.

I'd prefer to stay here, with his hand laced in mine, but I can tell that it isn't going to happen.

"Fine. I'm sure Grayson will get me a room."

"As long as it's not with him," Kaden mutters, quick with a snappy response.

I shake my head immediately. That's the last of his worries at the moment. "You owe your life to that man," I tell him, truthfully.

Slowly, he slides down deeper into the bed, and motions with his head for me to leave. Instead, I lean down over him and kiss his forehead. As I pull away, he holds the sides of my face and guides me down to give me a whisper of a kiss. Our first real kiss.

"You can go now," Kaden says, smiling.

Chapter Twenty-Two

I wake the next day, feeling terrible. All I want to do is curl back up and sleep for another few hours. But I know I shouldn't. I force my eyes open and am surprised to see someone sitting on the edge of my bed, grinning.

"What are you doing out of bed?" I demand, staring at my mate with what I hope is a disapproving expression on my face.

I shouldn't be surprised really. Instead of resting, healing like he's supposed to, Kaden is up and about, and here with me. The look on his face suggests he's had enough of being in a hospital bed by himself.

"You've slept thirteen hours straight. I thought I'd better come and check on you," he tells me.

That wakes me up. Thirteen hours?

He's dressed in a puffy blue robe, which looks ridiculous on him. Never in my life would I have expected to see him dressed in such a thing. He sees I am looking at it.

"They're making me wear it," he grumbles, his face screwed up. He does look rather comical.

A silence settles over us as we consider each other. His eyes no longer seem cold and distant, but familiar and warm. I feel him take my hand in his as he shuffles closer up the bed.

"I just wanted to tell you that I understand why you stabbed me. I kind of deserved it," he says softly.

"Yeah, you did. Especially for keeping the fact that we are mates from me," I agree. I'm not sure why I've brought it up, but I suppose

I deserve to be told how long he's known. And why he decided to keep the biggest part of my life from me.

He sighs deeply. "I should probably start from the beginning, shouldn't I?"

I nod slowly.

He lies beside me. I turn on my side so I can watch him as he talks.

"Four years ago, I boarded a train in the Purity Pack. It was back when my father ruled. I loved the Purity Pack then..."

I frown. I don't remember him ever saying he once loved my pack.

"I sat next to this beautiful young girl, with the palest of hair and the bluest of eyes. And we touched – but she was asleep and didn't notice the sparks," he says softly.

"Do you mean it was me? How could you know what my eye color was if I was sleeping?"

"Maybe you slept with your eyes open."

"I doubt that..."

He stirs restlessly. "Will you listen?"

"Sorry. Continue."

He collects himself and runs a hand down his abominable, blue outfit.

"Okay. So I freaked out and ran. You were right when you first met me to call me a coward. For three years I managed to expel you from my mind. Until, one day, the urge to find you grew too strong. I had to lay eyes on you."

The look in his eyes is warm but I squirm uncomfortably. What if he saw me do something embarrassing? I shake the stupid thought from my mind.

"I would watch you walk to school at least once a week," he informs me. He pauses when he notices my expression.

"Isn't that stalking?"

"I'm your mate – it's not stalking, it's observing," he corrects me.

I roll my eyes at him, but let it pass. He pats my thigh and doesn't take his hand away.

"It became so hard to be away from you that I began to grow anxious. Other boys were starting to notice you. They would watch you as you walked along, talking about all the wicked things they would do to you."

I shake my head vigorously. "Purity Pack members don't do that."

"You truly are ignorant, my love."

As he talks I am glad we have managed to close the gap between us. It's something we've achieved without even knowing it like an unknown force has drawn us together.

"I admit I was jealous," he tells me. "So, in the end, I stole you in the night and took you back to my estate to keep you away from prying eyes. I know it's stupid, but I had no other choice. I would have killed myself if I hadn't been able to have you near me."

Kaden's fingers draw soft circles on my bare thighs. I try to concentrate on the information I'm being given. Everything he says makes sense.

"I would have liked to know," I whisper.

He looks apologetic. "I know. And the worst thing is, I never planned to tell you."

I see the defeat and fear in his eyes. I sense there is a compelling reason he has kept his silence until now. A darker reason that even now he is reluctant to share.

I am seconds from asking him about it, but he surprises me by leaning forward, kissing my lips and stilling my unspoken words.

To feel his lips on mine is pure pleasure. They have already explored every inch of my body, but now they press against my own lips, and I am complete.

I expect him to pull away but instead, his kiss becomes fiercer. I respond, hoping this kiss will never end.

Kaden leans over me. I feel defenseless before his merciless passion and my hands press against his back. His muscles are hard against my fingertips through the fabric of the blue robe he has on.

I've never wanted to strip the clothes off a man as much as I do now.

Kaden must be feeling the same, as he lifts his lips from mine, breathing heavily. His eyes are alight with an ardent fire that burns straight into me. It seems to light a path as he takes in my entire, panting body.

"Do you know how hard it was to keep my hands from touching every inch of your body?"

He leans down again, his hot lips covering my neck with feverish kisses. My fingers drift up into his hair, wrapping themselves in the soft, dark strands.

"It was almost impossible to contain my imagination when I could be ravaging you," he murmurs against my neck, his hot breath like oil to a fire.

I want to shake my head. Of course I don't know what it felt like – yet now, in this very moment, I experience the same longing he did then.

"From now, until our death, I will not stop making up for those moments," he promises.

Reminding me of that one experience – only a few nights ago – Kaden tears my shirt off me and lets it fall by the side of the bed. This time I am wearing a bra, however.

What made me think of wearing that to bed? Idiot.

Kaden licks my collarbone as his hands slip behind my back to undo the clasp.

Then someone comes in.

"Is Kaden – oh dammit – scarred for life!"

Kaden is off me like a spring, falling back onto the bed so he can size up whoever has spoiled the moment between us. I cover myself with the sheets and see a mortified Alpha Grayson at the door.

"What do you want?" Kaden snaps, maddened at being interrupted.

I remain silent as Grayson shields his eyes. Does he seriously think that's going to erase his memory? Poor man.

"The doctors need you back downstairs," he says gruffly to Kaden.

Then he's gone, pulling the door closed after him.

Kaden sighs and runs a hand down his face. "I would rather stay with you than go see a couple of doctors."

I take a deep breath. "They want you for a reason, Kaden. You're their patient and obviously you're not completely healed yet. I'll come with you."

He narrows his eyes at me. "All right, I'll go if you're coming too. But only if you promise I can kiss you the next second we are alone."

I smile. "I promise."

There are two doctors waiting for us in Kaden's room. They take their time unwrapping Kaden's bandages and examining the wound.

"It doesn't look as though the wound is healing," one of them concludes solemnly.

I stare at the damage I have managed to do to Kaden's chest. The wound still seeps blood and appears swollen and purple. Even though it looks terribly painful, Kaden doesn't seem at all fazed. He seems more irritated than anything else.

"I am an Alpha," he protests. "I should be healing quickly."

The other doctor pushes his thick-rimmed glasses up his nose. Apparently, these two are Grayson's best, though they look nervous of Kaden. I don't blame them since I am a little too.

"We have been considering a possible reason why you're not healing at a sufficient rate..."

Kaden and I exchange apprehensive glances.

"We believe that it may be because this was inflicted at the hands of your mate," the first doctor goes on.

I flinch. "Me?"

"Indeed. Perhaps, Kaden, you should consider marking your mate."

My hands run through my hair, yanking at it so I can get some sense of what is real and what is not. Kaden must mark me in order to heal that vicious wound on his chest? Of course... the mark on my neck would seal everything in our relationship. I would be his, and he would be mine.

To my surprise, Kaden has gone very pale and the panic in his expression is unmistakable. But why?

"What's wrong?" I ask, taking his hand.

He searches my face as if he's looking for a refuge within my eyes, but his jaw tightens when he can't find it.

"I–I can't mark you," he stammers.

I ignore the jab that that reply sends straight to my heart. *What does he mean?*

"Why not?" I hear myself asking.

"He will hurt me! He will hurt me by hurting you!" he answers, glancing over my shoulder as if expecting to find the person he means right there.

"Who, Kaden? Who?"

"My brother."

I raise an eyebrow "Kace?"

He swallows deeply before taking in a shallow breath and shaking his head.

"No. Coen."

Chapter Twenty-Three

It takes three frightening minutes to console Kaden and calm him down.

I don't dare question him further. Instead, I just sit on the edge of his hospital bed, running my hand slowly down his back. The fear in his eyes has chilled my blood. To see someone like Kaden, who is usually so confident of his authority, be so genuinely scared scares me, too.

Coen? The polite companion with the warm smile, the friend who once helped me attempt an escape – how could he possibly be a source of such fear?

As for him and Kaden being brothers – they're not remotely alike.

"Why would Coen hurt me?" I inquire.

His breathing has gotten calmer the more I touch him.

"Because you're a pawn."

A pawn?

Kaden twists his head and notes my confusion. "I love to win my games, Mara. Coen prefers the process of the game. The manipulation that is involved. Using every piece as a weapon."

His words hardly make sense to me, but the look in his eye suggests he's deadly serious. I want to unleash the torrent of questions in my mind, but I allow Kaden to talk first.

"You may have thought Coen liked you, but he didn't. He used you to get to me."

His words hit me like a punch to the chest. *He never liked me?*

"Tell me how."

"Coen is my twin brother, only minutes younger than me. Mother said he was what was unleashed from Pandora's box. Even though she loved him, she described him as the epitome of envy."

"He was jealous of you?"

I can only imagine what Coen had to go through, seeing his brother getting the title of Alpha, while he, only a few moments younger, was forced to pursue an ordinary life in the shadow of his success.

"And now... now I've lost all control over him," Kaden mutters, looking frightened again.

I tighten my grip on his hand, letting him know that he can share anything with me.

"What do you mean when you say that I'm a pawn?" I press him. The question has been lurking at the edge of this conversation.

Kaden swallows. "Coen has been using you against me. He threatens me with your life. I have no choice but to comply."

My mind whirrs as I try to absorb every shred of information he's giving me.

"You're an Alpha. Why don't you just... kick him out?"

Kaden shifts on his bed but winces with pain. I place my other hand on his arm, wanting to feel more contact between us. He seems to relax at the sparks that we share between us.

"He's the..." He breaks off, squeezing his eyes shut. "He's the only one who knows where my parents are."

My heart skips a beat as I attempt to fight my way through my haze of confusion and make sense of what he's telling me.

"You told me your parents are dead," I remind him, my voice strained. It isn't the fact that he has lied to me about that – I couldn't care less about that – it's the fact that I have been assuming his parents weren't alive, when really they are. Which means he has been carrying this burden the whole time I've known him.

"I had to. If I even touch Coen, I'll never see my parents again."

131

He no longer shakes with fear nor gazes over my shoulder as if someone is haunting him. Instead, his gaze is hard and his expression stony.

"Everything I have done was under his orders. You think I wanted to kill Althea's child?"

I feel the blood pound against my temples as I try to make sense of it all. Kaden didn't want me to hurt Althea... it was Coen all along. Of all the things I've heard, this fits the best in my mind.

"And Kace?" I ask.

"The same. Why would I ever willingly let my mate marry my brother if it wasn't for the price I'd have to pay?"

I'm beginning to understand everything now. "Then why let me go and risk putting me in danger?"

"I had to... I couldn't physically keep myself away from you any longer. As long as Coen doesn't find out that you know we are mates, we should be okay," he breathes.

"You're saying we have to go on with our lives without ever becoming mates?" My voice rises as my outrage reveals itself. There is no way I could agree to such a compromise. It'll have to be tackled somehow. Even if I have to strangle Coen myself.

"I don't see another way..."

"Of course there is another way. There has to be," I inform him. "Don't worry. I will find out from him where your parents are."

Kaden frowns and I suddenly feel a burden has settled heavily on my shoulders. Kaden clearly doesn't like it.

"You're not—"

"I will manipulate him, exactly like he has been doing with us," I promise him.

Standing up, I feel empowered by the simple idea of helping Kaden. If I can do this for him, maybe I will finally have found the reason why I am on this earth. Maybe I will feel like I belong for once in my life.

"Kaden, I'm going to get your parents back."

***

"Were the games his idea?" I ask Kaden a few hours later, as we sit in the back of Grayson's car, being driven back to the Vengeance Pack. One of his hands is clasped in mine, while the other clutches his chest. What lies ahead will not be easy for him, but it's something we shall at least face together.

Coen can't know about us, however.

"No," Kaden concedes. "I do enjoy a game. And perhaps a good riddle from time to time."

"So... Milly?" I continue. I don't want to bring it up especially, but now seems a good moment.

Kaden seems startled to hear me mention the name of the girl he has presumably murdered. I remember how he taunted me with a riddle I couldn't answer, leading me to feel I had failed her.

"I sent her home long ago. There was never a time when I wanted to keep her there. It was Coen's orders."

The tension that has been threatening to shrink my heart relaxes and I can breathe properly again.

"I still have a lot to tell you. But right now, I just want to enjoy these last moments with my mate, and openly show her my admiration," he says warmly.

I feel my cheeks heating up, but at the same time his words sadden me. From this point on, we will be sneaking around. Kaden and I haven't spoken about how I'm going to manipulate Coen yet, but I think we have a pretty good idea.

Which I'm sure he isn't too happy about.

My thoughts are blown away as the man I know as my mate reaches for me. He kisses me softly and I savor the bliss that overwhelms me. I wish I could lock this moment away in a chest so I can come back to it any day in the long-distant future.

"Coen can't keep me from you," Kaden whispers against my ear, his hot breath making me shiver in delight.

"Yeah, but I could drive this car off the next bridge," I hear Grayson grumble from the driver's seat.

133

We pull away from each other. Grayson is watching us in the rear-view mirror and his expression is one of both disapproval and disappointment. But I am grateful to him for agreeing to drive us to the Vengeance Pack. Apparently, it will look better to Coen if we show up with another Alpha.

"You don't have to look," I retort, while smiling at an unamused Kaden. Something tells me he didn't want to be disturbed.

"We're nearly there, anyway," Grayson tells us.

I look out of the window and see he's right. The Vengeance Pack walls are closing in on us at a fast rate. Almost as fast as my heart rate is speeding up.

Kaden tugs gently at my arm and holds up a black cloth. Right. I was forgetting I agreed to be blindfolded. It's another way to convince Coen I've been brought back unwillingly.

Kaden ties the cloth loosely over my eyes, coating my world in darkness.

"This would be nice, in another situation," Kaden whispers in my ear.

I can't help but smile at the sly tone in his voice. I know exactly what he means by that.

A few moments pass by before I feel Kaden's lips by my ear again.

"I have a riddle for you," he murmurs.

Great...

"You shall be asked it when Coen is around – and you'll need to answer correctly," he insists.

My heart sinks. I am terrible at riddles – and he knows it. I lift the edge of my blindfold up so I can meet his gaze.

"Will you give me the answer?" I ask.

I frown as he shakes his head.

"I will give you a single guess now, as a practice," he says. The look in his eyes suggests he's excited to see if I can decode it.

"An unfortunate soul, can spin quite a tale.

Words weaved like a needle, with string like fire.

Cracks between the lines are memories;
A pair of eyes, she admires, the holder.
Blessed with one, but not granted solitude.
Living in fear, such a novelty.
Creating it, a hobby."

Chapter Twenty-Four

I don't get the opportunity to answer.

Once we pull up everything happens in a matter of seconds. As soon as we are identified I am dragged from the car and handcuffed. Kaden's hand on my arm is the only thing keeping me calm as I stumble about in the darkness of the blindfold. Fear blooms in my chest, threatening to spill out. I lose my bearings completely as I am hurried deep into the maze that is home to the Vengeance Pack.

The feeling of Kaden's fingers pressed against my neck make me gasp. I know what he plans. I don't bother fighting it as I feel myself slip into a state of unconsciousness.

I awake, tousled and weak. My blindfold has been removed and I am bound to a chair in the room I was first imprisoned in.

It's like everything that has happened since then has been a dream.

Kaden leans against the wall at the other end of the room. A smirk of vicious amusement dances across his face as he contemplates me. I am about to say something to him when I notice Coen by the door.

I remember I'm supposed to hate Kaden.

"It seems as though our game has come to an end," Kaden says, coming closer.

His voice is taunting and merciless and I am reminded of the fear I once had of him. This is Alpha Kaden, not my mate. And I am not his mate. I am Mara, his captive.

"It's a shame," he continues. "How I did enjoy pursuing you."

He gives me a long, lascivious look that goes slowly down my body. I feel exposed and vulnerable like my bare legs are spread wide for him.

"Let me go," I say hoarsely. It's a lame attempt, but I'm sure Coen buys it. At least I think so, as I cast a quick glance at him.

He stares blankly at us both.

Kaden is very close now and kneels in front of me. The corner of his mouth rises playfully, daring me to make a snarky remark. I am reminded again, of his other self – the self that is a sinful, mischievous Alpha yet to grow into his title.

I glance down at his hands and see they are covered by those wretched gloves. He runs a fingertip under my chin, watching me shudder with a look of utter pleasure.

"Oh, Mara... you thought you could escape me?"

The way he says it suggests it's more than an act. He's teasing me with the fact that he *did* find me. And he *did* win. Even if he almost died in the process, not that Coen has to know that.

"You always told me no one escaped twice," I spit back at him. "What I shame I played you."

He reaches out suddenly and grips my chin almost painfully. Almost.

"I have a riddle for you..."

Here we go. The riddle I am supposed to provide an answer for. Now I am on my own to decode it. My heart sinks.

Kaden stands and glances casually at Coen. The latter remains quite still, watching with curious eyes. Just looking at him makes me want to gag.

"An unfortunate soul, can spin quite a tale.

Words weaved like a needle, with string like fire.

Cracks between the lines are memories;

A pair of eyes, she admires, the holder.

Blessed with one, but not granted solitude.

Living in fear, such a novelty.

Creating it, a hobby."

He lets out a deep breath as he finishes. Caught in his gaze, I see a flicker of sympathy, but he smooths it over immediately.

What will he do to me if I fail to answer correctly?

Pushing the thought from my mind, I try to concentrate on the riddle itself. Instantly, I get a few ideas swimming about in my mind, which is a better start than last time at least.

An unfortunate soul, can spin quite a tale.

At first, I think of myself. I am in an unfortunate situation, that's for sure. But I discard the idea as I am the worst at spinning a tale.

Next, I consider the brothers. Kace, Coen, Kaden. Each is, unfortunately, a good liar, and has undergone terrible things.

The next line also relates to their abilities to hide these things from me.

Cracks between the lines are memories;

A pair of eyes, she admires, a holder.

Instantly, I delete Kace as a possible solution.

Coen, though... once, I sought friendship, trust, and a refuge in him. Despite the memories he keeps from me and the lies he tells.

Or Kaden. His eyes – I use them to read his emotions.

Blessed with one, but not granted solitude.

Coen lost his mate. Kaden can't be with his mate, at least just yet.

My head begins to hurt.

Living in fear, such a novelty.

Coen must fear his life... living without a mate can prove deadly over a long period of time. Kaden, of course, fears for his parents' lives.

Creating it, a hobby.

Both men radiate fear. But which should I choose?

Kaden raises an eyebrow. He awaits an answer I am unsure about. I must go with what my heart tells me.

"You. You're the answer."

Kaden pauses for a moment, then he smiles.

Not being able to move, I have to wait as he approaches me slowly. The intent expression on his face makes me shiver with delight. He bends down toward me till our faces are nearly touching.

"I'm always the answer, Mara."

And with that, he slashes the ties from my wrist, freeing me.

Gasping, I examine my wrists and see they are tainted by flaring red marks. I quiver with the closeness of Kaden, who is just inches from me.

He places his mouth next to my ear and whispers to me. "I shall meet you in your room tonight and I will make love to you with my mouth, like I did before."

I close my eyes in ecstasy.

"And this time, I'll give you *exactly* what you've been craving."

***

The longer I have to wait for Kaden to come to my room, the more nervous I get.

My body twitches with anticipation as I lie on my bed and imagine him stalking in, shirtless, to claim me.

When my door finally opens, however, it is Coen who stands there. I nearly faint from disappointment.

"Mara... you're okay!" he exclaims.

I'm immediately on the alert. He still thinks we are friends. He still believes I trust him more than anyone in this place. And that's how it needs to stay.

I get up and run to him, my arms outstretched. I wrap my arms around him and he gently responds with a hug of his own.

The scent of him makes me feel sick to the stomach, but I push it down, then force a flawless smile onto my face.

"I'm sorry I didn't tell you I was leaving," I breathe into his shirt.

Pulling away, I try to imagine myself in his eyes. Do I look happy enough? Or is my hatred of him obvious?

"You were stupid to try it," he mutters disapprovingly. Obviously, he doesn't seem to have had much faith in my ability to make a success of it. More importantly, he was probably worried he had lost his leverage over Kaden.

Secretly, I hope I truly had him scared...

"Well, I'm back now," I murmur.

Coen takes a couple of steps back and closes the door. The simple movement fills my heart with dread. He's never done that before. I wonder if I should give this up and call for Kaden.

No... first I need to seduce him into telling me where he's hiding their parents.

Slowly, I remove my jacket and drop it on the floor beside me. I am aware of Coen's eyes fixed on me. My shirt isn't too risqué, but now the jacket's gone there's enough on show to make him swallow.

"I did miss you though," I confess, quietly. *No, I didn't.*

Coen breathes in deeply, his eyes wandering over me. I turn on my heel and walk slowly over to my bed. Perching on the end, I give him the most suggestive look I can manage under the circumstances.

I hate myself so much for doing this.

"Is it too forward of me to say that you're looking extremely... good today," he inquires cautiously.

Yes. Far too forward.

I picture the expression that would appear on Kaden's face were he to walk in right now. He knows my plan, but I'm glad he's not here to witness it being put into action.

"Not at all. Come over here," I order softly, wondering if I sound as erotic as I hope I do. It's obvious Coen is nervous about Kaden. Or perhaps he is just worried that he is in danger of compromising his hold over his brother.

Whatever the case, he obeys and sits on the bed beside me. I force myself to relax, as I find myself tensing away from the man.

"It must be lonely for you... without a mate," I suggest.

My fingers cross behind my back. Did I just go too far?

His eyes blaze, but then he nods. I've got him. He's completely locked in on me; he's hypnotized.

I reach up and gently trace the outline of his chin with my fingertip. The stubble that I feel and the slight sweatiness of his skin is repulsive. This is not the man I want to spend my night with.

"So… how do you satisfy your sexual needs?" I ask him.

Yuck, I feel sick!

Coen looks uncomfortable. "I don't…"

"Oh… what a shame."

We are close, disturbingly close. If I wasn't acting, I would have slapped some sense into him by now. Instead, I have him exactly where he is most vulnerable.

Coen leans abruptly forward, trying to plant his mouth on mine. I stop him by bringing my finger up to his lips.

"Not now," I murmur, "not with Kaden so close. We'll find another time."

Coen nods, coming slowly back to his senses.

After he's gone I feel an inexplicable giddiness sweep over me. This is the first time I've successfully seduced a man into complete submission. I just hate how Coen had to be the subject of it.

Leaning back on my bed, I wait once more for Kaden.

Chapter Twenty-Five

Staring at the clock on my wall, I watch the hands tick by steadily. I have been sitting in this exact position for much longer than I expected. What is Kaden doing that can be more important than this?

Then again, I suppose he said he would visit me in the night, and the clock clearly shows that it is far from morning yet.

Slumping back onto my bed, I let out an irritated groan. My reason for being this *inspired* is all Kaden's doing. Damn him for arousing me like this. What if he was just saying he would visit me to taunt me? Perhaps he doesn't plan to come at all.

I heave my body off the bed and wander over to my window. There are secure bars on either side, stopping me from opening it more than a couple of inches. It lets in just enough air for me to be able to breathe. The lights are off in the room, so I can look through the glass without a reflection. Moonlight streams into the room.

City lights glow and flicker in the distance, teasing me with the freedom I no longer have. I make a quick mental note to ask Kaden if I can visit the main city of the Vengeance Pack some time.

I am leaning close, breath fogging up the glass, when I hear the soft creak of my door opening. I don't dare turn around in case it's not him.

"Riddle me this," a soft voice murmurs.

My hands clench on the window sill.

"If I were to take you up to my room, right now, how long do you think it will take until this whole place hears you scream my name?"

A shiver runs down my body. Slowly, I turn around and meet Kaden's eyes. The light from the moon falls eerily across his face, framing him as more of a predator than anything else. If my heart didn't belong to this male then I would be terrified. His expression is feral, hungry.

He raises a hand and I stare at the leather that encases it as it reflects the moonlight. It dawns on me that he is cautious about Coen, still.

But what I see is a proposal. And a promise.

I slide my hand into his firm grip. As my eyes flicker to his, I catch the provocative leer he doesn't bother suppressing within them. Wordlessly, he leads me from the room, his hand never leaving mine.

"Why not my room?" I question hoarsely.

Kaden glances down at me as we walk. I see amusement in his regard and begin to regret even asking him.

"Your bed is hardly large enough for what I plan to do to you," he murmurs.

My heart skips a beat. "Whose fault is that?" I mutter under my breath.

Kaden raises an eyebrow at me.

I shrug. I didn't pick out my bed. He did.

Kaden lifts the red velvet rope for me to slip past into his quarters. As we near his room, my nerves spread from the pit of my stomach and extend trembling fingers to every part of my body. I am still not sure what he plans to do, but I can't bring myself to ask.

The moment I set foot in his room, however, my worries vanish. Only a floor lamp in a corner of his room illuminates the space; it casts an intimate, sensual glow that entices me in with welcoming arms. I spare hardly a glance for the dark furnishings in the room. Of much greater interest is the massive bed against the opposite wall.

I hear the sound of Kaden clicking the door shut behind me. A moment later he wraps his arms around me from behind. I inhale his intoxicating scent. He nuzzles into my neck, his lips close to my ear.

"Tell me, Mara... why do you smell so strongly of Coen?"

I go still. He knows. Of course he damn well knows, he's an Alpha...

143

"I–I initiated the plan," I murmur, cringing as his grip on me tightens.

He turns me round and I see anger in his face.

"What plan?"

"The plan to find your parents..."

Kaden's eyes narrow dangerously. "I didn't agree to him having his dirty hands all over you," he growls.

He pushes me backward onto the bed. The way he stands over me is so intimidating, I can't help shuddering. Then I see how his eyes are ferociously poring over my body.

"I'm sorry about that, but do you have a better idea?" I demand.

He's clearly mad that I'm challenging him. He stares down at me, slowly peeling the gloves from his hands. Every move he makes is like an unspoken promise. A promise to inflict as much pleasure on my body as possible.

"Let's get rid of every trace of him off you," he says quietly, although his tone is still hard.

I lie back on the sheets and watch my mate strip off his shirt, revealing the hardened, tattooed torso beneath. The sight makes me press my thighs together.

I reach my arm out, beckoning him to come closer. All I want to do right now is dig my nails into his back and forget all about Coen.

Kaden leans over me, his strong arms bracing his weight. His lips, so enchantingly close, get even closer, and a moment later are gently pressing on mine. The soft whisper of a kiss surprises me. Moments ago, he was almost shaking with rage. Now, it's as if he has flipped a switch and reverted to his more gentle self.

"And what do you plan to do?" I ask provocatively as Kaden caresses my neck with his needy kisses.

I sense him smiling against my neck, and I respond by dragging my fingers through his hair. I had to ask. Whatever he wants, I want to know before we jump in.

"You will keep your purity tonight, my love," he mumbles softly.

144

I'm surprised at myself as I feel a slight dash of disappointment. To hide it, I summon my strength to push Kaden to the side. He falls on his back and I'm quick to straddle my legs over his hips.

His raised eyebrow tells me he's nothing but amused.

I scowl at him, then pull my shirt up and over my head. This gets his full attention and he watches me with renewed curiosity.

Next I undo my bra, letting the straps slide off my shoulders. Kaden licks his lips, and the intensity of his gaze upon my breasts stains my cheeks red.

"Don't be shy. Not in front of me," he breathes.

His words give me a surge of confidence, and the sincerity on his face prompts me to pick up his large hands and place them firmly on my breasts.

Instantly Kaden begins massaging them, a glazed look in his eyes. The feeling is like no other, I realize, as I lean my head back and pant with desire. My hands still grip his wrists, my nails probably leaving marks on his skin.

Inspired by the seductive response I'm getting, I decide to turn the spotlight on him. I pull his hands off me, much to his disgust, then I slide down between his legs.

The wary look Kaden gives me makes me smirk as I slowly unbutton his pants. My hand hovers above his swelling crotch, but before it can descend Kaden grabs it.

"Not now. Not when I'm still livid about Coen touching you," he says sternly.

I tilt my head, confused.

He registers my expression. "My self-control is limited right now."

I roll my eyes and place the tips of my fingers on the evident bulge in his pants. His grip on me tightens and his eyes squeeze shut for a moment. His reaction makes me suddenly hungry for more.

"Mara, I'm serious. I am one move away from removing every trace of your purity against that wall. And not gently either," he growls, so fiercely I jump.

145

He's right. He's an Alpha, and their self-control is limited. But still, I can't help but feel a little disheartened.

Kaden notices and pulls me back up so I'm crushed against his warmth.

"There is always next time. For now though..."

He breaks off, slowly flipping us over so he's on top. Staring into his eyes, I see the spark of dominance I've gotten so used too. He's in his domain now.

Swiftly bending down, his lips caress the bare flesh of my breasts. I relax and allow Kaden to slide my pants down my legs and off.

He goes lower. His lips are so soft and supple, yet his kisses are firm and needy. After what happened with Coen, it is obvious he wants to take his jealousy out on the most sensitive parts of my body.

My eyes close instinctively and I feel Kaden hook his fingers under the edge of my underwear. A moment later they are off, too.

The last time I was in this situation I had no idea who sat between my legs. I open my eyes again and see Kaden staring appreciatively at my exposed flesh. I feel so vulnerable that my legs begin to close, but Kaden intervenes. He splays a large hand over my hip to keep me still and then nestles down between my thighs. The sight almost makes me orgasm then and there.

Kaden looks up at me. I see love, lust, and hunger in his expression. I'm sure my own face betrays exactly the same emotions. Then he grins wickedly at me and ducks down between my legs.

This is nothing like last time. Last time he teased and experimented. Tonight, however, he has been clipped off whatever leash that was restraining him and delivers a full assault on my senses.

Stars explode in my vision the moment his tongue meets my sensitive skin. My heels dig into his back and my hands grip his shoulders so hard the knuckles turn white. Every sweep of his tongue against me makes me release an uncontrollable moan of pleasure. Never have I felt this way before; it's like Kaden is consuming me with every movement his tongue makes. Eventually, it's too much for me and I lose it completely. Lurching forward, I experience something I've never experienced before – the sweet release of an orgasm.

A chuckle from Kaden vibrates across the sensitive bundle of nerves at the apex of my thighs as he refuses to remove his mouth from me.

Spent, I slump backward. As I blink down at Kaden through bleary eyes, I can tell he isn't done yet.

"This time you will scream my name," he warns me.

I'm almost frightened at the idea of being put through that inexplicable torment of pleasure again. But my anxiety fades to nothing the moment I feel his index finger gently caressing me.

Slowly, he moves up my body till his face is directly over mine. He keeps his hand below my waist, toying with me.

"Beg me," he whispers, kissing both corners of my mouth.

I'm not sure exactly what I'm begging for but I comply. "Please..."

Abruptly, in one smooth movement, his finger slips all the way inside me and I'm left gasping for air. He places soft kisses on my neck as I get accustomed to the unfamiliar sensation.

The moment his finger begins to move gently inside me I feel a new rush of pleasure consume me. I fasten on his shoulders, unsure of how I should express my pleasure.

"Tell me how much you love it," Kaden demands in my ear, quickening the pace as he adds another finger.

"Don't stop!" is all I manage to choke out.

He smiles wickedly but follows my instructions. All too soon, I feel like I am teetering on the edge of the cliff again, and I beg Kaden for a release.

And he gives it to me, whispering sensually in my ear as I come apart beneath him.

As I catch my breath, Kaden removes his hand and flops down beside me. When I turn my head toward him, lulled by pleasure, I see he is smiling warmly at me. He reaches up and brushes a stray hair from my cheek.

"I love you, Mara," he says.

My heart floods with emotion, and I sigh with content.

"I love you too, Kaden.

Chapter Twenty-Six

The next morning, I wake in my own bed. A delicious tenderness between my legs reminds me of what happened to me last night.

I twist in my bedsheets and stretch out. Kaden must have carried me back here last night so Coen wouldn't get suspicious when he came to collect me for breakfast.

The thought of Coen, and what my plan is, instantly kills my elated mood.

I slide from the bed and quickly shower and gather some clothes together. Although Coen is no Alpha, I am still worried he might catch Kaden's scent on me. Once I am dressed, I spray on some perfume, praying it will be enough to mask the scent of my mate.

I am brushing my hair when there is a knock at the door. Coen waltzes in without even waiting for me to summon him. Good, I tell myself. This is a sign that he is getting comfortable with me. Not long ago he wouldn't even have walked over the threshold to my room. Now he strolls in like he owns the place. Things have definitely changed.

I have to admit, he doesn't look too bad. He has his warrior clothes on, by the look of it. He appears dark and dangerous like he's about to go to war.

"Good morning, beautiful," he greets me, a half-smile forming on his face.

I try my best not to vomit. "Here to escort me to breakfast?" I ask, trying to keep the atmosphere light and friendly, rather than dark and sultry. I'm not sure how best to deal with him if he comes on to me now, not with Kaden so prominent in my mind.

At breakfast, I sit facing Kace. He doesn't meet my eye and I have a feeling Kaden has told him that I know we are mates. I know Kaden wants me to continue with the marriage plans until he finds his parents, but I would like to know whose side Kace is on – Kaden's or Coen's?

"I need a favor," I say pointedly.

Coen lifts his head when he hears me speaking to Kace. Kace just stares at the milk swirling around his spoon.

"What kind of favor?" he inquires.

"I want you to take me to the Vengeance Pack city."

Kace looks up, his dark eyes meeting mine at last. They flicker with some sort of emotion – fear maybe?

"I don't think so," he says. He picks up the newspaper in front of him like he's sealing the conversation shut right there. I pull the edge of the paper back down to the table.

"Why not?"

He sighs. "It's not safe down there. Some very bad people reside in the city."

I purse my lips. *Does nobody here think I am capable of looking after myself?*

"That's why I'm asking you to take me," I persist. "As your fiancée, I feel as though you should demonstrate to the world that I am your responsibility and no business of anyone else's."

It's a subtle approach and I am rather proud of having thought of it.

Kace narrows his eyes at me, sensing the challenge I have laid before him. "Fine. I'll take you to the city then," he replies, rather flatly. "Then you'll see precisely how bad Kaden is."

His words give me pause. Why does he maintain that Kaden is so bad? How bad could this city be to make me think differently about him? By the look on Kace's face, he already seems to regret saying it.

150

I'm about to question him more about it, but Kace stands and pushes his chair back noisily.

"Tomorrow, Mara, we shall see the city." And with that, he leaves.

I spend the rest of my day in my room. Not once do I hear from Kaden. Instead, I read a book and wish I was someone in it, without all these confusing issues to deal with.

When I do get a visitor, I am dismayed to find it is Coen.

I sit up and lay my book down. The smirk on his face is sickening as he stares at me. I'm glad I've picked something modest to wear, so there's less for him to slaver over.

"Am I disturbing you?" he asks politely.

I shake my head and swing my legs off the bed so I'm in a less vulnerable position. "What brings you here?" I inquire, trying my best not to cringe from him.

He steps fully into the room and closes the door firmly behind him. Thank the Moon Goddess he doesn't lock it, or I might start hyperventilating.

"I want to talk," he tells me.

He comes over and sits beside me on the bed. It sinks under his weight, and I try my best not to fall into his lap. Hopefully, he doesn't catch on to how tense I am right now.

"It's hard not having a mate," he begins, ominously, "and it can't be easy for you here, I know…" He licks his lips and looks earnestly at me. "I want you to know that I'm always here."

I start as he lays his palm on my upper thigh. I stare at it for a movement, wondering if I should slap it off or take advantage of it to further the plan that I've formulated in my head.

"That is," he resumes, "if you ever need… a release."

It's a struggle to keep my smile going as I gaze into his eyes. I think I see a flicker of pain there. It dawns on me that he's lonely. He's lost his mate, and it has turned him into a bitter, destructive person. I resist the temptation to feel sympathy for him. He kidnapped his own parents before he was rejected. He proved himself to be a sadistic freak long before Althea came into his life.

151

"I've always seen you as the only person I can trust here," I confide in him. It's almost true, as I did trust him in the beginning, at least.

He smiles at this. "Like I say, you can come to me for anything."

I refrain from asking him there and then where his parents are. I know he'd never tell me in a million years. I just need to keep to the plan.

However, I'm taken by surprise when Coen suddenly leans over the bed and kisses me full on the mouth.

At first, I'm surprised. Then disgusted. Then nauseated.

As Coen moves his lips against mine, I notice how roughly he is going about it. My heart falls as I realize *he's* the one who wants the release.

I nearly gag right there, but I stop myself, even as his other hand moves up to caress the side of my face. I squeeze my eyes shut as I try to endure the revulsion that threatens to empty my stomach.

Without warning he pushes me backward onto the bed and gets on top of me.

Fear kicks into first gear as he runs the tips of his fingers down my side. *Is he crazy?* I silently beg for Kaden to burst in, but he doesn't come.

His lips move from my mouth to my jawline. I draw in a deep breath and place my palms against his shoulders to stop him getting any closer than he already is.

"I don't think we should be doing this!" I hiss.

He ignores me and kisses my neck feverishly. They are not soft kisses. These kisses will leave bruises.

"Coen!" I persist. "What if Kaden walks in?"

He growls low in his throat but seems determined to ignore my very reasonable anxiety. Why should he care about Kaden finding us, anyway? Kaden isn't supposed to have any particular feelings toward me one way or another. Besides, Coen basically commands the man.

The moment his cold hands slip under my shirt, groping at my belly, I begin to freak out. I push at his shoulder and repeat that he needs to get off me in case we are discovered. To no avail.

152

The clammy fingers of dread wrap around me. I'm pinned under a man much bigger than me. Does he plan to bed me without my consent? That's rape...

I take a breath to scream, but Coen covers my mouth with his before the sound even makes it to my lips.

Suddenly my bedroom door crashes open and a familiar scent invades the room. The feeling of relief is vast as I feel Coen being pulled off me.

I struggle up to see what's happening and see Coen sprawling on the floor with Kaden standing over him. As I watch, my mate picks his brother up by the collar of his shirt and lifts him till their faces are level and the latter's feet are clear of the ground. It worries me that, despite Kaden's glare, Coen is smiling.

My heart stops for a moment. Kaden may have him dangling inches off the ground, but Coen has so much leverage over his brother. It is like he is hanging his parents' lives right in front of Kaden's face.

Instead of hurting Coen, like I'm willing him to, Kaden thrusts his brother away from him. Coen stumbles backward into the wall. Kaden gives me a final glance and storms out.

The look in his eyes kills me. It's full of regret. Anger. Pain.

Coen, on the other hand, looks beyond triumphant. He doesn't seem interested in me anymore and leaves without a word. Perhaps he's got the message.

I shower and brush my teeth vigorously. Then I brush them again, still imagining the taste of Coen in my mouth.

The book I was reading lies on the floor by the bed. I can't bear even touching it as I'd just reach a big romantic scene. Instead, I shove my face down in a pillow and pray. I pray for the Moon Goddess to help me. Or at least to ensure that the red marks on my neck fade quickly, so Kaden doesn't have to see them.

That night, I almost cry with happiness when my mate comes through the door.

But then I see his face.

His cheeks are stained with tears as he stares right at me. In a second, I am out of bed and begging him to tell me what the problem is. He answers by turning around on the spot.

The back of his shirt is torn to shreds. Through the rips, I can see dozens of bleeding wounds. It's all I can do to keep from fainting.

My mate has been violently lashed with a whip. That much is obvious as I help him remove the remains of his bloodied shirt, pulling it gingerly over his head.

He falls to his knees. I know without asking why he has received this punishment.

For interrupting Coen.

The wounds are angry and red and I know what pain he must be in. I do what I can to tidy him up, then guide him to the bed. He falls face first on it, completely ignoring the other wound on his chest, and groans loudly into the pillow, using it to smother his pain.

It's clear that Coen has a lot more power over us than I imagined.

154

Chapter Twenty-Seven

My knees are numb under me. I've been in this position for a good fifteen minutes now, my head bowed as I kneel in front of my brother.

I don't move. I could take him down in one hit. But I won't.

Coen strolls casually across the room, a long whip curled in his hand. The smirk on his face burns into my mind as he crouches in front of me.

"Mother always liked you the most," he says, grabbing me underneath my jaw in order to lift my head up.

I stare into his cold eyes, embracing his words.

"Don't know why," he mutters. His fingers dig sharply into my jawbone, but I try not to flinch. I don't even pull away. Giving him that satisfaction is not an option.

Instead, I use my eyes. Glaring deeply into his own, I express my utter hatred for him. He doesn't address it though. Instead, he turns my head to left and right, examining me closely.

"And you always got the girls," he mutters.

He lets me go, letting me move my mouth to readjust my jaw. He's right, of course. That's why he orders me to kidnap girls from the Purity Pack. For his own amusement. Because no one else will have him.

He turns away and paces about the room. He doesn't need to tie me down to keep me where I am. The weight of his unspoken threats is enough to dissuade me from swinging my fist at his face.

"Your mate is gorgeous," he says into the air.

My hands clench into fists.

"It's a shame you interrupted us," he continues.

I hate this. The fact that he thinks Mara is interested in him truly makes me want to throw up. She's doing this for me, but as much as I want to tell him that, I can't.

"I'm sure she would have enjoyed what I had planned."

I make to stand, shifting my feet underneath me, but Coen presents the whip as a threat and I settle back down again.

"Dear brother. You have overstepped your place here, and I'm afraid I have to take action on this," he announces as if he is addressing a crowd.

My gaze settles on the whip. The scars on my back are proof that this isn't the first time I've endured his sadism. But I shall sit here and take it. For my mate. For Mara.

"How about a lash for every thrust I was planning to give your little mate...?"

I grit my teeth. In my head, I am cursing him bitterly, but I don't dare move a muscle.

"The day I find our parents, Coen, will be the day you die," I mutter under my breath, so silently he does not hear.

***

I run my thumb gently across Kaden's face, where his tears have now dried. He has filled me in on what he has just endured. His wounds are bathed and dressed to the best of my ability.

Kace has given us what help he can, and my fiancé is now perched at the end of the bed. Now he knows everything. To say he doesn't care about Kaden and me is an understatement. He hardly even bothered to shrug when I told him I knew Kaden was my mate. I think he is too engaged with his anger toward Coen to be bothered about me.

"I've finalized my plan now," I tell them both. "I'm so close to finding your parents."

156

Kace looks satisfied with that. "And then we won't have to get married."

I pull a face. "Glad to know that's such a big relief to you, I'm sure..."

Kaden takes my hand. "I can't *bear* to think of you and Coen together!"

"Just think for a moment, Kaden... the chances are, he has the location of your parents written down somewhere, right?"

Kaden tilts his face, not quite understanding where I'm going with this.

I get to my feet and push away from the bed. I have all their attention now, as I try to express the thoughts surging around my mind.

"When Coen helped me escape through the wall he told me he had a bad memory."

Kaden and Kace exchange glances, as if trying to recall something they've forgotten. Kaden's face is full of pain, but it's clear he's remembering something.

"He was always forgetting things as a child," he tells me.

"And I was always picking things up after him," Kace adds.

My excitement grows. They are on the same page as me, so now all I need to do is explain my plan before I lose them.

"Exactly. He's so scatterbrained he's sure to have written down the coordinates identifying where your parents are. Otherwise, he knows full well he'll forget them."

They both start nodding in agreement. My theory obviously makes sense to them.

"So we just need to find out *where* he wrote them," Kaden mutters.

I smile at him. I've cracked it. I'm about to lean down and give my mate a kiss when I remember something else.

I turn to Kace. "This is all fine, but we have somewhere to be... remember?"

I'd almost forgotten about my planned visit to Vengeance Pack City.

I am conscious of Kaden giving us both a curious look.

"You still want to go there?" asks Kace.

"Yes. I have to."

Kaden is looking displeased. "No, you don't."

Kace gets up abruptly, sensing trouble, and shoots me a warning look as he slips out of the room, signaling that he will wait outside.

"I've forced Kace to agree to take me," I tell my mate.

"You're not going."

Kaden is determined to shut the idea down, but I have good reason to disappoint him.

"I need to go down there," I explain. "You said yourself that Lexia, Grayson's mate, is living there."

Kaden shakes his head and takes my hands in his, holding them tightly. A warning grip.

"That place is riddled with gangs and villains of one kind or another. If they get so much as a glimpse of a pretty Purity Pack member like you..." He breaks off as a flash of pain overwhelms him.

"I'll be careful," I tell him, "but I've got to save Lexia."

I try to make it sound final, like the conversation is over. I know he wants to continue the argument, but he's in no state to pursue me. I withdraw my hands forcibly and take a step back. He can't even get up.

"By the time you get back I will be healed," he gasps, as if I should be as frightened of him as I was when I first came here.

"And what does that mean?" I ask, rather cheekily, as I take a few more steps backward.

"You'll see," he growls.

I don't stick around to see if he has anything else to say. He could easily make it too hard for me to leave and do what I have to do.

Chapter Twenty-Eight

"You're not wearing that."

I cross my arms over my chest and glare pointedly at Kace. "Since when did you start choosing my wardrobe?" I demand.

I don't think I look *that* bad. My shirt is white and lacy and my pants are a dark blue. I consider myself to look normal, approachable. Certainly more so than he does, in his scruffy dark leathers.

"You don't understand what it's like where we going..." he complains.

"At least I don't look like I've crawled on my hands and knees out of a coffin."

He sighs and then deftly unbuttons his dark cloak, his eyes never leaving mine. He pulls it off and arranges it on my shoulders instead.

I glare at him as he buttons it up, ignoring my attempts to stop him.

"What?" he queries. "I can't have you looking like a Purity Pack member."

We are moments away from stepping into the car that will take us down to Vengeance Pack City. Kace's overreaction to everything so far is making me nervous.

"And the hair," he murmurs. He flips the hood of the cloak over my head, tucking my blonde locks under it so they can't be seen.

I'm going into this city as someone else.

The car ride is a good twenty minutes. Entering the city is easier than it should be. Maybe that's why so many "bad" people live here.

As we enter – Kace in the driver's seat and me alongside him – I take in the sights. There are skyscrapers and wide thoroughfares crowded with people. Then we pass into a quieter district with mostly modern, private houses.

I'm puzzled. This isn't how this place was described to me back in the Purity Pack. In fact, everything here looks new. I find myself looking in awe at the people enjoying the sun on the sidewalk.

But this affluence doesn't last. The beautiful, modern homes thin out and their place is taken by slum buildings. They look old and run down, and some are apparently abandoned. This, I guess, is where those at the bottom of the Vengeance Pack hierarchy spend their daily lives.

"You think we'll find Lexia here?" I ask Kace. The buildings are crammed so tightly together it's hard to imagine anything more different to the open scrubland of the Freedom Pack. Had Kaden truly banished Grayson's mate to this forbidding place?

"It gets worse," Kace mutters, staring straight ahead. He looks anxious, and I suddenly appreciate why he didn't want to bring me here.

"Kaden has a special place for his least favorite people," Kace tells me.

I sense that he's being diplomatic about it.

Aesthetically, the surroundings don't get any worse. In fact, they improve somewhat. The district we enter seems cleaner, but the darkest of shadows shade the alleyways we pass by and there's nobody about, despite the time of day.

I imagine a poor, defenseless Lexia being dragged from her home pack, and her family, and being brought to this daunting place. The thought of her alone among these shadows fuels my concern for her.

I have to save her and return her to her mate.

Kace pulls the car smoothly to a halt in front of an abandoned-looking tenement. It looms over the car and I can't help swallowing as a feeling of intimidation overwhelms me.

I prepare to get out, but Kace grabs my arm to stop me. "We have to be careful out here, okay?"

160

"We'll be fine," I assure him. "I just want to check the place out and then we can leave." I've been hoping to convince him that finding Lexia isn't terribly important. I know he's wary about her – I see it by the look in his eye – and I don't want him ruining this for me.

We step out of the car and I'm hit with a cool breeze. It seems as though the sun barely breaks through in this part of town. I pull Kace's cloak closer to my body and am suddenly glad he has made me wear it.

"This way," Kace instructs, leading me toward an open alleyway. It's not the most threatening we've seen so I don't feel too apprehensive about following him.

But we've hardly entered it when I realize we may have made a big mistake.

Four masked figures emerge from the shadows with small but deadly-looking daggers in their hands. They stand as though guarding the entrance to the alleyway.

Kace doesn't flinch, however. "Let us through, fools. I am your Alpha's brother," he demands, his voice icy and low. The glint in his eyes suggests he's willing to take on anyone who doesn't obey his orders.

The men step away, but then another figure comes forward and stands squarely in our way.

"Stay where you are, boys. Looks like we have company." It's the voice of a woman. I wonder who on earth it is.

As if reading my thoughts, the woman steps into the light. She is dressed like an assassin, with dark leather pants and a black cloak, and I see the glint of a blade tucked in her belt. But her face, framed by thick blonde hair, is delicate and beautiful. Her eyes, which are a sharp emerald green, assess us with a mixture of curiosity and wariness.

"X, he says he is Kaden's brother," one of the men tells her.

X? Is that what they call her? How strange.

The woman's eyes focus on my companion. "Kace, isn't it?" Then she turns to me and raises an eyebrow. "And this must be your fiancée." Her eyes are as green as the forests and have flecks of gold in them. I hate how they are now trained on me.

"We are only here for a brief visit, woman," Kace says gruffly. "Let us pass."

The woman's expression darkens. Something tells me she doesn't appreciate the way he's talking to her.

I step in before things get out of hand. "Yes, I am his fiancée."

The woman called X inspects me from head to toe. Then she contemplates the hand I have thrust out for her to shake. She grunts and ignores it.

Instead, she closes the gap between us and pulls the hood back from my face. My hair, a striking contrast against these dark walls, spills out for all to see.

"How amusing," X murmurs. "I had a feeling you were a Purity Pack member. I could smell the worthlessness radiating off you."

I scowl but Kace interrupts. "We didn't come here for your taunts, X, or whatever your no-hoper followers call you."

His remark doesn't go unnoticed. X's face clouds with anger and her hand moves toward the knife in her belt.

"Tell me *exactly* why you're here, and I may consider letting you past," she comments coolly.

I glance at Kace and read the belligerence in his stance. Time to step in again.

"We are here to retrieve a girl who has been held captive here for many years," I tell her quickly.

The woman's hand comes away from her belt as she absorbs what I have said.

I wonder if I've done the right thing being so honest with her.

"Everyone here is a captive," she counters. "We could escape, but do you think any of us want to?"

I pause. I haven't thought about that. No, Lexia is from the Discipline Pack, a pack with morals that I doubt she could forget. I just have to get past this narrow-minded hoodlum to find her.

"The girl we are seeking has a mate waiting for her outside this pack, an Alpha—"

X bursts out laughing. The sound would be delightful were it not so sarcastic it hurts. She holds her stomach, looking at me with humor in her eyes.

"Mate? Nobody here wants a damn mate! And an Alpha? You've got to be kidding me... seriously, tell me you're joking."

I stare at her blankly. Is she out of her mind?

"News flash, sweet cheeks," she giggles, noticing my expression, "I don't know a single soul here that wouldn't kill an Alpha if they had the opportunity."

She's definitely crazy. Her eyes blaze insanely, and it dawns on me how institutionalized the people are here. I'd quite like to know how long this woman has been stuck in here.

"Look," I suggest patiently, "let's strike a deal..."

My mind flashes through all the games Kaden has dared me to play. But no, this is different...

X shrugs while I ponder what to propose and then cuts me off short. "Tell me the name of this girl, and I'll find her for yah. I own these streets as much as Kaden or anyone else does. No one enters this place without my permission – and no one leaves." She shoots me a wicked grin. "I'll know her, that's for sure."

Kace gives me a warning glance, but I can tell we aren't getting past her without her wanting us to. The best bet seems to ask her outright for Lexia.

"Her name's Lexia and we'd like to take her back with us. Please." I speak respectfully, as if she's an Alpha herself.

My words have an instant effect on her. She pales, all blood draining from her face. Her eyes glaze over for a moment as they lock on me in utter shock.

The moment of silence between us extends. Then, without warning, she grabs me and spins me round so she can hold her blade against my throat.

"Tell me how you know my real name!"

Chapter Twenty-Nine

Lexia sits in front of me, leaning casually back in her chair as she picks at her nails. Her eyes, so green, stare at me without warmth.

We are in a big warehouse – her home, she tells me. She has invited me back here after I insisted it was quite unnecessary to cut my throat. So now I sit on a chair opposite her, undergoing what feels like an interrogation. Maybe it's just the fact that the rest of her little friends are standing immediately behind her, also staring at me with undisguised hostility and suspicion.

"So, explain yourself," she demands, her eyebrows raised in expectation.

"Your mate told me your name," I say honestly. I can feel Kace's eyes on me.

Her face twists. I've gathered the fact that she doesn't like the concept of having a mate. I'm not sure what this pack can have exposed her to, to make her feel this way... Whatever it is, it can't be good.

"And how does he know I am mates with him?" she queries.

Her question stumps me. Alpha Grayson never told me how he knew.

Lexia's mouth twitches into a smile as she registers my expression.

She leans forward in her chair. "You know what I have learned while living here since I was fourteen?"

I slowly shake my head.

"Never trust an Alpha. Ever," she mutters.

My mind whirls. Grayson is going to have a great time taming this one.

"You need to go home," I murmur. I decide to hold back the fact that my mate is an Alpha. If she knows that, the little trust that she has in me will fly straight out the window.

She yawns. "Not happening. I belong here and no one is going to take me away."

I catch Kace's gaze from across the room and see him shake his head. Did he know she would do this? I scoot my chair a little closer to her.

"Lexia, listen—"

"No, you listen. I have spent the last six years fighting my way to the top of the ranks here. This part of the city runs like a business. If you're not at the top, you're not worth a thing," she says viciously, taking me by surprise. "Anyone who comes here is quickly beaten into their place. Do you know how long it took me to gain the respect of these people? These criminals?"

Of course I don't.

"And I won't let some Purity Pack member come in here, taunting me with a mate I don't want..."

Cringing, I lower my gaze.

"Now take that silver spoon out of your privileged mouth, so I can hear you properly," she finishes, sitting back in her seat.

I swallow, despite my dry throat. She's knocked the breath straight out of me and I'm not sure how to respond. Should I explain to her that there is nothing she can possibly do? If an Alpha wants you, that's it.

"I'm trying to help you," I say, trying to convince her.

She pulls her knife from her belt and, for a moment, I fear she's going to stick it in my chest and be done with it. Instead she twists the handle, admiring the blade as it shines in the light.

"I don't need your help," she informs me scornfully. "I suggest you leave and never come back."

I stare at her hopelessly while she just sits there, pretending I don't exist. Then I stand, my chair scraping on the ground.

"When your mate comes knocking at your door, don't say I didn't warn you..."

And with that, I walk out.

***

Once we are back at the Vengeance Pack I go in search of Kaden in his quarters.

I feel I've done all I can to help Grayson, but it's clear to me that it's too late. Lexia is now a member of the Vengeance Pack.

I hope Kaden will tell me how we are going to break this to Grayson. I'm sure he won't be too pleased.

"Going somewhere?"

I spin round to see Coen standing behind me. His eyes drag down my body and I can't help the shiver of disgust that runs down my spine. I have a powerful urge to punch him square in the face.

"I hope you're not trying to sneak into Alpha Kaden's quarters," he teases, as if such a notion is impossible.

I take a deep breath. "I was just passing by."

"Would you care you to join me then?" he responds, his voice smooth as oil.

I remind myself of the plan. All I need to do is find out where he is hiding the co-ordinates describing where Kaden's parents are and I won't have to worry about this creep again.

At that moment I spy Kaden watching us from the top of the staircase behind his brother. He looks devilishly handsome, but I notice that his lips are set in a grim line. He surreptitiously taps a few times on his watch, then motions over his shoulder. He wants to meet me in his bedroom when I'm done.

And I will.

"So," I mutter, returning my attention to Coen. "Why don't you and I talk about this in your bedroom?"

166

The idea seems to please him and he leads me upstairs. Kaden has vanished from sight. When we reach Coen's bedroom he plumps himself down on the bed and clearly expects me to join him. Instead I wander round the room, trying to make it appear that I'm innocently fascinated by my surroundings. In reality I'm scoping the place for the information I need.

"Have I ever told you that you're beautiful?" Coen asks lazily from behind me.

I screw my face up, glad he can't see as my back is to him. The papers on his desk suggest nothing but the fact that he lacks artistic skill when it comes to drawing animals, or anything else.

"Maybe," I murmur in response, moving on to continue my search. The room is surprisingly mediocre for a mass murderer and sociopathic kidnapper, though it occurs to me that an impartial observer might find it not dissimilar to my own, which is just as minimalist really. Of course, I try to enliven mine with a few pictures for decoration, whereas he just sticks up these horrendous drawings of his.

"Well, you are beautiful," he insists.

The next moment he's right behind me, his arms around my waist. I flinch, feeling his chest press against my back and his lips caress my neck.

"How jumpy you are!" he taunts me, laughing in my ear.

I let out a breathy laugh as well in an attempt to keep the atmosphere light.

"I'm just a bit nervous Alpha Kaden might come in again," I reply, my hands bracing against the desk as he pushes me forward as though he's thinking of seducing me on it. I wonder for a second whether grabbing the papers on the desk and throwing them at him would give me time to escape but almost as quickly I dismiss the idea.

"He won't," he assures me as he attempts to nibble my ear. "I think he might be okay with us now, anyway."

First of all, there isn't an "us". Secondly, Kaden would not be okay with it...

I keep my mouth shut.

Coen seems to change his mind about how things are to proceed and prods me toward the bed. I sit nervously on the edge of it, while he lounges full-length, eyeing me with interest.

I try desperately to think what to do next as removes his shoes and socks. Then something on his ankle catches my eye. It's a tattoo of some kind, done in thin, black ink across his Achilles heel. It appears to be a bunch of zeroes and ones compacted together, in a form I don't recognize.

Coen sees where I'm looking. "Oh, you like this?" he asks, rolling up his pant leg. "It's binary."

Binary? What's that?

"You'll have to explain," I tell him, switching on my most innocent, shy smile.

"Binary arithmetic. The simple use of two numbers can be used to translate anything," he explains cryptically.

I blink as I fight to understand what that means.

He laughs. "I know – I never grasped much as a kid either. My father taught me this before he... died."

Died. Yeah, right.

He examines the tattoo as though seeing it afresh. "It has many uses. This one right here is my way of remembering something I never want to forget."

My heart skips a beat as he thumbs the tattoo and my mind races.

"Can you tell me what it means?" I ask, hoping for the best.

Instead of just telling me, he shakes his head and grins. "No can do. It's a secret."

I glance into his eyes and come to a realization. Then I stand up.

"Where are you going?"

I shoot him a sweet smile. "Just going to the ladies' room. I'll be right back."

Like heck I will. I may have just found a way to get Kaden's parents back.

Chapter Thirty

I knock softly on the door to Kaden's room, hoping Coen gives me at least a couple of minutes before he begins to wonder where I am. I lean against the wood and make out a shuffling noise coming from within.

"Hold on a second," I hear Kaden say.

I check the coast is still clear, then put my ear to the door again to see if I can hear if Kaden's coming. All I can make out is more mysterious shuffling.

"What are you doing in there?" I hiss.

I think I hear him chuckling.

"I'm getting changed," he says.

I try the doorknob, only to find it is locked. *Has he seriously locked me out just because he is getting changed?*

"I need to come in!" I urge in as loud a voice as I dare. "Let me in. I'm your mate!"

A groan of frustration on the other side of the door startles me.

"What are you doing?"

I'm beginning to get anxious now. Kaden hinted that he wanted me up in his room the moment I was done with Coen. And now he's locked me out? If he doesn't open this door soon his brother will spot me...

"The button of my pants is stuck," I hear him admitting in irritation.

I slap my hand over my mouth as I fight the impulse to giggle. This isn't the time, or the place. But... I have to see this. I turn the door handle again and this time, I find it unlocked. I push it open, then close it swiftly behind me and lock it. When I turn back I can't help but laugh out loud at what I see.

Kaden is standing in the middle of his room, his pants unbuttoned and his fingers grappling to sort himself out.

He glances up at me, looking embarrassed. Despite how comical he appears, I can't help but admire – just for a second or two – his impressive shirtless torso. All I can think about, suddenly, is sex, which is not something a Purity Pack member like me should ever be thinking about.

"How did you manage that?" I ask, trying to replace the humor in my voice with concern.

He sighs deeply. "I knew you'd come. I wanted to look nice for you..."

"So you're telling me that the most notorious Alpha in these parts has met his match in a button?" I can't keep the smile from my lips.

He scowls back at me. "And a zipper."

I stand in front of him, asking him with my eyes if I have his permission to attend to his unfortunate predicament. He allows me to kneel down before him and untangle his button from his zipper. When I'm done I remain where I am.

He gazes down at me, frowning. Slowly, he reaches a hand to me and cups my chin. His palm feels warm against my skin.

"I hate that I can smell Coen on you," he murmurs.

I sigh and slowly rise. "Way to ruin the moment," I tell him.

He pulls me to him, his mouth at my ear. "Finally. Some alone time."

I wrap my arms around Kaden's neck and relish the kisses he begins to bestow on me. I'm dying to get between the sheets with him, but I have to tell him about Coen first, and what I found tattooed on his foot.

"Can we talk?" I ask breathlessly as his lips assault my neck and his proximity makes me feel weak at the knees.

170

He groans with annoyance and redoubles his attentions. I feel his hands wander down my body and round to the back of my thighs. Getting the hint, I jump and allow Kaden to hold my legs around his waist.

"How about later?" he says.

He walks me over to his four-poster bed and lays me down on it. The silk sheets caress my skin deliciously. Then he looms over me, his eyes blazing with the intensity of lust and passion that I feel myself.

"What if I told you I may know where your parents are," I murmur.

He hesitates a bit at that, but then resumes the kissing and licking that he does so well.

"Mmm?" he mumbles against my skin, implying that I can go on talking, even though he isn't.

I pause while he rids me of my shirt and bra so he can press his bare skin against mine. His hands stroke my waist and breasts, stimulating me in a way I never have been before, while my own hands explore the ridges of his exposed back. At least his wounds seem to be largely healed now.

"Coen... has a tattoo," I whisper as I tug at Kaden's pants. He sits up and slips them off.

"A tattoo? What does it show?"

I'm about to tell him but the touch of his mouth against my breast makes me jump in surprise and then moan with pleasure.

"Binary," I murmur, trying to think straight. "Although I'm not sure how to decode it."

I run my hands through Kaden's hair as he lifts my hips high enough to slide my pants and underwear off.

"I know someone who can decode it for us," he replies as he lowers his face to mine. "But for now, will you let me worship you?"

I grab his face, preventing him from going anywhere until I allow him to.

"You know I love you, right?" I say, almost choking over the sincerity in my words.

His gaze softens and he nods slowly.

I'm not sure what has come over me. What disease of desire and want has taken over my brain, banishing all rational thought? Kaden has completely consumed me, and I can only lie here and accept it.

"I don't know if I will be able to stop myself from..." He breaks off, his fingertips grazing across my neck where a potential mark would go.

I grab his hand and squeeze it gently.

"Come on," I plead, raising my hips up so they press against his.

The disease of lust has spread throughout my body and is now beyond my control.

Kaden exhales and I can see the last restraints of his composure snapping like rubber bands.

"Only if you promise to become a Vengeance Pack member," he insists, his lips brushing against mine.

That makes me pause. *Become a Vengeance Pack member?* The moment he marks me, I will be his Luna, anyway... I feel myself nodding, and his face lights up.

"Perfect," he purrs. "Then I shall hold back nothing."

He removes the last of his clothing and mounts me. His eyes have already drunk in the sight of me. Now I want to see him.

What I see makes me gasp.

"Are they all that big?" I squeak, alarmed.

He just smiles and kisses my forehead. "I'm an Alpha, remember?"

I swallow nervously. I am utterly defenseless under him, with my arms by my side and my legs spread.

He kisses my neck softly. "I promise I will be gentle."

This is really happening. There is no going back now... I clench my jaw and nod my head. "I trust you, Kaden."

And I do, even as he slides into me and my nails dig involuntarily into his muscular arms. The pain I feel is nothing that I've experienced before. It's not unbearable, but enough to make me hiss in surprise.

Kaden gazes down at me, concern in his eyes, as he pauses. "I know it hurts. I can stop if you want me to."

I see the way he keeps glancing at my neck, and the way his muscles strain. He's holding himself back. Holding himself back from the feral, primal urge that I know he longs to give in to. He remains entirely still until I shake my head at the idea of stopping. I want this. I want nothing more than to be close to my mate, and have him forever.

I wrap my legs around his waist, drawing him closer as I feel the fullness of him within me. Tentatively, he rolls his hips deliciously against mine, and the pain begins to fade.

As I feel his body pulse against mine, the feeling of him thrusting into me makes me moan loudly. If Coen should hear, I couldn't care less. All I care about is this pleasure Kaden inflicts on me.

As his speed steadily increases, much to my excitement, I feel his lips brushing against my neck. He's resisting the urge to mark me as his. I capture his lips with mine, distracting him as we make love under the moonlight that streams through his window.

And as I suddenly fall, my mind consumed only by thoughts of my mate, I dig my nails into his back and cry out helplessly. Only one thrust separates us, as Kaden follows close behind.

Spent, I feel Kaden pull out and roll over. I turn my head and smile at him, ignoring the lingering pain between my legs.

I love him.

Chapter Thirty-One

Again, I awake in my own bed.

Sitting up, a strange tingle between my legs reminds me of last night. Kaden has decided, for a second time, to carry me back to my room once I have fallen asleep so that Coen won't suspect anything.

After showering, Coen takes me to breakfast. He refrains from mentioning my desertion of him last night – perhaps he puts it down to girlish nerves. The whole time I am eating, Kace is watching me. I sense that he wants to talk.

We have to wait until Coen has left the room to eat his own breakfast.

The moment he has gone, Kace is on his feet. I follow suit, leaving my breakfast half eaten on the table. He thrusts a hand out for me to grab and I take it.

What is he planning?

The room Kace leads me to is one I've never noticed before. He knocks a few times on the door before walking in, taking me in with him. As soon as we are in the room, he lets go of my hand. Then I see Kaden.

He's at the far end of the room, hands clenched in his thick black hair. He looks beyond stressed, as he stares at a computer in front of him. It's just one of several computers set up on desks around the room. He hears me approach and seems to lighten up a little at the sight of me.

"Mara," he murmurs warmly, coming to meet me.

Kace retreats as Kaden wraps his arms around me. Instantly, the sparks that engulf me bring me peace. I glance over his shoulder and see we are not alone.

"So this is Mara..."

Kaden pulls away and stands beside me so I can see who I am looking at. There is a girl sitting behind another computer, her black boots casually propped up on the desk. She has dark hair and dark eyes beneath dark eyebrows. Definitely Vengeance Pack.

She stands swiftly, a slight smirk on her features as she notes my expression.

"She's exactly what I assumed she would be," she says to Kaden.

I blink, not sure what she means by that.

"Mara, meet–"

"Excuse me, Alpha, we are perfectly capable of introducing ourselves..." the girl interrupts.

Kaden looks a little irritated, I notice out of the corner of my eye.

"Quinn," she says, holding her hand out for me to shake.

I stare at it for a second. Black ink crawls up her hands like vines. For a moment, I wonder if it will hurt to shake her hand. As I slide my hand into hers, I realize I'm wrong.

"You already know my name," I reply cautiously.

She twists around without another word and saunters back to her chair behind the computer. Kaden tugs on my arm, regaining my attention.

"We can trust Quinn," he assures me. "She's going to help decode this binary."

Quinn stares at me as if she's challenging me to question her.

I keep my mouth firmly shut for fear I might say something I will regret.

Kaden leaves my side and I wonder for a moment how he knows Quinn. Is she a servant here? The leather she wears so confidently suggests otherwise. Perhaps they are friends?

"Tell me you remember the code," Quinn says, more like a demand.

I breathe in. As it happens, as I waited outside Kaden's room and he struggled with his pants, I had time to memorize the binary numbers tattooed on Coen's leg by repeating them several times over. Now, I am fairly confident I know the simple numbers off by heart.

I go closer to her and wait until she has pen and paper ready before repeating them to her.

"010100000111010101110010011010010101110100011110010010 11100010000001000100011011110111011001100101001000000001 00110001100001011011100110010100101110."

"That's a lot of numbers," Kaden murmurs, looking over my shoulder. Obviously, he can't believe his own brother managed to hide such a large tattoo from him. Yet it wasn't really large at all and it only covered a relatively small patch of skin.

Quinn grunts. "It's not that long. It should only take me a few minutes."

I step back, giving her some space. Curious to see how she does it, I watch over her shoulder as she begins circling random numbers and writing letters beside them.

She glances at me and frowns. "Strange," she mutters, inspecting my neck, "you're mates with Kaden, yet he hasn't marked you."

I purse my lips. "We can't have Coen knowing about us."

"That's dangerous," she says, glancing at Kaden.

She looks genuinely worried about the fact that Kaden and I aren't officially mated, but I don't understand why.

"Why is it dangerous?"

"Kaden knows the danger of having an unmarked mate," Quinn murmurs absently.

I don't know what to make of that and she seems to register my confusion.

She chuckles. "You don't know?"

She exchanges a glance with Kaden. Then her lips crease in a wide grin. "Oh, Purity Pack members are so innocent!"

I see Kaden give Quinn a warning glare. Something is going on here that they aren't telling me about. I get to my feet and put my hands on my hips, glaring at them both so they get the message that I'm waiting to be told what they're on about.

"Werewolves aren't used to not being mated," Kaden explains slowly. "When they aren't, but they could be, they go a little... crazy."

I can tell from his shifty expression that he's not telling me everything.

"They call it a Heat," Quinn says, smiling devilishly.

"A what?"

"The burning, insatiable need for–"

"It's nothing," Kaden interrupts. "Don't worry about it. Mara. That won't happen to you."

Quinn winks at me before turning back to her work.

I still don't understand, but I can see I'm not going to get any more out of them. But I'll find out eventually. I just need to–

I jump as Kaden's arms wrap around my waist. He rests his chin on my shoulder and lets his warm breath caress my neck. Despite Kace's wary eyes on us from the other side of the room, I allow myself to lean back into him. The mystery over the Heat thing quite vanishes from my mind.

"I enjoyed last night," I whisper under my breath, so that neither Kace nor Quinn can hear. I've been waiting to tell him that.

Kaden gives my waist a squeeze. "So did I. I'm sure a repeat is due in the near future," he murmurs gently.

His fingertips dance across my bare arm. I wish he wouldn't do it when there are other people in the room, as I'm not sure I will be able to restrain myself.

"Craving more already?" I whisper hoarsely.

"Mara, I could take you on every surface in this room, against every wall in this estate, and I still wouldn't be done with you."

His words melt my insides. I don't even have the power to say anything in reply.

"I think I have the answer," Quinn exclaims, drawing me out of the trance Kaden has managed to put me in.

We move a little closer so we can see what she has written down. What I read makes me gasp.

Purity. Dove Lane.

"I'm not sure what it means, though," Quinn says, tucking a strand of dark hair behind her ear.

But I do. "I live on that street," I say softly.

I feel dizzy with confusion as I attempt to work out why Coen should have this, of all things, tattooed on his ankle.

Kaden's hand touches my shoulder. "How can my parents be there?"

My mind spins. *How can Kaden's parents be at my home?* Then it dawns on me. "We have a cellar..."

Kaden frowns, as does Quinn.

"We've always had a plan to hide there in case war is initiated by this pack. But no one's been down there for years. My mother always said she thought teenagers snuck down there to hide from their parents. Maybe..."

Kaden steps back and I can see the doubt in his eyes. Doesn't he believe me? I'm not even sure if I believe myself right now... but it makes sense.

It's another sick way for Coen to use me against Kaden.

"We need to go there right now," Kaden insists.

I stop him before he storms off. "No! You have to stay here. If Coen catches you there, it will ruin everything." I look over at Kace. "Kace and I will go."

***

I bundle up the last bit of paper in my fist and toss it into the bin. *Why do I even bother drawing?*

A gentle knock at the door makes me pause. Quinn, my substitute mate, crosses the threshold into my room.

I hold my arms out and invite her to sit on my lap. She wraps her arms around my neck and smiles wickedly down at me. This plan we have been weaving has been going so well.

178

"So? Did they fall for the binary?" I ask her.

"Indeed. They are heading for the basement right now," she tells me, leaning down to nibble my earlobe.

I can't help but smile. Perfect. Everything is falling into place.

Chapter Thirty-Two

A knock on the door distracts me from my preparations to leave.

Kaden stands in the open door, casually leaning against the frame. He's smiling, and between his fingers he dangles a tiny bottle filled with black liquid.

"Come to wish me luck?" I ask. Kace and I are just an hour away from going to find Kaden's parents. I can't thank Quinn enough for being able to decode it.

Kaden continues toying with the strange little vial. "I can go in your place, if you're worried–"

"No, we can't arouse Coen's suspicions."

He comes inside and closes the door behind him. Then he sets the bottle down on my desk.

"What is that?" I inquire at last.

A flicker of some emotion flashes across his face but he smothers it quickly. Now he just looks awkward. "We didn't use protection last night."

My mouth drops open as I realize what the liquid is for. I pick the vial up and peer closely at it. Is this how the Vengeance Pack ensure pregnancy doesn't happen?

"You want me to drink this?" I ask hesitantly.

Kaden steps a little closer to me, still looking embarrassed. "It isn't that I wouldn't want a family with you, Mara. But now... it's not the best time."

I see the pain in his eyes, but his words are practical; they make sense. He strokes my bare arm with a warm hand. He knows the sparks between us will comfort me. And they do.

"No, you're right," I say, sucking in a deep breath.

The thought of drinking the liquid swirling around the vial is intimidating. I spin the lid off quickly before I have the chance to think too much about it.

"And," Kaden murmurs, "I plan to repeat what we did last night... a lot. That medicine will last a month."

Closing my eyes, I toss the liquid straight down my throat. It tastes like vanilla and charcoal.

I lower the empty vial and wipe my mouth. Kaden is watching me and I wonder if I detect a shadow of regret in his expression.

"What's wrong?" I ask.

He shrugs and takes me in his embrace. Instantly it is as though my worries wash away and all I can concentrate on is my mate with his arms around me.

"Nothing's wrong," he murmurs into my hair, though his tone suggests otherwise.

I decide not to question him further. All I want is his lips on mine. He responds to my unvoiced need and kisses me softly. No more doubts. Just my mate.

***

I stand in front of the familiar front door, unable to lift my hand to knock.

Inside this house are my parents. The same people who have trained me to hate the man that I love. The same people I had sacrificed myself for, to save them from Kaden. It feels like a long time since I last saw them...

Kace stands beside me and gives me a reassuring smile. He doesn't know what he's in for...

The door bursts open before I can knock again. Mother stands there, dressed in her best church clothes. She is clearly about to go out. She looks at me, her blue eyes locking with mine. I watch her eye twitch and a flicker of shock course through her. Then her gaze transfers to Kace and she takes in the dark hair, dark eyes, dark clothes. The whole Vengeance Pack look. She screams and retreats inside.

"Mother! Wait! It's okay!" I insist, following her into the house.

She's at the shelf, sorting violently through the things on it. I watch in disbelief as she pulls out a packet of incense.

She doesn't seriously believe that will keep him out...?

Kace strolls in casually after me and looks mildly amused by my mother's reaction.

"Calm down!" I urge my mother. "I'm home."

She stares at me for a few moments before dropping the incense and falling into my arms.

"Thank the Moon Goddess you escaped that evil man!" she whispers into my neck.

My heart falls. She means Kaden.

Kace clears his throat from behind us. Mother glances over my shoulder at him and pulls away, still bothered by his presence.

"This is Kace," I tell her. "He... ah... he helped me escape," I lie through my teeth. I've sinned so much lately I hardly care anymore.

Mother sizes him up. When I turn around, Kace gives me a meaningful look. Right, we are running late as it is.

"Do you have the keys to the cellar in the back yard?" I inquire.

Despite my desire to hug my mother and have a good cry on her shoulder for all the times I've missed her, I can't. Not until Kaden has his parents back. And Kace too, for that matter.

"They're on the wall–"

I go to where the keys usually hang and sort quickly through them till I find the right one. Then I snatch Kace's hand and drag him outside. Mother doesn't follow, and I have the feeling she's about to dance around with that incense and pray that her encounter with Kace won't have too much of an effect on her.

The cellar is tucked away right at the back of the yard. Mother always told us that Alpha Rylan of the Purity Pack owned it, and we weren't to go near it. Was that Coen's doing?

The cellar lies behind a large metal door that I've never seen opened. Kace grabs my arm to stop me.

"I should go first."

"Why?"

He rolls his eyes at me as if he hardly needs to explain. Then he takes the key from me and twists it in the lock. He looks at me for a moment before swinging the door open.

At first, I don't see anything inside the small room, which is pitch black.

Kace steps forward and I'm about to follow suit when I see his foot trigger a small wire stretched across the entrance, near the floor. There's a loud click from somewhere. Kace is in the act of spinning round, a look of terror on his face when a gunshot rings out.

He crumples to the ground.

I scream. I haven't seen so much blood in my life. And I've never seen someone die before. Kace has fallen face first into the grass and is most likely dead. I have to hold myself back from vomiting.

It's a trap. All I can do is repeat it over and over in my head as I back away from Kace's body. Then another thought pushes its way in. *He needs help.*

Glancing one last time at Kace, I am inside in a second and grabbing the home phone to call Kaden while ignoring my mother's frightened expression. He picks up almost immediately.

"Kaden, you need to get down here right now!" I insist.

He starts to question me but I slam the phone back down. I need to get out there and help Kace.

I run back outside, heading back to the cellar. But what I find makes me scream even louder than I did when Kace was shot.

There's just a puddle of blood. No sign of Kace. He's gone!

***

My head hurts. That's all I feel at first.

When I open my eyes everything's blurry. There's a bright light shining on my face. I don't even remember what has happened, or know where I am. Then it starts coming back to me.

Shot. I've been shot. I glance down at my stomach and see it is covered in gauze. There is no pain. I must be on strong pain medication...

"He's awake," I hear an unfamiliar voice murmur. The accent is familiar, though... Wisdom Pack.

"Good job, Sherlock," another voice replies, sounding a little closer to me.

All of a sudden I am alert and looking around. The light no longer bothers me and I see who's in the room with me.

There are two men, both dressed in dark clothes and staring at me curiously. The closest one has thick hair pushed back from his face, all blazing red and different to anything I've seen before. His eyes are so blue I'm quite unnerved.

The other man leans against the edge of the table I'm on, arms folded across a broad chest. He has dark blond hair and the same colored eyes as his companion, though perhaps a little darker. The red-haired man closest to me seems calmer and his stare is impassive. The other has a wolfish grin on his face, as though he's enjoying the situation.

"What's going on?" I rasp, finding my voice. I am tied down, and I feel a surge of anger sweep through me. I tug at the restraints but cannot get free.

"Calm down, Kace," the redhead says. "We're just trying to help you." I see he is wearing a thick belt round his slender waist and there are several blades in it.

Are these men assassins?

"My brother is an Alpha," I warn them.

The blond man laughs. "You're still in your pack. Just not where you might expect."

184

That makes me even madder. *Wait until Kaden gets his hands on these fools! Don't they realize that kidnapping me is the biggest mistake they could make?*

"You can trust us. We're here to help you," the redhead repeats. "My name is Reilly, and my brother behind me is Adrian. Ignore him."

"Does it look like I care what your names are?"

Someone grabs my hair from behind, yanking it backward, and I realize there's someone else in the room. Looking down at me are a familiar pair of emerald green eyes.

Lexia.

She smiles wickedly down at me, still grasping my hair painfully.

"I need you to tell me one thing, Kace," she murmurs.

I swallow. There is no doubt in my mind that I should have killed her the moment she intercepted Mara and me.

"Is my mate really an Alpha? If so, where is he?"

Chapter Thirty-Three

I press my face deeper into Kaden's chest, trying to find comfort in his nearness. His arms tighten around me as if he's trying to console himself at the same time.

I'm in his lap, on the floor. He's trying to be strong for me, but I can feel his tears running down my neck. He just lost his brother. And I witnessed it.

"He just... just disappeared," I whisper in a voice that sounds half-choked.

Kace has gone. I turned my back for a few seconds and he vanished into thin air like it was a magic trick. Someone has to have been behind it...

"I know," Kaden murmurs. But I suspect he has no better idea of what happened than I do. And I know how worried he is about it.

I'm not sure how I made it back to the Vengeance Pack. Perhaps Kaden brought me. It's all a blur. I just want to blank it all out. But I'm grateful I'm not stuck back at home, where my mother would surely only make things worse.

I pull away slightly and look up at Kaden. He's stopped crying now and his expression is hard. Vengeance flickers in his eyes and I know that whatever happened to Kace, things will be resolved. And not in a nice way either.

"You must be devastated," I mutter, feeling stupid for crying in front of a man who has just lost his brother.

He shakes his head, chasing my tears away with his thumb.

"Why should I be? He's alive."

He seems very sure of it, but I have my doubts about that. Kace looked in a very bad way when I last saw him. Whoever took him would have to have gotten him medical help straight away. That is if he was even still alive...

Suddenly Kaden frowns and looks down at me. He lifts his hand and cups my cheek. The tips of his fingertips are cold against my inflamed skin.

"You look flushed," he observes, his eyebrows creasing.

All of a sudden I am aware of how warm I feel. Perhaps it's from being pressed up against Kaden; he does tend to have that effect on me... Or maybe I am red from all the useless weeping I have been doing.

"I'm fine. I think I'm just tired," I assure him. I'm not uncomfortably warm but now that he's pointed it out I'm hyper-aware of it.

Kaden brushes a piece of hair back behind my ear, still looking a little worried. "I have something to tell you."

I sit up properly. We are only on the floor because I collapsed in a heap the moment we walked through the door and were safe from being spotted by Coen.

"I'm going to be away from the pack for a few days," he tells me.

I am stunned. He's going away? *Now?*

"Why?"

"I'm worried about an uprising within the pack. I'm going to find help from the only two Alphas I think can make a difference," he says gently.

The concern in his eyes is inescapable. He's genuinely worried about this.

"And who may they be?" I ask.

"The Alpha of the Love Pack..." He pauses. "And your old Alpha."

I freeze. Alpha Rylan. Once upon a time, I did everything under his orders. The mantra we chanted in school was created by him, and central to it was a reminder of the evil represented by Kaden. I've never met him, but I'm positive he won't be very happy about me leaving his pack. Especially for this one.

Alpha Malik of the Love Pack I know to be very different. He is reputed to be the one man on this earth who will give himself over to anyone if it is in the act of love. I have heard he's a little crazy. And attractive. At least that's what the girls of the Purity Pack always say, wishing the Moon Goddess would pair them with him.

"What makes you think they will help you?" I ask Kaden. His idea sounds deranged. He wants to ask the two Alphas who despise him the most to help him? Maybe he's the crazy one...

"It has to work. All I need is a few days, and then I'll be back," he tells me, trying to sound confident. But I detect uncertainty behind his words.

I sigh and rest my head on his chest again. Is my neck stinging? Or am I imagining things?

"When do you leave?" I ask quietly.

"Today. The sooner I bring them back here, the better. I also need them to help me find Kace," he adds.

I trust him to know what to do for the best, but I'm not happy about it. He's going to leave me here alone, with Coen.

It's as if he can read my mind; his response surprises me. "Grayson will be here in an hour. He's agreed to look after you while I am gone."

I feel my eyes widen? Grayson? Of all people, he's sent for Grayson?

"Is this because of Lexia?" I ask.

"Grayson doesn't know about Lexia. It would devastate him if he found out his own mate doesn't want him."

I see that. It would make him mad with anger.

"He has the right to know, though... he will want her either way," I argue.

You can't just keep an Alpha from his mate. Kaden himself proved that to be impossible. And yet he still sits here, looking doubtful.

"Mara... not now, not yet. We wait till this is cleared up. Then we tell Grayson."

I nod reluctantly. I'm not sure if the heat burning in my cheeks is because of him, or the frustration I'm feeling.

"What about Grayson's... condition?" I inquire. Kaden hasn't yet explained to me how his family cursed Grayson, making him change into a beast every night against his will.

Kaden doesn't appear ready to talk about it. I remind myself that he has enough on his mind already.

"His brother, Evan, will be accompanying him," Kaden tells me, ignoring my question.

Evan... I remember his kindness and feel a little reassured.

"The babysitter needs a babysitter?" I joke.

Kaden's brief smile in response doesn't reach his eyes.

I kiss him swiftly on the lips, taking him by surprise. Before he can respond, I pull away, however. I'm not playing with his emotions, but it feels like my skin's burning from the inside and all I need right now is a cold shower.

"You promise you will call if anything happens while I am gone?" he asks.

"I will. Just get back as soon as possible."

He nods. I stand up, my tears now dried and my self-esteem salvaged. But something doesn't feel right. I wipe the sweat building on my forehead.

Kaden notices and stands up beside me. "Are you okay? You seem a little... off?"

"Kaden, I'm fine. I just witnessed Kace being shot and then vanish. I think it's just a fever," I tell him.

He looks doubtful.

"Now go," I insist, pushing him gently toward the door.

"I'll be back as soon as I can."

I smile. I trust him with that. Despite the look of longing in his eyes, he turns around and walks out the room.

I head for the shower, wondering why I feel like I'm about to burst into flame.

***

Lexia sits before me where I lie on the table, studying me.

She's seriously crazy. The look in her eye is untamed and wild. Grayson is going to have a great time with her, I'm sure.

"For someone from the Discipline Pack, you're a little unhinged," I muse.

Her jaw clenches, as do her hands in her lap.

"The Discipline Pack taught me how to be a leader. Do I look like a leader?" She demands, with a little growl in her voice.

I look her up and down. I have to admit she does look like a leader. The two assassins behind her are like dogs on her leash, waiting for her command. Adrian looks bored with our conversation and sits sharpening two knives. Reilly stands behind Lexia, staring at me with his arms crossed and his eyes impassive. I find him particularly unnerving. I think it's the blue eyes and the fact that he's from the Wisdom Pack.

"You look as if vengeance helps you sleep at night," I tell Lexia.

Her eyes narrow. Did I upset her?

"You're right," she murmurs.

She leans forward and looks at me directly in the eyes. Her own eyes are glowing green jewels. They could fool any inexperienced man.

"I want to know who my mate is," she says.

Adrian sudden ceases his knife sharpening and sets the knives down on the table before strolling over to Lexia's side. He kneels down, his hand resting on her thigh.

"We want to know who he is, so we can kill him," he grunts.

Then it clicks. Adrian and Lexia... they're lovers.

"Her mate is special," I respond coolly, looking at Adrian. "An Alpha. You're an idiot if you think you can challenge him."

Sure, Adrian is well-built, and he obviously knows how to charm the women, judging by how he's wrapped Lexia around his finger.

I'm sure it didn't take much. I have to admit that he's more attractive than I am.

But Grayson... Grayson will crush this man and not think twice. I've witnessed the beast Grayson turns into at night and it's not pretty.

"I'm going to take him down," Lexia interrupts sourly. "Both of them. Kaden. My mate. And anyone else who stands in my way."

I allow myself a hollow laugh.

"You just wait, Lexia. You may think you're on top of this hierarchy right now. But soon you'll be face to face with your mate. And that will change everything."

Chapter Thirty-Four

Cool water from the showerhead dribbles down my bare skin, but it does nothing to quell the heat within. As I look down at my arm I half expect to see the water evaporating on contact.

I'm going crazy, I've decided.

It's as if the sun is beating on my back, rather than cold water. I give it up and step out of the shower. Obviously, it's doing nothing for me, which means that whatever is wrong with me, is probably in my head.

Maybe it's because I'm missing Kaden already? No… I felt this before he left. If I had told him how I was really feeling he would have stayed – but he needs to see to matters elsewhere.

I towel myself dry and get dressed, though it's an effort. The fabric feels like sandpaper and even the soft cloth of my shirt makes me squirm uncomfortably. I settle on a sleeveless, light-colored dress instead.

Perhaps this is an allergic reaction to something? Or grief... the thought of Kace lying on the grass makes me ache with sadness. But not with heat.

I sit on the edge of my bed, wishing my heart didn't feel like a furnace inside me. I need a glass of water...

I head downstairs and hear voices coming from the main entrance, very familiar voices, I realize.

All of a sudden, Grayson and his brother Evan appear around a corner. Thankfully they are both fully clothed. Grayson's mercury-colored eyes light up when he sees me. I swear he looks different from when I last saw him – more filled out, his hair silkier, and his smile...

I shake my head. What am I thinking? I have a mate, and I'm perving on Lexia's? There's definitely something seriously wrong with me...

"Interesting choice of clothes considering its quite cold in here," Grayson remarks, looking me up and down.

He's right. I should be shivering in this dress, but instead, I'm on fire. And getting hotter by the second.

"Yeah..." I break off and avert my eyes as I catch myself admiring how tight his shirt is on him. I've seen him naked before, of course – yet the sight of him in clothes has suddenly turned me on?

Evan steps forward, a smile on his face and his arms outstretched. "It's good to see you Mara!"

The pleasure in his voice makes me want to hurl. Not because I don't like him – heck, he's one of the nicest guys I've ever met – but something about how happy he is, in contrast to how I'm feeling, just does my head in. The very sight of him fills me with rage.

I stumble back a few steps, much to his confusion.

"I'm sick," I tell him, to stop him getting any closer.

I don't want Evan anywhere near me – yet Grayson's welcome to come as close as he likes. *What's wrong with me?*

I close my eyes for a second and take a deep breath. This isn't me... I would *never* entertain thoughts like these normally. I'm just tired. I need sleep, and when I wake up, everything will be okay.

"Oh. Is there anything we can do?" Grayson asks, standing beside a rejected-looking Evan. There's concern in his face, but all I can focus on is how handsome he is. The glint in his eyes is enchanting.

I force myself to nod. "I'm fine. Just need some sleep. Do you mind if I go up now, and I'll see you for dinner later?"

Evan and Grayson exchange uneasy looks but both nod anyway.

"If you need anything, just let us know," Evan offers. I see the genuine anxiety in his eyes. But my body still doesn't want to be anywhere near him.

Before I can say or do something I'll regret, I turn and bound up the stairs to my room, where I lock myself in and try to extinguish my vulgar thoughts about a man who isn't even my mate.

***

I'm sure something was wrong with Mara when I last saw her. She didn't seem at all well. I'm not sure if it's because of Kace, or something else.

I exhale slowly. My heart constricts every time Mara appears in my mind. How could I leave her when she's ill?

My reverie is interrupted when the door opens.

I'm in the Love Pack. Alpha Rylan of the Purity Pack has agreed to meet me here. The whole place makes me feel sick, what with all the doe-eyed girls and the atmosphere of casual flirtation pervading everything.

Glassy blue eyes stare at me from a familiar face. Malik. For an Alpha, he looks scruffy and unkempt and I notice that the top three buttons of his shirt are undone.

Nice to know he wants to look good for our meeting.

He slides into a chair in front of me and looks at me with a cocky half smile on his face. I don't like him.

"Well, well. Kaden," he murmurs. His words slur together in that strange way these love freaks always speak.

Another figure appears at the door, a young-looking girl. She peers in and winks at Malik before withdrawing her head. It's pretty obvious what her wink means.

"Does your pack know you fuck young girls like that for fun?"

Malik's smile doesn't falter, but his blue eyes remain cold.

"I make love," he corrects me.

I shake my head. What he does is sinful. Sinful and shameful. And to think he's older than me.

"You think it's okay if you call it love?" I ask him, mildly amused.

He shakes his head and leans closer over the table. Malik is stupid, but the other Alphas like him.

194

"I think it's okay because I don't have a mate. It's four years since I was supposed to find her. I'm tired of waiting."

He doesn't understand. I get it. I was like that once, before I accidentally touched Mara on the train that day. It changes your life forever. I'm sure his mate, whoever she might turn out to be, wouldn't be pleased if she found him in bed with another girl.

"Surprisingly enough, I'm not here to talk to you about your sex life," I tell him.

Malik slides a hand over the top of the table and I watch him carefully. This man knows what I am like. He's been an Alpha for a long time, and I believe that he sometimes thinks he has the better pack.

"Right. So what has attracted the Alpha of Vengeance to my humble abode?" he inquires smoothly.

I blink a few times. I'm normally a very forward person, but his weird eyes make me shiver. He uses them to strip you down and see into your soul. Not that I have one anymore.

"I need your help," I admit, forcing the words out through my teeth. It's not easy for one Alpha to request help from another. Especially one from the Love Pack.

Malik grins. He's loving this.

"And how may I assist you?"

Before I can answer, the door opens again and in walks Rylan.

If anyone lives up to the word pure, it's Rylan. Not because of his morals, more just the aura that comes off him. Everyone feels it, sees it, tastes it. It surrounds him and it has everyone bending at the knee for him.

Except me, of course.

"Kaden, my old friend," he says.

He sounds like Mara. He has that same sweet, musical accent. They even share the same light blond hair and blue eyes. Except, at the same time, they are nothing alike of course.

"Rylan," I murmur.

He doesn't shake my hand. Instead, he just pats Malik's shoulder and sits down beside him. Instantly, I feel slightly intimidated, but the front I put on is intended to convey otherwise.

"He needs our help," Malik says bluntly, crossing his arms over his chest. He isn't interested in the brooding looks Rylan and I exchange.

We are complete opposites, Rylan and me. For my part, I respect justice and honor. For his part, he respects morality and goodness.

"How so?" Rylan asks.

This is the hard part – convincing two men of such different character to help me.

"I believe there is a risk of an uprising within my pack."

"Is this another one of your games?" mutters Malik, leaning further back in his chair. "I'm sick of being a player on your giant chess board."

"You can be the queen," I say smoothly, sparking a smile on his lips.

Rylan continues to stare at me without giving anything away. I've always preferred Malik to Rylan. At least he's open-minded and has a sense of humor.

"This isn't our problem," Rylan says stonily. "I will not have you drag my pack members down."

I notice he doesn't bother mentioning how his pack members have been disappearing.

"What if I agree that if you help me, I'll leave your entire pack alone?" I suggest. I mean it. It's not as if I wanted to steal those girls anyway. I only did it for Coen, who expects it of me.

Rylan's eyebrows lift. I've got his attention.

I'm about to speak further when my phone rings suddenly in my pocket. Malik jumps and I flinch.

"One moment," I say, stepping away from the table.

If it is Mara that is in trouble, I cannot ignore the call. I answer the phone.

"Kaden? Listen..."

The voice isn't familiar in the slightest, and that makes me frown. Whoever it is, he has my phone number, and he sounds stressed.

"Who—"

"It's Mara," the man at the other end tells me. "Her heat has started."

Chapter Thirty-Five

I stare at Grayson's back as he gazes out the window. The sun is setting across the horizon, bathing the room in deep orange and red hues. A normal person would find it comforting, but I am anxious. It could be only minutes from now that my brother turns into a murderous werewolf. Minutes from when he could fully turn on me.

Grayson seems to be in some sort of trance. I figure he's staring out to the Vengeance Pack city, wondering about his mate. It's a brilliant view from this room within Kaden's estate. A perfect view of the life his mate has to live.

It's easy to sense that he wants to go straight down there and whisk her away to his pack. But he can't do that, and he knows it. If she resists, his entire plan for a calm mating process will go out the window. And if she is willing, which I am sure she most likely is, will Kaden let her go?

"I think it's time to be tied," I say, slicing the silence between us. From my angle, I can see the side of Grayson's face and I note how his jaw tightens. I can't help but wonder what his mate, Lexia, would do if she found out about this problem of his... Surely the thought has run through his head before.

This condition affects him greatly. Now he's turning to me, a shadow flickering across his face. His eyes are gleaming like I've never seen them before. I didn't inherit those silver eyes from my mother. He did.

My brother wanders over to the bed, muscles stiff. For some reason, he looks tenser than he does most nights. Usually he is happy enough to be bound to his bed. In fact, it was his idea to be bound when we first found out he was cursed. But tonight he seems reluctant.

"Is everything okay?" I ask.

After Mara acting strange, and not coming to dinner, I've been on edge. Now Grayson looks like he's in a dazed trance, his eyes wandering around the room like a crazy person.

He doesn't answer. Instead, he slides into the bed and holds his wrists up. It takes a good five minutes to secure him to the bed. It always does. He's an Alpha, so he's stronger than most metals. He doesn't mind the silver, he tells me. Sometimes I don't believe him.

Only, today, I don't have the silver. Instead, I am securing the thickest chains around his arms and legs, hoping they'll be enough to stop him escaping.

I pull up a chair and wait for the sun to go down, waiting for him to shift. The silver keeps him from shifting on a normal day, and it's making me nervous knowing we're powerless to stop him transforming. As long as he doesn't escape...

However, as the sun goes down further, disappearing beyond the horizon, Grayson doesn't change. He just lies there, staring blankly at the ceiling. I stare at him in confusion.

"Grayson? Why isn't it happening? What's wrong?"

Again, he doesn't answer. *Why isn't he shifting?* Panic rises within me. This has never happened before. I glance out the window. He should definitely be changing into his wolf form by now.

I go to him and see that his forehead has a thin sheen of sweat on it. When I touch him, he's ice cold. Something is clearly wrong, and I feel a strange frustration at the fact that I can't do anything to help him.

"Gray?" I mutter, shaking him.

His eyes snap to me. I retreat in shock as he takes a deep breath and suddenly growls. It's a growl like nothing I ever thought could come from a human throat. So feral and wild.

"Mara," he rasps.

He's glaring at me now, and his wrists start to jerk frantically at the chains. Why he has spoken Mara's name, I'm not sure. But, whatever his reason, he sounds desperate.

"Mara isn't here," I tell him, trying to keep my rising voice steady.

He lurches upward, pulling at the chains like an untamed animal. Except he is not the animal I expect him to be. Instead, he strains his biceps and glares at me again.

"Get her!" he growls, so deeply it doesn't sound like his voice at all.

Why is he so desperate to see Mara? Then it dawns on me and it's like a bucket of ice-cold water has been dumped on my head.

Her heat has started. Shit.

No wonder she wanted nothing to do with me earlier. The thought of being with a mated wolf can make one in heat sick to the stomach. And, to make it worse, I saw the glimmer in her when she looked at Grayson. Now he is reacting to the primal need within him. I can't let him make that mistake...

"Gray... listen," I insist, trying to get his attention despite his eyes being clenched shut, "you need to calm down."

When his eyes reopen they are almost glowing. He is completely out of control, I realize, as he continues to yank the chains restraining him. When his gaze settles on me I see he is begging me to let him go.

But to do what? If I find Mara for him and he claims her, Kaden will go berserk. He is with another pack right now, with no knowledge that his mate is so vulnerable. If Grayson escapes the chains keeping him to his bed, I don't doubt Mara will welcome him into her bed in the state she's in. Thoughts of Kaden will be driven right out of her mind.

"I swear that if you don't let me go..." Grayson grinds out, his eyes glittering. His threat goes unfinished as he arches his back and his naked torso rises into the air. I'm holding his wrists now, trying to stop the chains cutting into his skin. Already, I am seeing dark red marks from his relentless struggling.

"You'll do what?" I retort.

"I will take down whoever I can..."

"So you can what?" I challenge him. "Go and fuck Mara meaninglessly until Kaden gets back?"

I'm doing my best to make him see sense, but it's no use. He's a desperate Alpha responding to Mara's need and that is all he can think about right now. I stare as he writhes desperately on the sheets. I know I have to call Kaden and let him know. Fast.

Ensuring the chains are still secure, I leave the room and get on the phone to Kaden.

"It's Mara," I tell him. "Her heat has started."

He sounds doubtful about it at first, until I mention Grayson.

"Who is this?"

"Evan. Grayson's brother," I answer hurriedly. "I don't think you understand the seriousness of the situation. An unmated Alpha around someone in heat is extremely dangerous."

As we talk I am on my way to Mara's room, trying to get there as quickly as possible.

"I know," he murmurs, sounding thoughtful.

The Love Pack is a long way from the Vengeance Pack. It's going to take time for him to get here. I begin climbing the stairs.

"Are there any other unmated males around your estate?" I ask, panting.

I hear his breathing cease at the other end of the phone, as if he suddenly realizes something terrifying.

"Coen," he whispers.

Of course. His brother. So Grayson's not the only threat to Mara around here.

"Please tell me he's bound just like Grayson is," Kaden says slowly.

I close my eyes. How am I supposed to admit to Kaden that I have no idea where Coen even is right now? As far as I know he's inside a compliant Mara right now.

"Just get back here as soon as possible," I urge him. "I'll deal with Coen."

201

The only trouble is, I'm not sure I will be able to...

I bang my head against the wall of the shower.

The water is as cold as I can get it and this is the third or fourth shower I've had, yet I'm still extremely hot. It's useless. I switch the shower off. I've tried sleeping several times now, but I can't handle the feeling of the sheets over me. All I want to do is tear my clothes off. Though it's not just that... it's the fact that every time I close my eyes, I am terrified by what I start thinking. I get vivid images of Kaden taking me up against the wall, on my desk and in my bed. Then I get the same with Grayson and the delectable body he flaunts so openly.

I throw myself down on the bed, in just my bra and underwear, my eyes wide open.

I'm not sure what time it is right now, but it's late. I couldn't go to dinner with Grayson there. If I leave this room, I'm worried I might jump him the moment I see him.

So, I stay where I am safe. Inside.

Until, a loud banging on my door makes me jump.

Chapter Thirty-Six

Before I can get up to answer the door, it bursts open violently.

I would never have thought there would come a time in my life when I would ever think this way about seeing Coen appear in my bedroom. But now, I stare at him as he pants and stares back at me and my lust for him keeps me pinned to the bed.

I see his bare hands as they tremor slightly at his side and wonder what they would feel like on my hot skin. Would they burn me even more? Or would I find that they cool the heat bubbling under my skin?

"Mara!" he murmurs under his breath.

I sit up in bed and let my arms, which I have instinctively crossed over my chest, fall. It is as if I have shunned all rational thought, as if I suddenly couldn't care less that Coen is a malicious megalomaniac who only wants to commit wrong against me. Such reservations are simply brushed into my subconscious, like a heap of leaves into a corner, and set fire to without ceremony.

"Coen," I find myself responding huskily.

He comes into the room, a look of determination blazing deep in his eyes. I watch with mounting pleasure as he pulls his shirt over his head, revealing a torso of hard muscle and sinew. How have I never looked at him this way before?

He kneels beside the bed and reaches for my face. At his first touch the feverish burning inside me suddenly dies down. A kind of gentle coolness douses my skin and soothes me in a way that brings me vast relief. At the same time, it makes me crave more.

Yes, I want more. No, I *need* more. Now. And I don't care who it is that answers my need. Right now, Coen is the only unmated man in my sights.

"Let me show you what it's like to be with me," he murmurs into my ear.

I raise my hips suggestively, as the desire between them grows and grows. I am inviting Coen to take complete control of me.

Then, all of a sudden, Coen's large body slumps over mine, limp and unmoving. It takes several seconds of convulsive struggling to get his unresponsive bulk off me. He rolls off the bed and onto the floor for all the world like an oversized rag doll.

"What...?"

Blinking, I see there's someone else in the room. I straighten up abruptly and recognize an amused Lexia standing a few feet away, wiping a blood-smeared baton against her leg. I stare at her in disbelief.

"How—?"

"You're welcome, by the way," she says breezily.

She nudges Coen with her foot, then withdraws it with a look of disgust. I want to question her. I want to ask her why she's here and how she got into my room. Instead, it seems as though my words are caught in my throat, which is starting to heat up again now Coen's hands are no longer on me.

"Say the word, and I'll kill him," Lexia offers casually.

She kneels on the floor and holds a small knife against the unconscious Coen's neck. I am out of the bed in a second, my horror distracting me from my burning skin.

"No!"

She pauses, glancing up at me and our gazes meet. Her emerald eyes are glowing with defiance and I wonder if she is going to kill him anyway, whatever I say. But she doesn't. Instead, she rises to face me.

"He can't die," I say feebly, hoping she doesn't ask for an explanation. Luckily for me, she changes the subject.

"Get changed before he wakes up. I need to get you out of here," she says, her expression suddenly serious.

I glance at my clothes on the floor and my skin crawls at the thought of putting them on again.

Lexia sighs and scoops my clothes up off the floor, then thrusts them at me.

"You're in heat," she mutters testily.

I frown. *What did she say?*

She seems to notice my expression. "Wow. I knew Purity Pack members were innocent..."

I glare at her as I slip my dress back on over my undergarments. It leaves a trail of fire across my skin. Does she think insulting me is going to make me any more grateful for what she just did? Interrupting me...

"Let me guess," she continues. "You feel as though someone lit a fire inside you and, moments ago, Coen quelled it. What you don't know, Mara, is that Kaden is the only one who can make it all go away once and for all."

I'm confused.

"Why? Why is this happening?" I ask her.

Lexia doesn't answer straightaway. Instead, she props Coen up against the wall and ties his wrists together with a shirt from my room. Then she stands up and gives him a sharp kick for good measure.

"Because, Mara, your mate is stupid and hasn't marked you."

"What do you mean? How do you know all these things, anyway?" I demand to know as she steers me out through my bedroom door. I resent her patronizing attitude toward me, but something tells me I should listen to her, especially since she just saved me from Coen. Although, I'm still not certain I wanted her to...

She glances over her shoulder at me as we walk. "I come from a pack that educated me. I knew you were in heat because the moment I stepped onto this property, the two unmated males I brought with me went crazy."

"So why are you here?"

205

Lexia notices how I am trailing behind and grabs my hand. As soon as her skin touches mine, it burns me like fire, and I am forced to snatch my hand away.

"I am here to make an offer to your mate," she informs me. "Obviously he isn't here, otherwise it would have been you and him I would have walked in on about to have wild sex."

I glare at her, but a part of me knows she's right.

"You don't have to put it like that," I mutter.

She nudges me with her elbow. "I know. But I like how pure your reaction is. Even when you're in heat."

I don't really understand this heat business she keeps talking about. I'm still not sure I trust her, even after what she did to Coen. Maybe it's the fact that she still holds that black baton thing.

"So what is this offer for Kaden?" I ask her.

"It's about his brother," she replies.

I stare at her in surprise. What does she know about Kace?

She sees the way I'm looking at her. "Don't worry. He is alive."

I can't help the relief that floods through me. He is alive, and that is all that matters. We walk on in silence for a while, until another question bubbles in my mind.

"Where are you taking me?"

I know I should have asked earlier, but I was too caught up in Kace. We are currently descending the same steps I took when I first found out what Kaden looked like. It feels so long ago...

"You'll see. I don't want your presence interfering with my plans. Anyway, you're in danger out here. You don't know how many unmated men are lying around here unconscious."

She says it casually, tossing her baton up in the air and catching it, but I can see she's not about to put up with any argument from me.

I follow Lexia further down. It is darker down here, and colder, not that it does much to ease the fire under my skin. I just have to trust my gut instinct that she is on my side.

"But why?" I ask her. "Why help me?"

Lexia stops at the foot of the stairs and exhales. "Because my sister was raped and killed while she was in heat. I'm not soulless, Mara. I have a heart."

***

My phone rings on the car seat beside me and I grab it quickly.

"Evan?"

I can hear him breathing heavily on the other end, making me nervous.

"Kaden. How far away are you?"

"Close."

"Well, I'm in Mara's room right now and she isn't here. And I'm not sure where Coen is either," he tells me anxiously.

That doesn't sound good. My foot presses harder on the accelerator. If he has her... No, I can't think like that.

"I'm not far away. I've got Alpha Rylan and Malik with me." I glance in the rear-view mirror and see Rylan gazing out the window and Malik lounging back in his seat, sleeping soundly. Rylan turns and meets my gaze.

Evan has gone silent on the other end. "You're not serious?"

"Yes, why?"

There's a long pause before he replies.

"Kaden, you are bringing two unmated Alphas straight to your mate. Who happens to be in heat!"

Chapter Thirty-Seven

I don't think I could have slammed the brakes on any harder, or ended the call any faster.

Looking in my rear-view mirror, I see Malik lurch forward in his seat, slamming his head against my headrest. Instantly, he's awake, gazing around in a dazed state. Rylan grabs the armrest and manages to brace himself as the car jerks to a halt.

"What's going on?" Malik asks irritably, rubbing his left eye with the back of his hand.

I park the car at the side of the road, half on the grass. A flicker of alarm passes through Rylan's eyes as I twist the keys from the ignition and turn in my seat.

"Care to explain?" Rylan inquires with exaggerated politeness.

I'm not willing to kick these two confused Alphas from my car as it is essential they make it to my pack safely. But Mara needs me. Even from here, I can feel her unspoken plea for my help, and it has me quivering anxiously.

"You need to stay here," I tell them, aware that I am not making much sense, but my rational mindset seems to have wandered off somewhere without its leash attached.

Malik's face screws up. His cheeks are tinted from the heat inside the car and it's obvious he doesn't want to remain cooped up in here any longer. Rylan slides forward in his seat.

"You're telling me you dragged us out here to leave us on the side of the highway five minutes away from your pack?" he asks. His

208

disbelief is evident in the way he gazes at me, though his expression remains as impassive as ever.

I nod, glancing out the window and wishing I was already on my way to Mara.

"If we stay here too long, people passing by might get concerned someone is giving birth on the side of the road," Rylan says blandly.

He turns his gaze to Malik, who responds with a look of indignation.

"Why are you looking at me?" he growls.

"That's where accidents happen, isn't it?"

Rolling my eyes, I push my door open and step out. Rylan follows suit, as does Malik, but probably only to feel included. At least it stops them squabbling.

"Kaden, tell us what's going on," Rylan demands.

Before I can speak a gust of wind blows up around us and I watch as Malik completely changes tack. One moment he's straightening his crumpled shirt. The next, he's staring down the road with darkened eyes, his muscles taut and his expression intent.

I instantly know the cause. Malik is sniffing the air now, as if trying to catch a scent in the breeze. And he is. My mate's scent. He reels forward, almost drunkenly. Rylan catches his arm and jerks him backward. Malik growls in response and tries to wrench himself from Rylan's relentless grip.

"He can smell my mate," I say.

Rylan catches my look and I fancy I see he is beginning to understand what is going on, even as he fights to restrain the other Alpha. I take Malik's shoulders in my grasp to stop him struggling any further.

"Heat," Malik grunts, his dark hair ruffled by the breeze.

Driven by the primal side of me that insists I should protect my mate from any man who threatens her, I want to beat him to a pulp, but something else stirs in my mind.

"How can he smell her from here?" I ask Rylan. "Even *I* can't smell her."

Rylan exhales but gestures for me to help get an absent-looking Malik back in the car. When he realizes what we're doing, he tries to break free, but together we get him inside and locked in.

Rylan and I catch our breath as Malik pushes wildly against the doors, his breath fogging up the window.

"We can't just leave him here," Rylan says, staring at the feral monster demanding to be let out of the car.

"He will be fine, unless you want me to wind the window down a tad for him," I mutter sarcastically.

Rylan scoffs, then turns his back on Malik and faces me. "I want you to take me with you."

"Not happening. My mate is in heat," I reply, irritated that I have to remind him.

Another uncontrollable Alpha around Mara won't help. Especially with Coen around – and missing, for that matter. What if he is in the same room as Mara? What if...

"Kaden, do you know who I am?" Rylan says patiently. "I am the earth's walking embodiment of all that is pure. I think I can handle myself around one excited female."

I grit my teeth. I know he is right.

"Fine, but one look in her direction and I won't let your rank dissuade me from pulling out the silver chains I have set aside for an Alpha," I tell him.

He nods respectfully.

Leaving Malik pounding angrily on the car door, Rylan and I shift before taking off at a fast run toward my pack.

The closer we get to my estate, the more I begin to tingle. I can feel Mara's heat now as if it was my own. All I want to do is run to her and soothe her obvious discomfort.

But the moment we have shifted back and I walk through the door, I am faced by the one person that I really don't want to be looking at. My brother, Coen.

His eyes flicker warily to Rylan as we enter. He wasn't expecting to be confronted by another Alpha, that's clear.

"Brother, we need to talk," Coen says evenly, in a way that is most unlike him, though I see through the façade he believes is concealing the malice in his eyes. He raises an eyebrow at me, daring me to ask Rylan to leave the room.

And I do. With a look of slight irritation on his face, Rylan briskly exits. Where he is going to go, I'm not sure. Not to my mate, hopefully.

"You made a mistake by leaving," Coen sneers.

The primal urge inside me claws at my consciousness, but I have to master it. I must listen to whatever he has to say. It's odd that he's here, though, talking to me instead of seeking Mara out. Unless...

"Just worked it out, have you?" he says, smiling mockingly. "Yes, I just got down with your mate... we had such a lot of fun." He folds his arms across his chest, enjoying the way I'm quivering with anger.

"You wouldn't," I growl.

Coen leans casually against the wall. I hate his cocksure attitude when we both know I could end his life with just one punch. How tempting it is...

"Oh, Kaden. She screamed my name so loud when I fucked her. Better than you ever did."

One second I am standing with my fists clenched in the middle of the room. The next moment I have Coen pressed up against the wall, my forearm across the base of his neck. He grins at me, but I see the faint glaze of fear over his eyes.

"Kill me...," he gasps, "and you kill the only chance you have of ever finding our parents."

I can hardly see through the anger that envelops me. Until I feel someone else's presence behind me. Coen glances over my shoulder and a look of utter disdain sweeps across his features.

"Kill him, Kaden," says a familiar female voice.

Lexia. *What is she doing here?*

"Trust me, you want to," she goes on. "End his life and accept the cold-blooded killer that you really are." Her voice is harsh, but somehow it makes sense, what with the pounding in my head and Coen's panting face before me.

Terror invades Coen's expression. He begins to struggle, but it is useless. My inner demon has risen to the surface. The part of me I usually let Coen control. The part of me that comes with being an Alpha...

"Look for another way to find your parents, Kaden," Lexia tells me. "Think of Mara..."

That's all I need to hear.

Coen is dead before he even falls to the ground.

I turn away to face Lexia. She looks shocked, like she didn't think I would actually do it. Then she offers me a small smile of congratulation.

"Good job, Alpha," she murmurs.

I don't want to look at my brother's corpse. I replace the mental image of my bare hands around his neck with one of Mara. Now that I am no longer threatened by Coen, I can finally be with her. But I need to ask Lexia one thing first.

"Why did you want me to kill him?" I ask. She sounded so desperate for me to end Coen's life.

She shrugs. "People like him don't deserve to live. I know this better than anyone."

The forlorn look in her eyes dissuades me from pressing her about it. She's hardly likely to share much with me, anyway, not after she thought it was me who wanted to kidnap her in the first place.

I start to walk away.

"Wait," Lexia says.

When I turn to look at her, she lowers her gaze and a warm blush spreads across her face.

"I have the key that will free Mara. Take me to my mate, and I will take you to yours."

Chapter Thirty-Eight

Lexia follows closely behind me as I lead her up the stairs.

Grayson will be in the spare room, no doubt struggling with Mara's heat. I feel as though there is an invisible force pulling me in the opposite direction toward Mara, but the rational part of my brain is telling me I won't be able to free her without the key in Lexia's hand. So I must take her to Grayson first.

"You don't want to see him," I find myself saying, a hint of warning in my voice.

Lexia doesn't reply for several seconds. I listen to the sound of our footsteps, counting every one that isn't leading me to my mate.

"Why not?" she says at last.

"Mara is in heat," I say. "Naturally, as an unmated male, he will be feeling the effects, too."

How will she react if she sees him like that? Feral... completely out of his mind. Grayson will lose all the trust I have won with him in an instant. He will never forgive me for letting Lexia see him like this. Especially when it is my fault in the first place.

When we reach his door, we both stop outside. Lexia stares at me apprehensively. I can see that she's doubting herself and the wisdom of going in.

"You're probably right," she decides suddenly.

Instantly, I see her expression change. She suddenly becomes impassive and remote. It's a mask, of course, to hide her emotions.

"Fate will guide your course, Lexia," I tell her gently. "You and Grayson will meet soon, when the time is right." I'm not sure if my words have any true meaning to them or not, but I hope they console her.

She nods curtly. I just hope Lexia will feel so calm about the Alpha of Freedom when she meets him – the commander of the night who holds a deadly secret...

"Here, take the key," she says quickly, after another glance at the door.

She grabs my hand and opens my fist so my palm is flat. Without a word, she places the key in my hand, then closes my fingers around it.

"Go, she's waiting for you."

I wish I could say something more to comfort her, to lighten the solemn look in her eyes. I want to tell her that her love hasn't even started yet and that she has a lot left to learn.

But I keep it to myself and walk briskly back toward the stairs.

***

I brace my hands against the shower wall once more, praying I'm going to make it out of this alive. This heat is relentless. It consumes my entire body without allowing any kind of refuge.

I've been in and out of the shower repeatedly, each time wishing it was colder. It feels stuffy in my room but the shower isn't much better.

With my eyes closed, I don't even notice when he walks into the bathroom. The first thing I know of it is when his arms encircle my waist and two large hands rest on my bare stomach. Instantly, I'm flooded with a cool sort of relief that has my knees weakening. I don't even have to question who it is.

Kaden.

I lean back, feeling his chest pressing against my back. If he is bothered by the ice-cold water, he doesn't show it. Instead, he gently caresses my wet skin with his fingers.

"Finally," I mutter, leaning my head back against his shoulder. I can sense his smile.

His urgency is obvious, as he trails his hands gently over my breasts, my waist and my hips. Each touch doesn't just leave sparks, but also an overwhelming sense that my craving is going to be satisfied at last.

"You have no idea how long I've been waiting for this," he murmurs in my ear, sending shivers dancing down my spine.

I twist around slowly. He's as naked as I am, I realize. And I can feel he wants me as badly as I want him.

I stroke his face gently, reveling in the smoothness of his skin as the water pours over it. There is a heady mixture of passion and lust in his shadowy eyes. He kisses me softly, but I haven't been waiting here in agony the entire day to be kissed like that. So, taking the lead, I grip his soaking wet hair between my fingers and force him closer to me.

He starts backing out of the shower, taking me with him. Dizzily, I manage to switch the water off before Kaden hoists me up by my thighs. I can't get enough of him. All I want is to get him to the bed so I can release my need.

He stands me up at the edge of the bed, before pushing me back by my shoulders so I fall onto the sheets. Right now, I couldn't care less that we are both soaking wet. Kaden is all I can think about, and all I want to think about.

He looms over the bed. Biting my lip, I admire his naked self, all glistening and wet. I spread my legs impatiently for him. "Coming?"

"Maybe," he replies, teasing me.

He leans down and, finally, settles himself between my legs. He kisses me again, but this time with a lot more energy. I respond as I feel his hands begin to caress my drying skin. When he enters me it's so sudden I have to pull away from our kiss and gasp for air. He leaves feather-light kisses on my jaw, trying to soothe me. But, despite my inexperience, I don't want him to go easy on me.

"Mmm, Kaden!" I mumble luxuriously as I focus upon the delight of feeling my mate inside me.

The sound of his name on my lips seems to inspire him. His pace increases, causing me to arch my back and moan with pleasure. The

215

feeling is indescribable and I don't want it ever to end. Resting his forehead against mine, Kaden looks deep into my eyes as he continues to quench my heat.

My fingernails dig into his back as I feel him begin to lose self-control. Now he is thrusting into me at a relentless pace.

"Beg," Kaden orders in my ear.

I'm nearing the edge but he has slowed down, his thrusts coming at half the speed that they did before. I'm desperate for him to finish me off. My fingers dig harder into his back, but he doesn't seem to care. Instead, he smirks down at me and carries on with lazy thrusting.

"Kaden!" I growl. I push my hips up to him, a silent plea for more, but he pushes them back down with one hand so he can continue at whatever pace he sees fit.

"That's my name," he murmurs. "Care to scream it?"

He moves his hand from my hips to caress the sensitive bundle of nerves between my legs and I almost combust. The feeling is beyond imagination, yet I hold back my scream for more and instead answer him with a deep moan.

"You like that?" he asks, his breath hot against my neck.

I find myself nodding and run hands up to his hair. The pleasure in his eyes is evident, as he continues to run his fingers gently across me while still thrusting slowly.

"Don't stop," I whimper, my hips answering the movement of his fingers against my will.

But he does.

He pulls his hand away and then pushes my hips down again. I squirm, but he just watches in amusement.

"You think this is funny?" I moan. "This is torture..."

He tilts his head and caresses my inner thigh with his hand, like the tease I am discovering he is. I want to slap him, but I think that would only encourage him more.

"Oh, Mara, I could keep you here like this for hours. Don't tempt me."

216

I stare into his eyes, blazing hot and terribly excited. He's obviously not getting the message. In frustration, I hook my legs over his back and force him closer to me.

"Fuck me hard, Kaden, or not at all," I command, all the purity I once had flying out the window.

Kaden stares at me in surprise for a moment, as if he can't believe what I just said. I can't believe it either. But as I feel Kaden's grip on me tightening, and his face light up with an inner fire, I know he likes it.

"I can do one better," he says, his voice rough.

He bends his head down, pressing his lips to my neck. Instantly, I know his intention, and it excites me. Especially as I feel him begin to move inside me again.

In one second, everything changes. I go from unmated to mated as Kaden sinks his teeth into my neck, and I scream – from the pleasure of his suddenly quickened pace or from the pain of his teeth piercing my neck I don't know.

The moment he is finished creating the mark upon my neck, he kisses it softly, which contrasts with the fast pace he is currently going at. He looks into my eyes, and I see the change in him. Dimly, through the vivid sensations of finally being mated to him, I read a new combination of relief and content.

He lifts my right leg up to his hip and angles his thrusts deeper into me. I have to bite my lip to keep from wailing with pleasure.

"Don't hold back," Kaden purrs in my ear. "I want to hear you."

I moan and yelp in response to his thrusts. This is why I know Kaden is my true mate – through what he does to me. He takes my body and possesses it fully, claiming me in the most exquisite, mind-numbing way. I can't escape. I'm his. Whatever magic he wields, it's intoxicating, and I feel myself losing all control over myself.

Ultimately, I erupt in an explosion of sensations. My climax renders me completely useless, as Kaden reaches his also, collapsing beside me in exhaustion.

The heat is gone. The pain is gone. And everything seems to fit perfectly into place when I turn my head and see my mate gazing lovingly straight back at me.

Chapter Thirty-Nine

When I awake in the morning, Kaden is still asleep beside me. I stare contentedly at his sleeping face, not being able to gather the courage to wake him from his peaceful slumber.

Eventually, I clamber out of bed and throw on some clothes before heading downstairs. Having not eaten since my heat started has really taken a toll on me. And I'm craving pancakes....

But when I walk into the dining room, I'm taken by surprise.

Two of the most highly esteemed Alphas sit at the table, casually eating breakfast. I halt at the door, inhaling sharply. Kaden has already told me about them being here, but the sight of them still almost paralyzes me.

Alpha Malik lounges back in his chair, looking irritable despite the name he takes power under. I mean, he isn't living up to the word love in the way he's shooting obvious daggers at Alpha Rylan, who sits opposite him.

Rylan's eyes flicker up as I enter. Something dances across his expression, but he manages to smother it before I can tell what it is.

"Good morning," he says softly.

I lower my gaze, unsure what I should do. Back when I lived in the Purity Pack, Rylan's name was a sacred utterance that you said with reverence or not at all. And now, as I stand here before him, my words stick in my throat.

After a few moments, I regain confidence and walk to my seat at the end of the table. Both men look at me curiously, as if I am some foreign creature they have never seen before. Until now I'd rather assumed men of such high rank don't bother with people of my caliber. Or lack thereof.

"Good morning," I croak. There is an empty plate in front of me, but I have suddenly lost my appetite. Especially with the way both men stare at me, not saying a word. When I glance up, something like guilt flashes in Malik's eyes, but he averts his gaze quickly.

"You look... fresh," Rylan murmurs, in a tone I can only identify as knowing.

My head shoots up. Has he figured it out? He stares at me impassively, without letting anything slip. Malik, on the other hand, has a slight smile on his lips, and I can tell instantly that he knows also.

"Fun, isn't it?" Malik says slowly.

At first, I'm not sure what he is insinuating.

"I didn't do anything," I lie.

The guilt I feel is undeniable, however. Rylan can tell if anyone has been impure, no matter who they are. My lie as probably as transparent as glass to him. Even Malik rolls his eyes at the way I try to protect myself.

Rylan suddenly drops his spoon in his bowl, making me jump.

"Why?" he breathes.

I frown, taken by surprise. "Sorry?"

Out the corner of my eye, I see Malik desperately trying to catch Rylan's gaze, as if he knows what he is going to say. I wish I did because right now I am completely lost.

"Why leave my pack?" he asks, his voice so soft I hardly catch it.

I go very still. My previous Alpha is asking me why I decided to leave his pack? How can I explain that Kaden has completely enchanted me and I no longer want to go back?

"My mate is here," I tell him, trying to keep my voice firm but respectful.

Rylan is still an Alpha, and still has influence over any decision I make. But, having said that, I will *not* let him separate me from my mate.

"You belong in my pack, with others like you," he insists. His look of calm has become troubled. I can tell he is serious about this.

"Others like me?" I splutter, not sure if I should be offended or not. "What is that supposed to mean?"

I glance at Malik for help, but he just sits there, cringing. He probably agrees with Rylan. Why would he care that Kaden got to stay with his mate? I am sure it would please him more if I were sent home, to leave Kaden to suffer without me.

"You don't belong here," Rylan continues. "You were born to be pure and spread the word of the Moon Goddess. Don't you get that?"

I flinch. Is that what he wants?

"That isn't me anymore," I explain apologetically. "I'm sorry, but I cannot live up to everything you want. This is my home now."

My hands tighten into fists. I am not the frightened, fearful girl I once was. Kaden has shown me a new life, and it is something I want to live.

But it is obvious Rylan doesn't feel the same way.

"Look at you, Mara... you look like a Purity Pack member and there is nothing you can do to stop that. You don't fit in here," Rylan tells me bluntly.

It stings. It stings because I know he is right. Stand me next to a Vengeance Pack member and the contrast would be obvious. I have nothing in common with the exotic beauty this pack has been blessed with. Not that the word blessed would be in their vocabulary.

"Rylan, that's enough," Malik cuts in, finally intervening in our conversation.

Rylan gives him a dark look, clearly warning him not to step into our argument.

I stand up and push my chair back. I have had enough; all I want to do is see Kaden and have all of this disappear. The moment I leave the room though, Rylan follows quickly after me, grabbing my wrist before I can make it any closer to Kaden. I twist around, ready to hurl all my anger at him.

"You're coming back home with me," he states sternly. "You are still my pack member."

My heart sinks. His grip on my wrist is like iron, and no matter how hard I try to rip my arm away from him, I can't get away.

"You can't take me anywhere!" I growl, still attempting to yank my arm away.

I'm tempted to punch him, but that level of disrespect toward an Alpha would land me in one of the prisons run by the Discipline Pack.

Malik has followed us out of the room and joins us in the foyer before the front door. I find myself glancing nervously at it as Rylan's grip on me remains unbroken.

He can't be serious about taking me straight home... can he?

Malik looks ill at ease. "Rylan, seriously, you need to let her go before–"

"What's going on here?" asks a familiar, knee-weakening voice from across the room.

Twisting around in Rylan's grip, I see a very confused, sleepy-looking Kaden coming down the stairs and looking as if he has just gotten out of bed. I drink in the sight of him with his disheveled hair and naked torso.

"Mara is coming back to the Purity Pack with me," Rylan declares, pulling me close in beside him.

The look on Kaden's face changes instantly from calm and curious to extremely angry. He makes a visible effort to restrain his rage. "I don't think that's a very good idea," he says, his voice deadly calm.

"Don't think for a second I am going to leave one of my pack members here for you to taint," Rylan exclaims defiantly.

Kaden shakes his head slowly from side to side as he approaches us. He has his eyes on Rylan, sparing only cursory glances for Malik and me.

So much for Kaden trying to keep things civil with the other Alphas.

"It's too late, Rylan," he says gently. "I have marked her. She is mine." He sounds as though he's breaking the news of someone passing away.

Rylan glances down at me, his eyes immediately searching my neck, although my hair covers it. It wouldn't matter, anyway... he obviously believes every word that Kaden says. He transfers his attention to me.

"Why stay here? Do you know who he is, and what he does?"

"That isn't Kaden," I tell him. "Kaden isn't like you think he is."

Rylan frowns, his forehead furrowing. All I can think about is how satisfactory it would be to strike him in the stomach and run over to Kaden. Instead, I stand civilly beside him, hoping he will let me go soon and then leave.

Instead, he smiles slightly. "Is that why he killed that man with his own bare hands? What was his name, Kaden?"

All eyes turn to Kaden, including mine. He stares at me, and instantly I can tell it is true by the look of defeat in his eyes. But *who*? I give him a questioning look, wanting to know exactly who he has killed.

"Coen. I killed Coen," Kaden mutters, his gaze cast downward.

For a moment, I don't know what I should say. I am appalled, but I am not sure why. I mean, Coen did nothing but terrorize Kaden and me. And now he is dead. Maybe it's just that I can't seem to wrap my head around it, at least not immediately.

"You see?" says Rylan.

"The only reason you are so worried about my mate is because you can't handle your own," Kaden says, rounding on him.

A deep silence settles over us. It is so tense, I imagine that cutting it with a knife would be difficult.

"Don't talk about her," Rylan growls deeply.

I blink a few times. I thought Rylan hadn't found his mate yet? At least, that was what everyone said back in the Purity Pack. But, by the look on his face, it seems Kaden has overstepped a very sensitive line.

"Why not?" Kaden presses. "She doesn't know you are mates because she is delinquent, and you can't handle it."

Kaden's words have triggered a sore spot in Rylan that I had no idea even existed. His grip on my wrist begins to loosen as his anger is directed elsewhere.

"Stop!" Malik says, interrupting both of them.

None of us move.

"Rylan," says Malik softly. "Use your eyes. Can't you see they are in love? I am the Alpha of Love, and therefore I have the authority to command you to let go of Mara... that is, if you truly are as pure as you claim to be."

It takes a few moments for Malik's words to sink in. Rylan looks at Kaden and then back at me and finally lets go of my wrist.

Immediately I rush into Kaden's arms.

Rylan regards us with glazed eyes, then turns and heads for the door.

Why he has gone so abruptly I'm not sure. Maybe it was because of this mate he supposedly has. I guess I will never know.

Chapter Forty

"So... what now?"

I stand in the corner of Kaden's office, my arms folded. The stress on Kaden's face is obvious as he sits at his desk, tapping a pen rhythmically against the hard wood.

Malik is on the other side, staring blandly out the window. It faces the west side of Kaden's property, where the view is dominated by the giant wall constructed to keep other packs out.

"Rylan's gone," Malik says, as if it's something we are just comprehending.

I haven't been told what Kaden's plan was regarding the uprising, but by the thoughtful look on his face, he's forming a new one now. Papers are scattered in front of him but I can't tell what any of them say.

"But you're still willing to help?" Kaden asks, seeming a little apprehensive.

I gather that this whole thing rides on Malik but, by the looks of things, he doesn't seem keen to play his part...

I've heard rumors. At first, I didn't believe there really was a sex tape showing Malik with one of his pack members. But then I learned that the Alpha of Love enjoys sleeping around. Just looking at him confirms my suspicions. If I wasn't mated to Kaden, I might admire his thunderous eyes and ruffled brown hair. I might even admire the tightness of his shirt and how it accentuates the hardened lines beneath.

I look out of the window before I get carried away.

"Of course," Malik confirms at last. "A civil war within any pack is no good for any of us. We should stamp on the fire before it grows."

He's not the youngest Alpha in the world – that would be Landon, followed by Isaiah of the Passion Pack – but he's politically smart and naturally rather clever. Too bad he wastes it on trivial affairs.

"Not to mention that my parents and my brother Kace are still missing," Kaden reminds him, his voice sounding a little strained.

I frown. Lexia has Kace... she told me so herself. But only Coen knew where his parents were. And now Kaden has killed him.

"I think I can help you with that..."

We all turn to the doorway and see Lexia standing there. How long she's been there, I'm not sure. She appears more than a little apprehensive.

"With what?" Kaden asks, equally as apprehensive.

Lexia comes into the office and closes the door behind her. As she does so, I catch her glancing at Malik. Maybe she had expected to find her mate here.

"I know where your parents are," she tells Kaden.

This takes me by surprise. I was assuming she would say she could help find Kace, but his name doesn't even cross her lips. But she knows where Kaden's parents are?

Kaden stands, instantly intrigued. That's one way to catch an Alpha's attention.

"Where are they?" he demands, desperate to find out where his parents are after all these years.

Lexia pauses and glances at me as if to request back-up for whatever she is about to say.

"I can also tell you where Kace is... but I want something in return."

Kaden frowns. Lexia is brave to suggest any kind of a deal with an Alpha, let alone the Alpha of Vengeance. I can see Kaden weighing up whether or not it is worth it to barter with her or otherwise simply to insist on knowing what she has to say.

Perhaps because I'm there, he decides to compromise.

"And what is it that you want?" he asks, his eyes narrowing ever so slightly.

Lexia stands beside Malik behind Kaden's desk, keeping her distance. She really doesn't like Alphas... it's just too bad her mate is one.

"I want to be the leader of the East Side of this pack," she proposes, her voice shaking slightly.

I blanch at her temerity. Kaden just looks confused.

He tilts his head. "You would like to own part of my pack?" he asks slowly.

But Lexia shakes her head, as if that is the most ridiculous thing that she has ever heard.

"I don't wish to own anything. I am from the Discipline Pack; we naturally enjoy leading, and I think I would do a good job of it if you were to let me. It wouldn't affect you at all, in fact, but it would stop this uprising they are planning."

This gets Kaden's interest. Lexia seems to gain confidence as she notices the spark in Kaden's eye.

And here I was thinking Lexia belonged completely to the Vengeance Pack! Clearly, she was born and bred in the Discipline Pack. Poor Grayson...

"How do you know about the uprising?" my mate asks her.

"I know everything about your pack. Why do you think I would be such a great leader? You think Mr Love over here is going to convince them?"

Malik shoots her a glare, but she only smiles coyly at him. It is obvious that she is only taunting him because he knows she is right.

"No offence, by the way," she adds.

"Whatever," Malik grumbles.

"So if I hand you the leadership of all those criminals, you will give me my brother and my parents?" Kaden asks, making sure he is getting *exactly* what he wants out of the deal.

Lexia hesitates and catches my gaze. She'd better keep her end of the deal because I know she kidnapped Kace.

"I will tell you where they are," she confirms, selecting her words carefully.

"And you can stop this uprising?" Kaden asks.

I want to consult him before he makes this decision. It isn't that I am worried about Kaden losing something to her — I mean, he will always be stronger than she will ever be — but it all just seems too easy...

She nods.

"Fine then. I give you the rights. It won't matter, anyway, as I am sure it won't be long before your mate comes for you," Kaden says, leaning back calmly in his chair.

Lexia frowns at this. I know how she feels about mating, so I am hardly surprised that his words bother her. She's about to give an angry response when Kaden cuts her off.

"Now tell me, where are my parents?"

Lexia hesitates with her response once again. The look in her eyes suggests that Kaden isn't going to be very happy about what she is about to say.

"Six feet under and somewhere between the Passion Pack and the Devotion Pack," she says solemnly.

Kaden freezes and my heart drops straight to my feet. *Dead?* His parents can't be dead... not after all the work we did to save them from Coen.

"They're dead?" Kaden whispers in disbelief, echoing my thoughts.

"I'm sorry, Kaden..." says Lexia.

Kaden doesn't respond to the news like I expect him to. Maybe I thought he would break down, but it is as if he has raised a shield to protect himself. He regards Lexia calmly. Perhaps it is Malik's presence? Or maybe he has already considered the idea of them being dead and isn't all that surprised at it being confirmed.

"And Kace?" Kaden asks, so impassive I wonder for a moment if it is really my mate behind the desk.

"He will return to you now that we have struck a deal," Lexia promises.

Kaden sighs with relief.

He dismisses Malik and Lexia and tells them they are free to go home. When they've gone, he closes the door behind them and it is just us left in the room. He turns to me, and I almost expect him to break down crying, but he remains composed.

"Are you okay?" I ask gently as he comes over to me.

He shrugs. "I don't think I believe it just yet," he confesses.

Despite how calm he is being, I detect a hint of despair in his eyes. I decide that now, more than ever, my mate is in need of distraction. I grab his face between both my hands and pull his mouth to mine. How I love the feeling of our lips touching. He responds almost immediately, kissing me back while gently holding my waist in his hands.

"Shall we go back upstairs?" I ask, tilting my head back as he kisses my neck.

I feel him smile against my skin.

"Nothing would make me happier."

***

I stare pointedly at Lexia's foolish assassin in front of me.

The blue-eyed redhead has tied me to a chair. Now he sits directly in front of me, staring deeply into my eyes in that creepy way of his. Reilly, I think his name is.

"Where's Lexia?" I demand.

"She isn't here right now. This is between you and me," he replies.

All I want is to get out of here, back to my brother Kaden and his mate Mara. I am beyond sick of being locked in the dark all the time, without knowing if I am going to be released or not. Right now, I can't tell if the slight smile on Reilly's face is good news or bad.

"Lexia is going to let you go back to your pack, but I want you to take a little message along with you," Reilly tells me.

My heart skips a beat. Am I finally getting out of here?

Reilly leans forward to whisper in my ear.

"Coen may be dead, but the masters behind him aren't."

Made in the USA
Lexington, KY
17 May 2017